PRISONER
of the
INQUISITION

www.**rbooks**.co.uk

Also by Theresa Breslin

DIVIDED CITY

THE MEDICI SEAL

THE NOSTRADAMUS PROPHECY

REMEMBRANCE

SASKIA'S JOURNEY

For junior readers:

THE DREAM MASTER

DREAM MASTER NIGHTMARE!

DREAM MASTER GLADIATOR

DREAM MASTER ARABIAN NIGHTS

For more information about Theresa Breslin's books, visit:
www.**theresabreslin**.co.uk

PRISONER
of the
INQUISITION

THERESA BRESLIN

DOUBLEDAY

PRISONER OF THE INQUISITION
A DOUBLEDAY BOOK 978 0 385 61703 1

First published in Great Britain by Doubleday,
an imprint of Random House Children's Books
A Random House Group Company

This edition published 2010

1 3 5 7 9 10 8 6 4 2

The Random House Group Limited supports the Forest Stewardship Council (FSC),
the leading international forest certification organization. All our titles that are printed on
Greenpeace-approved FSC-certified paper carry the FSC logo. Our paper procurement
policy can be found at www.rbooks.co.uk/environment.

Mixed Sources
Product group from well-managed
forests and other controlled sources
www.fsc.org Cert no. TT-COC-2139
© 1996 Forest Stewardship Council

Set in Garamond

Random House Children's Books,
61–63 Uxbridge Road, London W5 5SA

www.**kids**at**randomhouse**.co.uk
www.**rbooks**.co.uk

Addresses for companies within The Random House Group Limited can be found at:
www.randomhouse.co.uk/offices.htm

THE RANDOM HOUSE GROUP Limited Reg. No. 954009

A CIP catalogue record for this book is available from the British Library.

Printed and bound in the UK by CPI Mackays, Chatham, ME5 8TD

A book for Annie Eaton – at last!

INTRODUCTION

In 1469, when Queen Isabella of Castile married King Ferdinand of Aragon, it brought together the two kingdoms. It was the great ambition of their lives to unite the rest of Spain and rule it as one country. Intensely religious, they also wanted all their subjects to follow the Christian faith. With fire and sword they carried out this mission.

The Holy Inquisition (1232–1820) was a judicial institution founded by the Catholic Church to discover and suppress heresy. During the reign of Isabella and Ferdinand, officers of the Inquisition (some priests, supported by soldier religious brothers) and officials of the State, combined – not always willingly – to persecute heretics. In Spain, under the regime of the Chief Inquisitor, Tomás de Torquemada, the Inquisition was particularly active. Torture was used during questioning of the accused, and extreme punishments, including burning at the stake while still alive, were inflicted on anyone found guilty – especially on those who had converted to Christianity and then relapsed.

In the year 1490 the mariner-explorer Christopher Columbus is seeking patronage from the Spanish monarchs for his ambitious plan to cross the Atlantic Ocean. By this time most of Spain has been taken back from the Moors – apart from the Kingdom of Granada. The armies of Queen Isabella and King Ferdinand are gathering as they plan to lay siege to the town of Granada and capture the beautiful Moorish palace of the Alhambra.

Meanwhile the officers of the Inquisition continue their work throughout Spain . . .

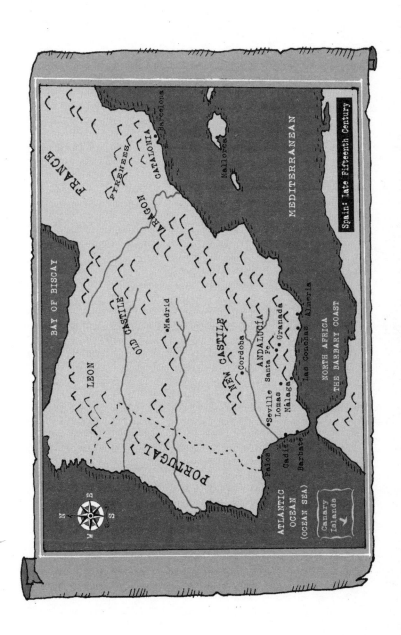

Prologue

She begged for a cross to hold.

They would not give her one.

Her body was bound fast with thick ropes to the central pole of the stake. Her arms and hands were free. She brought them together. She laid the thumb of her right hand across the forefinger of her left. She pressed her lips to the intersection of this cross and cried out in a loud voice,

'In the name of the Blessed Lord Jesus who died for our sins!'

The flames began to rise around her.

Was it true that in some cases they dampened the firewood so that the condemned would roast more slowly? Her figure became obscured by the smoke, her form a writhing shadow within the fire.

She could not be seen, but she could be heard now, screaming; and the crowd called to her: 'Recant! Recant!'

A young man shouted out, 'For the love of God, let her die! Let her die!'

It sometimes happened that the executioner would go in and swiftly garrotte a heretic before the flames reached them. But she was shown no such mercy.

Her screams lessened, to be replaced with worse – a croaking agonized babbling.

The man bent his head, sobbing, his hands covering his ears.

The stink of burning flesh lingered in the square for hours afterwards.

PART ONE
AN EXECUTION

Summer 1490
Las Conchas, a small port in Andalucía
in southern Spain

Chapter One
Zarita

We did not see the man who followed behind us.

For in the summer of 1490, before the Holy Inquisition brought fear and suspicion to our town, I did not glance constantly around me when I went about my business. After all, I was Zarita, daughter of a rich and powerful magistrate, and I could go where I chose. And on that day in August, a day so hot that even the cats had slunk from sun to shade to find some coolness, I was escorted by Ramón Salazar, a handsome young nobleman who had declared he would die for love of me.

Ramón sauntered at my side, his new sword of Toledo steel swinging at his hip, as we made our way along an unpaved street in the old port. He took his role as my protector very seriously, pulling his face into a frown and giving severe looks to every passer-by. We were here because I wanted to visit the shrine of Our Lady of Sorrows, which was situated in a church close to the sea. At sixteen Ramón was only a year older than I and had never fought a duel, yet he swaggered along beside me like any experienced soldier.

Ramón stayed by the main entrance while I went to the side altar. I wanted to ask the Mother of God to intercede for the lives of my mama and the baby son she'd just delivered with much pain and blood. It took several minutes for my eyes to adjust to the gloom.

I didn't notice the side door open and a figure slip inside. He stood in the darkness, this man, and watched me as I walked towards the statue of the Virgin. He waited behind a pillar while I lifted my veil, lit a candle and knelt to pray.

Then, when I opened my purse to take out some money for an offering, he darted forward.

Chapter Two
Zarita

'Señorita, I beg you. One coin only.'

'What?' Startled, I stood up. The man was bigger than me, his eyes enormous, brown seeping to almost black in a face that was gaunt and grey with unshaved stubble.

'I need money,' he said. 'I've walked all morning and found none. I cannot go home empty-handed to my wife and my son.' He held out his hand, palm up.

I was suddenly aware that I was alone with this ruffian inside the empty church. I pulled my veil down over my face and took a step back.

He came forward – so very close to me. His mouth opened, showing blackened and missing teeth. An overpowering foul odour. His outstretched hand brushed mine.

I shrieked in alarm.

Ramón came running down the aisle from the main door.

'My son is hungry. My wife is very ill. She needs medicine. One coin would buy something to ease her discomfort,' the man gabbled at me.

But I paid no heed to his pleas. The smell of him and the contact of his fingers, with their roughened skin and broken fingernails, repelled me. That a peasant would go so far as to try to grasp the hand of a woman of my status was outrageous.

'He touched me!' I screamed. 'This man actually *touched* me!'

Ramón looked at me in horror. His face turned red with fury. 'You assaulted this woman!' he yelled at the beggar.

'N-no!' the man stuttered in confusion. 'I was only asking for a coin.' He looked at me, as if I might verify what he said.

In fear, I shook my head and sobbed again. 'He touched me.'

'For that you die!' cried Ramón, and tried to pull his sword from its scabbard. But he wasn't practised enough to do this in one movement. It caught on his tunic, and he swore and snatched his dagger from his belt.

The beggar turned and rushed out of the side door.

Ramón gave chase, and I, terrified to be left on my own, gathered up my skirts and ran after them both.

Chapter Three
Saulo

I had watched my father enter the church through the side door.

I bit my lip in embarrassment as I realized that he was too humble and afraid to go in by the main door. He didn't know that I was there; that I'd tagged after him for the last hour or so as he trudged through the town, begging. He would have been shamed if he'd known his son had witnessed people spurning him, and one grandee pushing him aside and spitting in the street as he passed by.

He thought I was with my mother, sitting beside the straw mattress where she lay, unable to move with the sickness that had struck her down a few weeks ago. I was supposed to stay beside her and try to keep her quiet, for last night she'd started to call out words in a language I didn't know. When this began, my father became very anxious and tried to hush her so that the neighbours wouldn't hear her speak in this strange tongue. And then he'd stroked her head, while murmuring, half chanting, some poem in her ear. It seemed to soothe her. When I'd asked him what she was saying, he told me it was the speech of angels. But I recognized his expression: I had seen it on his face before, in other places we'd lived, when he decided it was time for us to move on – the look of a hunted animal when it scented danger.

All my life we had travelled from town to town. At the time I didn't think much about the reason for this. There was never enough money. Any we had my father used to buy medicine, for my mother's health was always poor, and often one of us would have to stay home to look after her. Our days were spent finding enough food to eat, and this was what occupied my mind now. I knew that I made a better beggar than my father. He would have been distressed had he found out that I sometimes resorted to begging for bread. But I'd done it before, taking advantage of the fact that I looked much younger than my years. When neither of us could get work, I would huddle down in a doorway until I saw some rich señora approaching, and then I'd whimper in a pathetic way.

But as I sat under a tree in the square outside the church on this sultry summer day, I was very hopeful that my father would be successful. When he left that morning he'd asked me to tend to my mother, but I had disobeyed him. My mother had fallen asleep so I'd trailed behind him as he followed the richly dressed girl and her companion. I figured out, as I imagined he had, that if someone like her was walking in this area, she could have only one destination. She would be going to the shrine of the Virgin Mary, which was inside the church on the cliff overlooking the sea. And if this girl was visiting a church to pray on a day not designated for religious observance, then it was likely that she had a merciful disposition. She seemed to be about my age, with the most beautiful long black hair caught up in swirls and curls with fine tortoiseshell combs. From time to time the young nobleman who was with her would turn to smile at her and reach out to touch her hair. She looked like a good girl, her face properly covered with a veil, kind and devout. She'd come to this poorer part of the town to visit the shrine, so it must mean that she sought some special favour, that she had a sorrow or a petition of her own.

I thought, *She will listen to my father as she expects her God to listen to her.*

I was wrong.

Chapter Four
Saulo

The side door of the church banged open and my father came scuttling out. He glanced to the rear of the building: the cliff wall surrounded the back, with no path visible. He turned and raced along the side of the church towards the front.

Right away I sensed danger. I stood up.

The church door opened again and the young nobleman who had been the girl's escort appeared, and then the girl herself, further behind, skirts clutched up in her hands, running.

The young man chased after my father, shouting wildly. 'Murder! Thief! Assassin!'

There were few people about, but those who were in the square stopped to look.

I beckoned with my hand. I thought my father had seen me but he veered away to the right, in the direction of a staircase going down to the sea.

My heart thudded in my chest. No! That way led to the shore, and the water would bar his way.

At the first step the young man caught up with him and lunged out with his dagger.

'Ramón!' the girl screamed. 'Be careful!'

My father carried no weapon. He shoved away the man called Ramón and sent him sprawling. But, in doing so, he himself fell backwards and tumbled down the stairs.

With the other onlookers I ran over to see what was happening.

Below us, my father scrambled to his feet. A few more seconds and he might have got free; found another alleyway or a cliff path to make his escape. But then a group of soldiers came marching along the quayside. From the top of the stairs his pursuer, Ramón, bawled at the lieutenant in charge.

'Arrest that man! He has just assaulted a girl inside the church and tried to kill me!'

The soldiers charged after my father, grabbed him and, with many blows and kicks, hauled him up the staircase to face the man, Ramón.

'Take him to this girl's father!' The young nobleman's face was twisted in rage. 'His name is Don Vicente Alonso Carbazón and he is the local magistrate!'

And so my father was dragged through the streets to the home of the magistrate and flung down in his compound. I ran after them, unable to think clearly about what was happening, so fast were these dreadful events unfolding. On the way there, more folk gathered behind the soldiers to watch the spectacle. They now crowded about the open gateway.

The girl went to hug her father as he came to the door of their house. She made to pull off her veil but he stayed her hand. He was without his jacket, and the collar of his shirt was undone. His hair was wild and his body trembled as he spoke.

'What is the noise,' he demanded angrily, 'that disturbs me at a time when I most need peace?' He held up his hand. 'Silence!' he roared. Then he pointed at the young nobleman. 'You, Ramón Salazar, tell me what's going on here.'

'Sir, Don Vicente – this beggar man attacked your daughter in the church in a most atrocious way. And when I went to restrain him, he attempted to kill me.'

Don Vicente took a step forward and struck my father in the face with his fist. My father fell to the ground, spitting teeth and blood into the red dirt of the yard.

'Sire' – my father tried to speak – 'most noble Don—'

Don Vicente aimed a kick at his head. 'Silence, you cur,' he snarled. 'If I had not more pressing matters to deal with, I would try you here and have sentence carried out upon you immediately.'

'We are in a state of war.' The lieutenant in charge of the soldiers spoke up. 'Queen Isabella of Castile and her husband, King Ferdinand of Aragon, have stated that they will tolerate no civil unrest while they fight to reunify all our provinces so that Spain can become one country again. A town magistrate can have a traitor executed by a military officer without formal trial. And anyone who harms a noble-man or a woman in a church must be guilty of treason.' He pointed to a nearby tree. 'We can hang him now and end the matter here.'

'Do it,' Don Vicente ordered. He swivelled on his heel and prepared to go inside his house. 'And get rid of that rabble at my gate.'

'Father!' I yelled as the soldiers began to close the heavy wooden doors to the compound.

I tried to push my way in but they beat everyone back violently with the flats of their swords. I pounded on the wooden surface; it wouldn't yield. When I heard the bolt being secured, I ran off and scoured the outside walls until I found a place for a toe-hold. I took a few paces back, then threw myself at this part of the wall, and scrabbled with nails and feet until I gained the top. Now I could see into the yard below. A groom from the stables had been ordered to bring a rope and it was slung over the upper part of a thick tree. My father's mouth was agape with terror and disbelief. Blood drooled from his lips.

'Papa!' The girl tugged at her father's sleeve.

Her papa, the magistrate, shook her off. 'Go you inside,' he said. 'You have disgraced our family.'

'Papa!' the girl wailed in anguish. 'Listen to me. This man does not deserve to die.'

But it was too late.

They quickly noosed the rope and cast it around my father's neck, and the soldiers hauled him high on the tree branch. And some of them grinned and joked as they did so, as if it were a sport to see a man kick out and frantically claw at his throat as he choked to death. But one soldier, a stocky red-haired man, went forward and pulled hard on my father's legs to end his agony.

My father's body jerked in a last spasm. His arms flailed sideways. To me it seemed he was reaching out to embrace me. I jumped down into the courtyard and ran to him, tears coursing down my face.

'Father! Father!' I cried. 'Father!'

Don Vicente stopped at the threshold of his house. He surveyed me with disdain. 'I should have known. Carrion like that always spawn more filth.' The features of his face drew together in lines of deep disgust. 'Better to wipe out the breed *and* the seed.' He waved his hand in a command to the soldiers. 'Let the beggar's son dance the same jig.'

The lieutenant nodded to the groom.

'Bring another rope,' he said.

Chapter Five
Zarita

My papa, Don Vicente Alonso Carbazón, was known in our town of Las Conchas for his strictness in dealing with criminals, but I had never seen cold hatred on his face until that dreadful summer's day.

Alerted by the commotion, he came to the door of our house. Upon hearing Ramón's garbled version of events, he hit the beggar so hard on his mouth that the man's face burst open like a pomegranate. The sight of the poor man grovelling at his feet seemed to inflame rather than appease Papa. I didn't know that he was maddened by grief and had lost control of his emotions.

'Papa.' I laid my hand on his arm, but he shook it off and dismissed me. And then: horror! They sent for a rope.

I looked to Ramón to stop this, but he was still furious at being humiliated in the church and having to call on the soldiers for help to capture an emaciated peasant. The grim satisfaction in his manner told me that there was no use in appealing to him to stay Papa's hand.

I staggered back into the doorway of the house as the soldiers did their grisly business. Then a young lad leaped down from the wall of our compound and ran towards us, sobbing and crying for his father.

One of the soldiers grabbed him by the waistband of his breeches and swung him up into the air. 'Another one for the crows to pick the eyes from!' he laughed.

And I heard vile words spew from my papa's mouth, and

he gave an order for the lieutenant to hang the boy alongside his father.

'*Papa!*' This time my screech got Papa's attention. 'The boy wasn't there in the church. He has nothing to do with this.'

'These thieves and brigands work in gangs,' Papa told me. He tried to usher me into the house. 'You are too young and innocent, my daughter, to know such things.'

'He is only a child.' I pulled on my papa's shirt sleeve. 'Look at him. Think of your own newborn son.'

'I have no son.'

I stared at Papa. And then I saw what I hadn't noticed before. He was not properly dressed and the hair of his head and beard was unkempt.

'Your baby brother died half an hour ago,' he explained.

'Oh, no!' Hot tears flooded my eyes. Nine pregnancies my mother had endured since my own birth, with all but this one ending in miscarriage. And now the boy child was dead. No wonder Papa was beyond reasonable thought.

'Father! Father!' Outside, the boy was still fighting and reaching out to touch the dead body of his father swinging from the tree. But the noose of a second rope went around his neck and the lieutenant slung the long end over the same branch.

'You'll be with your father soon enough,' one of the soldiers mocked the boy. He began to pull on the end of the rope and the boy rose into the air, his legs kicking as his father's had done not five minutes since.

I went down on my knees before my papa. 'Think of Mama,' I pleaded. 'She is a kind and gentle mother to me. She wouldn't want this boy to die as well as her own son.'

My father's face crumpled and he placed both his hands

over his face. 'Your mama—' he began, but he could not continue. Sobs racked his body.

'Mama?' My breath froze in my lungs. 'Mama! Tell me that nothing has happened to her. Please, Papa. Tell me that she lives.'

'She lives,' he said, 'but it will not be for long.' He hesitated, and then he motioned to the lieutenant. 'There has been enough death in this house for one day. I will spare the boy's life, but see to it that he is sent away where I will never see him again.'

In some disappointment the soldiers let go of the rope and the boy crashed to the ground, where he lay twitching, stunned but alive.

'We are on our way by ship to join the armies of Queen Isabella of Castile and King Ferdinand of Aragon in siege against Granada,' the lieutenant told my papa. 'I'll give this beggar rat to the first galley boat we meet at sea. He can be their slave until the end of his days.'

Papa nodded, but I barely heard this exchange. I pushed past him and ran upstairs to my mother's bedroom. My aunt Beatriz knelt beside the bed holding my mother's hand. And I knew then that my mother must be dying, for my aunt was an enclosed nun who did not leave the cloister except in extreme circumstances. She had set her nun's veil aside and I could see how her features resembled my mother's, except that she was much younger. She was talking to her sister in a soothing voice, telling her how her trials of this life would soon be over and she would find her rest and reward in Heaven.

'No!' I said in a loud voice. 'Don't say that! Mama cannot die.' But I could see that my mother's cheeks and eye-sockets had sunken in, and that every breath was a struggle for her.

The local priest, Father Andrés, who stood at the end of the bed, tried to offer words of solace, but I was not to be placated. I shouted at him, 'I went to the shrine of Our Lady of Sorrows to pray and make an offering so that everything would be well. I lit a candle and asked that Mama recover after the birth. But there was no one in Heaven listening to me.' I was angry with his God who could ignore my pleas for mercy. 'What use was there in my doing that?' I berated the priest. 'It was all for nothing. Nothing!'

Father Andrés' face registered shock at my words but he spoke to me kindly. 'You mustn't say things like that, Zarita. It's wrong to question the Will of God.'

My aunt Beatriz said, 'Zarita, child, compose yourself. Your mother is slipping away. Let her do so in peace with quiet words of love from you.'

But I could only think of my own need, my own sorrow. I cast myself across Mama's body where she lay on the bed and wept tears and cried, 'Do not leave me, Mama! Mama! Mama! Do not leave me!'

Chapter Six
Saulo

On that day I swore revenge.

My dazed stupefaction at the stark and savage cruelty of the actions of this day was replaced by venomous hatred. Before the soldiers bound my hands and hauled me through the streets to the docks, I stared hard at the face of the man who had wronged me and vowed I would not forget him.

I, Saulo, of the town of Las Conchas, determined that I would bring ruin upon Don Vicente Alonso Carbazón. I would chop down the tree upon which he'd hung my father. I would scatter his livestock and poison his wells. I would burn his house to the ground with goods and furniture inside and trample them to dust. I would destroy him, his wife, and all his children.

Chapter Seven

Towards midnight, inside the church of Our Lady of Sorrows, situated high on a cliff overlooking the Mediterranean Sea, the candle lit that morning by Zarita del Vicente Alonso de Carbazón flickered and went out. Twenty minutes later the life of her mama also ended.

Thus the simple lighting of a candle began a chain of events that would bring disaster to those involved that day.

PART TWO
THE ARRIVAL OF
THE INQUISITION

1490–1491

Chapter Eight
Zarita

Whereas my papa, the magistrate, was respected in the town of Las Conchas, my mother had been loved.

People came onto their balconies to watch her coffin-carriage, drawn by four black plumed horses, make its stately way through the streets, and they threw down flower petals as it passed below them. In addition to being known for her almsgiving, Mama had helped fund a hospital to care for the destitute; here her younger sister, my aunt Beatriz, had established a religious nursing order. Heavily veiled, with the cowled hoods of their habits drawn up, the nuns stood in front of the building to watch the funeral procession, and many of the poor lined either side of the dirt track leading to the cemetery on the hill above the town. My father's business friends also attended, and a smattering of the local nobility. Although rich, my father was not of noble blood, but he was respected by the lords and dons, who knew that he enforced the laws that kept them safe.

The family tomb had been opened up and Father Andrés, robed in black, stood by the cemetery gate. He was attended by a dozen acolytes wearing white surplices over black cassocks and holding long thick candles of solid beeswax. I'd heard my father order our farm manager, Garci Díaz, to have these made up specially,

'Spare no expense,' he'd said. 'I want the best for my wife and my son.' Papa's voice had broken on this last word, and Garci had reached out his hand to my father but then withdrawn it before touching him.

Now, the driver of the hearse pulled the horses to a halt and the priest came to meet us.

And suddenly it was real for me. I'd lived the last few days crying and sobbing through what seemed like some awful nightmare, but as I watched the men lift the wooden coffin that contained Mama's body and that of my newborn brother, raw emotion wrenched through me. The blinding sun pierced the black lace of my mantilla and seared my vision. It was true; not a dream from which I would awaken. My mother was to be put in this cold dark place and she would not return home to us again.

The horses shifted, and their bridles and traces jingled. Father Andrés began to intone the prayers for the dead: '*Out of the depths have I cried to thee, O Lord. Lord, hear my voice.*'

He led the way. The men with their burden followed, and then family and friends. I could hardly move. My old nurse, Ardelia, put her arm around my waist to support me. She was weeping sorely, for she'd been my mother's nurse too and had loved her, as did any who knew her. Her shuddering sobs reverberated through me. Tears began to fall again from my own eyes.

Years ago, when he'd first been appointed magistrate, my papa had our family vault erected with pillars and statues and the fancy embellishments that he deemed fitting for his new rank. At this moment he appeared to be carved from the same cold marble, and my heart chilled as I saw his face. He'd spoken less than a dozen words to me since the day my mother died.

Ardelia had tried to explain: 'Don't fret about your papa's manner,' she told me. 'It's understandable that he behaves in such a way. You resemble your mother so much that it must break his heart to look upon you.'

In my darkest thoughts I fretted about this. Had I been a boy, would Papa be so grief-stricken? Did he mourn his longed-for baby son more than he did my mother? He hadn't made any sign of sympathy to me to help me bear my loss. That first evening after Mama had passed away I went to kneel by his chair, as I often did of an evening, when he would stroke my hair and talk to me. I'd intended to share my thoughts with him; we might speak of Mama and console each other. But as I knelt down before him to rest my head in his lap, he stood up abruptly and left the room.

'*Remember, man, that thou art dust, and unto dust thou shalt return . . .*'

We paused at the entrance to the tomb, and I noticed that there was another here who had not addressed me or given me any kind words since the day of my bereavement.

Ramón Salazar stood to one side. I tried to catch his attention but his gaze was moving among the group of women. I fancied he couldn't look at me because it pained him to see me in distress. His face was composed in a suitably sombre expression. Yet I could not help noticing that he wore a brand-new braided doublet with pin-tuck stitching in the Italian style. It was velvet of deepest black and topped with a collar of crisp white lace, and I wondered if he'd had it specially made for the occasion and chose the style to set off the aristocratic angular lines of his cheekbones. All at once I needed the warmth of a man – this particular man who had so often professed his undying love for me. I desired his nearness and craved his strength to uphold me. Impulsively I stepped towards him. He glanced at me and then studied my appearance more closely, and I saw a glimmer of faint distaste on his face. I clutched at him and tried to lay my head upon his chest.

He took a tiny pace back.

Not one week before, Ramón would have sought any excuse to enfold me in his arms, but now he patted me and then let his arms fall down to his sides. Was I so ugly in my grief? I knew that my eyes were red from weeping, my cheeks blotched, my mantilla askew as I'd scratched and pulled at my hair.

Ardelia drew me gently to her.

'*May hosts of Angels lead you into Paradise . . .*'

The time of committal had arrived. The immediate family entered the mausoleum. The smell of death came into my nostrils. The lights flickered on the walls.

'*Eternal rest grant unto her, O Lord.*'

Eternal rest.

Eternal.

For ever.

I would never ever see Mama again.

I felt my senses swim and a thundering rush in my head.

Then a strong arm was around my back and a hand supporting me under my elbow. For one giddy second I thought it was Ramón, come to my aid. But it was my aunt Beatriz who was beside me.

'Zarita' – she spoke firmly in my ear – 'conduct yourself with dignity. Your mama would have wished it so.'

I bit down on my lip hard enough to taste blood in my mouth. I straightened up and raised my head high. On my other side Ardelia squeezed my hand in her large one and whispered words of encouragement in my ear.

They buried Mama with the baby boy she had borne; the boy my papa so desperately craved to follow in his footsteps, to manage the farm and be the proud landowner he was, and perpetuate his name.

Afterwards Papa was weary; he retired to his room as soon as we returned from the cemetery. I was left to tend to the mourners who had accepted the offer of food and drink at our house.

Ramón was there, but he did not stand by my side as he might have done to help me greet and then thank the guests for attending and offering their condolences.

My aunt Beatriz took her leave after an hour or so. She held me close as she kissed me. 'To lose one's mother is an overwhelming grief, Zarita. Know that I share your sorrow, and take comfort from that. I loved my sister, for she was beautiful both in looks and in nature. She is gone – we hope to a better place than this.' Aunt Beatriz made the sign of the cross upon me, touching my forehead, my heart and across my breast. 'Each person upon this Earth has their own hill of Calvary to climb, Zarita. I can give you but small advice. Do as your mother would have done. Continue her work. Be active in your almsgiving. Take an interest in those amongst us who have nothing. Think if there is anyone who might need your help. You may not even know who this might be. It is up to you to make time to seek them out.'

My aunt's words were in my mind as I began to light the lamps against the darkness. Everyone had left apart from Ramón Salazar, who sat slumped a chair by the window, a goblet dangling from his hand. His handsome face was flushed with too much wine and I recalled how happy we'd been only two or three days since. A sudden memory of the beggar in the church came to me, and with it another thought. I went over and sat in the chair opposite Ramón and asked him if he recalled the words the man had uttered. But Ramón didn't want to remember that day. He tried to brush aside my question and was reluctant to engage in conversation about the incident. Yet I persisted: the shame of my lack of charity to the beggar, which had caused the resulting horror of his execution, made me speak.

'He mentioned a wife,' I said.

'What?' Ramón drank more from his wine cup. His words were slurred. 'Who has a wife?'

'The beggar man,' I repeated. 'When he asked me for a coin in the church, he mentioned that his wife was ill, and that she could die.'

'So?' Ramón yawned.

'I just wondered' – I spoke very quietly – 'what might have become of her?'

Chapter Nine
Zarita

Among the people who came to our house to pay their respects in the weeks and months after the death of my mother was the Countess Lorena de Braganza. She was twenty, barely five years older than me, and only a passing acquaintance of our family, yet she stroked my papa's arm as if she were his closest friend, and purred sympathy into his ear.

At first I paid her little heed, for I was concentrating on business of my own. I had discovered a purpose, a special mission of charity to undertake. I thought that if I could find the beggar boy's mother and rescue her from poverty, then I could be like my own mama and thus be near her even though we were parted. I saw myself now as an angel of mercy and hoped that it would expiate my wrongdoing and relieve some of the guilt I felt over the beggarman's death.

I knew that I would have to go into the poorer areas of the town, and for that I must have an escort. I did not ask Ramón Salazar. I didn't think he would agree. In any case his visits to my home lately often coincided with those of Lorena de Braganza when his attention was distracted by her conversation and witty remarks and there was no opportunity for me to speak to him privately for any length of time.

I decided to ask help from Garci, our farm manager. I was confident that he would assist me: from when I was small, he could refuse me nothing. He and his wife, Serafina, had never been blessed with children of their own, and they doted on me, so I could beg him for anything and he complied with my wishes. Therefore I was taken aback when I outlined my proposal to him and he shook his head,

'No, Zarita. I won't go with you into the slums of the town. We cannot have another incident where your father has to deliver quick justice to control thieving and violence.'

'Justice!' I exclaimed. 'That wasn't justice, Garci. You cannot mean you condone what my papa did in hanging the beggar without trial!'

'I wasn't there,' Garci replied slowly. 'As you know, I was at the horse fair in Barqua.' He looked at me severely. 'And that's the main reason why you were able to leave this house accompanied only by Ramón Salazar. Had I been here, I wouldn't have opened the compound gate for you to go to the streets of the old port without more of an armed escort, and a female companion.'

I shifted uncomfortably. Garci had guessed that I'd taken advantage of the turmoil in the house that day: my papa and Ardelia and Serafina, our housekeeper, had been occupied with Mama, and I'd managed to slip out with only Ramón as escort.

'So, as I didn't witness the situation myself,' he went on, 'I will not judge your father's actions. He is a rigorous man.' He paused. 'And now that your mother has passed away, who is there to remind him that mercy is a God-given virtue?'

Garci had mentioned my mother and I saw his weak spot. 'Mama would have wished this,' I told him. 'She would have been horrified by the beggar's death and would have made sure that his wife was cared for.'

A few moments elapsed before Garci replied. 'You are right,' he said. 'Your mama would have done as you say. I will go with you and look for this poor woman.'

* * *

32

Garci understood that Papa was not to know of our expedition, so we waited until one afternoon when he was absent from home visiting the Countess Lorena's father's house in the nearby hills. I had the sense to dress very plainly, wearing neither fine clothes nor jewels and covering my hair and face completely. Yet before we even reached the outer *barriadas* of the town Garci wished to turn back. 'These slums are no place for any decent person,' he told me.

'Yet there must be good people who live here,' I said. 'Or do you think poverty makes one indecent?'

This was one of my mama's sayings: she would defend her almsgiving to my papa when he declared that, in his opinion, the poor brought misfortune upon themselves. Garci didn't reply; just made a clicking noise with his tongue to show his disapproval.

'I am performing an act of charity,' I added in order to appease him, and then I reminded him, 'My mama would have approved.'

'Ah, your mama,' Garci said. 'She was the kindest of women.' He sighed, and I knew that there were tears in his eyes.

After this he became more amenable to knocking on doors to enquire the whereabouts of any ill woman who might be on her own now, but had previously had a husband and a boy looking after her. However, we could find no trace of the woman. A great number of doors remained shut against us, and the people who did open up were hostile and suspicious. Finally Garci stopped in the middle of the street.

'It's hopeless,' he said. 'The beggar's wife could be in any room in this warren of buildings, too sick to rise up to answer our knock.'

There was an old woman sitting on a doorstep. I went over and knelt in front of her. 'Mother,' I said.

She looked at me with the milky white eyes of the very old. 'I have no daughter,' she replied. 'I had three fine sons, but they went to war and I never saw them again.'

'I call you Mother because I have none of my own,' I told her softly. The old woman reached out a gnarled hand and touched mine. I asked her if she knew of anyone who might be the woman we were looking for.

'I know of no such person,' she said.

In despair I sat back on my heels. Then I felt in my purse and took out a coin and gave it to her. She hid it in a fold of her clothes, and I wondered how many days' bread that would give her.

As I stood up, the old woman raised her head and said, 'There may be one who will help you. There is a man, a doctor, who lives in the house at the far end of the street. He goes to those who are sick but have no money.'

I walked quickly to the house she'd indicated. But when we drew near to the door, Garci hung back.

'This is the house of a Jew,' he said, and he blessed himself.

'It is the house of a doctor who might be able to help us,' I replied.

A man opened the front door and stood in the entrance. 'Why do you stand in the street staring at my home?'

Garci put his hand on my arm to guide me away. The man seemed amused by this and made to go back inside. I spoke up briskly. 'I'm looking for a woman, a particular sick woman.' I described all I knew of the beggar's wife.

'I may know this person,' he said. 'Some days ago I was called by a neighbour to attend to a woman whom she'd heard was gravely ill. The neighbour told me that the woman's husband had been executed and her son had disappeared and not returned home, so she had no one to look after her.'

I pulled out my purse and thrust it at him. 'You can have any money you need to buy her medicine and pay for your time in curing her.'

He tilted his head on one side and surveyed me. 'Is this an act of mercy, or of a guilty conscience?' he asked quietly.

Behind my veil my face flushed in shame and I could not reply. Had he heard the story of how the beggar had died? Did he recognize me as the daughter of the magistrate?

'No matter' – he seemed to come to a decision – 'I will take you to her.'

The woman lay on a pallet of straw in a room on an upper floor of a house two streets away. When we entered, something scuttled away in the far corner, and she stirred and cried out.

The doctor bent over her and spoke to her rapidly in a language unknown to me. By the door Garci blessed himself again.

The doctor raised her up and helped her drink some liquid from a bottle he'd brought with him. Then she sank back down on the makeshift bed, her body not much more than a bundle of bones.

'Does she know you?' the doctor asked me.

I shook my head.

'It wouldn't make any difference,' he said. 'She's too far gone to recognize anyone.' He pulled the blanket about her and then ushered us outside.

Again I offered him my purse.

'The woman is dying,' he said. 'I cannot cure her. No one can. The good neighbour brings her some thin soup and water each day for she can eat nothing else, and I come every evening and give her enough opiate to ease her pain for the night.' He raised his eyes and stared at my own behind my veil. 'Keep your money and spend it where it might help the living.' He glanced up and down the street. His implication was obvious.

When he left us, I turned and spoke to Garci. 'We must take her out of here, away from the vermin in this building.'

'If you move her she will die,' Garci said.

'She will die anyway. Let us help her die in better conditions than this.'

'We cannot bring her to your house!' Garci was aghast.

I knew this. My papa wouldn't suffer such an intrusion.

'No,' I said, 'we'll take her to a peaceful place where she will be cared for with love.'

So it was in the convent hospital of my aunt Beatriz that I helped nurse the beggar's wife during the last weeks of her life.

Chapter Ten
Zarita

At one time I might have been able to wheedle my papa into allowing the dying woman to be brought to our house – if only to the servants' quarters above the stables – for I'd often coaxed him into agreeing to something he'd initially forbidden. But my influence was waning as the Countess Lorena de Braganza became an almost constant presence in my home.

I was so preoccupied with my visits to the convent hospital to nurse the beggar's wife that it was a month or so before I realized the extent of Lorena's power over Papa. One day I came home to find that our black mourning curtains had been taken down from the windows. I went to speak to Serafina and found her packing them away in boxes. Her face showed no emotion when I asked her why she had done this. 'It's only the middle of December,' I said. 'Not yet six months since my mother died.'

'Not my idea,' she replied. 'Your papa ordered me to do it.' Then she added, 'I believe the Countess Lorena de Braganza might have suggested it to him. She thinks the house needs cheering up for Christmastide.'

Then, to my fury, I discovered that Lorena had been giving Papa advice about me – saying that I was not capable of running such an important household as his; that I was a foolish girl and had shown myself to be such by going out without a chaperone; that the incident in the church had sullied my reputation; and that I should be sent to a convent or married off quickly to anyone who'd have me. I also noticed that she cultivated Ramón Salazar, talking to him at length, pretending to solicit his opinion on the most trivial matters. I wasn't overly concerned, because Ramón had always been besotted by me and only me. For over a year he'd pursued me and sought out my company, so much that he'd become like a family member. I believed it was only a matter of weeks before he spoke to Papa, and our families came to an arrangement for us to be betrothed. I thought that Papa would approve the match. He wanted me to be happy but he also had aspirations to nobility, and Ramón Salazar was of noble blood. My father was conscious of his status in society, and his daughter's engagement to Ramón Salazar would further enhance his own reputation.

In the spring of the following year a wedding *did* take place. But it wasn't for my marriage to Ramón that awnings were erected in the compound of our farm, arches of flower garlands strung over the doorways of the house, long tables laid with white linen cloth and sparkling glass, and a priest summoned to perform the ceremony.

It was for my father.

My father and his new wife, the Countess Lorena de Braganza.

I'd disliked her from the moment I saw her; this countess with her glittering eyes and tiny tongue that darted between small teeth. A tongue as sharp as a pin and eyes that poked and pried. A tongue that was never still for long, and occupied itself with spiteful remarks and sly suggestions. Eyes that roved over our ornaments and silverware, assessing their value, and calculated the price of all they saw.

The gowns she wore were cut low to expose the swell of her bosom, and she leaned forward and laughed when men in her company spoke, even if their remarks were not in the least amusing. For my part I sat and glared at her, for she made the silliest conversation I'd ever heard.

I didn't want her to marry my father. I didn't want her in my home. On the evening when their engagement was announced, she came to my room to speak to me and I saw that she was wearing my mother's coral necklace. The necklace my mother had promised I should have on my sixteenth birthday.

'That's mine!' I snatched it from her neck. The catch broke and the beads flew off, spilling and rolling onto the floor.

She screamed, and her maidservant and my father came running.

'Help me,' she whined, holding her throat. 'Zarita took some kind of fit and scratched me.' She took her hands away to reveal a bright red weal across her neck.

I gasped. She had pressed her own nails into her neck to make the mark!

'I didn't do that,' I told my papa.

'Zarita, you must apologize at once,' said Papa.

I stood in sullen silence.

'At once!' Papa repeated. 'Or I will lock you in your room until you do.'

I muttered an apology, but when my father left, I said to Lorena, 'You made that mark yourself.'

To my surprise Lorena did not deny my accusation. She waved her maid away and said, 'You can hardly complain when you employ the same methods yourself to get attention.'

'I don't know what you mean.'

'Of course you do.' She looked at me intently. 'I saw you when you came from the church the day the beggar was supposed to have assaulted you.'

39

'He *did* touch me.' I spoke in a low voice, for that day was one I preferred to forget.

'Oh, I know he did. You were heard to say so.' Lorena smiled, and it was not a friendly smile. 'He *touched* me.' She imitated my voice. 'This man actually *touched* me.'

I recoiled from her. How did she know what I had said inside the church of Our Lady of Sorrows?

'Everyone believes the beggar attacked you,' Lorena went on, 'yet your bodice was not torn nor your gown damaged in any way. What was the poor man trying to do? Get a penny from your purse or snatch your money from your hand before you put it into the coffers of the priests? Good luck to him, I say. I've spoken to the fop who was supposed to be your protector, Ramón Salazar, and found out what took place. I expect Ramón was happy to play along with the pretence of an assault – it made him look more of a man to leap to your defence. But it was you' – Lorena came near and hissed into my face – '*you*, in your spoiled petulance, who caused a man to go to the gallows because he brushed against your hand.'

I fell back under her onslaught, the truth of her words stripping my soul and leaving me naked.

'So don't put on airs with me, my dear sanctimonious miss. You must live with your own deceit and the consequences of your actions.' Lorena lifted her skirts to leave. 'An innocent man is dead. And his son too, most likely.'

Chapter Eleven
Saulo

But I was not dead, though for many days and nights after I left Las Conchas I wished that I were.

The soldiers soon dispersed the crowd gathered outside the compound of Don Vicente Alonso Carbazón. Then the lieutenant yanked the end of the rope and hauled me out through the gate and off down the road. His soldiers came after, cuffing and kicking me all the way to the dockside until they found the ship on which they'd booked passage.

'I'm minded not to have the bother of finding a galley boat to take him as their slave,' the lieutenant commented when I tripped and fell as we mounted the gangplank. 'I don't want this piece of scum still with me when we join up with the armies of the king and queen.'

'We can throw him overboard with the rubbish when we quit the harbour,' one of his soldiers suggested.

The lieutenant grunted. 'Mayhap his corpse would float ashore and reveal what I'd done. I'll not risk the anger of that magistrate if he finds out I've killed the boy when he decided his life should be spared.'

The ship's captain, who'd been listening to the discussion, said, 'If we don't meet a galley boat between now and next landfall we'll tie him to the anchor as we drop it down.' He winked. 'We can say he got caught up in the rope and was dragged over the side.'

He grabbed me by the hair of my head, ran me across the deck and flung me into one of the open holds. I hurtled downwards, banging arms, legs and head against bales and boxes of cargo until I ended up on the solid wooden floor. I'd scarcely recovered my breath when the opening was battened down and the light extinguished. This was a new terror for me. I'd not experienced extreme darkness before; blood surged behind my eyes as I groped wildly with outstretched arms to find something to hold on to. The ship shuddered as the sailors made ready to leave. Suddenly the world moved under my feet and the whole universe slid away. My mind was seized by a fit, for I'd never been on a boat. The sails cracked out and we began to make headway from port. As the wind lifted, the swell took us, and the spine of the ship arched against the sea. Terrified by the primeval power of the elements, I lurched about, screaming in the blackness, while the ship rose and fell, borne up and brought down by the hand of an unknown gigantic creature. I vomited, heaving up again and again, until dry retching cramped my stomach with excruciating pain, and I fell down, exhausted, and lay there whimpering.

There was no way of knowing daylight from darkness. Deprived of sight, the noises I heard sounded loud in my head – the scuttling of rats and the groans and creaks of the wooden hull as it forced its way through the water. I thought the planks would split asunder and I would be cast into the Deep, so I cried out piteously for my mother and my dead father.

And within the ferment of my mind I saw them again: my mother left alone, sick and dying, and my father, his body swinging at the end of rope.

The weather worsened, the ship pitched and rolled, and the huge boxes and bales of the cargo began to shift. I feared I should be crushed. I crawled about until I found a space among the struts, where I wedged myself along the ribs of the ship. There I clung, while outside the waves battered and crashed, seeking a way in to overwhelm me. I remained without moving for what seemed like days, until I became so weak I could hardly lift my head.

It was the red-haired soldier, the one who'd shown my father mercy by pulling on his legs to cut short his last agony, who finally opened the hatch. A rope came tumbling in and he swung down to take a look at me. Then he bawled to whoever stood at the top waiting for his report, 'He lives!'

He returned a few minutes later with a jug of water. 'Twice now you have cheated Death,' he said as he forced open my mouth and poured the water down my throat, 'for, by rights, you should have expired here for lack of water.' He went aloft again, coming back with a hunk of bread and a wineskin full of rough red wine. Breaking the bread into pieces, he moistened it with the wine and watched as I managed to swallow. He grunted as he helped me stand up. 'Perhaps you were born under a special star.'

A small Spanish trading galley boat had been spotted on the horizon. The lieutenant didn't care if I was alive or not: even if I had been only halfway dead he'd have dropped me over the side, but now he saw that he might trade me for some alcohol to drink.

One barrel of cheap wine was all I was worth. And even that was grudged. It was more in a spirit of appeasement that the captain of the galley boat agreed to the exchange, for the soldiers had their weapons trained on the smaller boat. Sitting low in the water with no covered quarters for the occupants, the galley boat was only partially decked, with rough sailcloth rigged as an awning at the stern and down each side to protect the rowers from the elements. It had one light cannon mounted up front, and although the few crewmen

carried long knives in their belts, they'd be easily overcome by
a larger ship equipped with guns and armed men.

The deal was done in minutes, and Fate decreed that I
became a galley rat.

The red-haired soldier came to bring me up to the deck.
The hatch opened again and sun dazzled in my face. I
squinted up as the rope came down.

'If you cannot climb the rope by yourself, then hold the
end and I'll haul you up,' he said, not in an unkind way.

I stumbled forward to grasp the swinging end of the rope.

Something glinted in the light.

Caught between the bindings of a cargo bale was a knife.
It was long and thin-bladed: the kind a woman would have
for paring vegetables. I found out later that it was of the type
used by government officers to cut the twine as they affixed
the customs seal on taxable goods. It must have become
entangled as the cargo was inspected before loading the ship.
I reached for it, and in a moment I had it in my hand. But
where to hide it? Bending over to block the view of anyone
watching from above, I slit the inside waistband of my
trouser and slipped the knife inside.

They strung a line from the military ship to the galley
boat to transfer the wine barrel. One end of a rope was tied
around my waist and the other end to this line. Then I was
tossed overboard. The galley crewmen hauled me across the
gap, but I was too weak to climb the rope up to their boat.
The ship cast off and I would have been caught in the under-
tow – except I heard a voice from the galley boat shout out,
'Pull him in! Pull him in!'

Spluttering and coughing, I landed on the wide platform
at the galley stern.

The man who had given the order approached me. He

was a strange sight, dressed in black shirt, breeches and hose, topped with a three-quarter-length fitted jacket of peacock blue, thickly embroidered with silver thread. He wore a fanciful hat, the like of which I'd never seen before – black with a purple feather and more elaborate than those worn by mummers and performers who play out pageants in town squares at Christmas and Eastertide. Buckles glinted on his shoes while flurries of lace frothed at wrist and neck. A golden hoop dangled from one ear, and on his tanned face he'd grown a moustache and a tiny goatee beard. By his dress and manner I knew he was the captain. He bent over me and stroked my hair.

I snapped my head to the side and sank my teeth into his hand – whereupon he struck out at me with the bamboo cane he carried. I backed into the corner like a wild animal. The galley captain sucked on the bite I'd given him but, far from being angry at my attack on him, he nodded in approval.

'I like a lad with spirit,' he said. 'It means you'll be good in battle and able to fend off any trouble from our own oars-men. Too scrawny to take an oar now, but you'll grow into it if we feed you.'

I stayed where I was for the remainder of the day, cowering in the corner. That evening we anchored in shallow water off an island so that the oarsmen could rest and eat. The captain gave me a piece of the goat that was roasting on a brazier set up on the deck inside an iron firebox to cook food. I ate greedily. It had been weeks, months perhaps, since I had tasted meat.

The captain chuckled as he watched me gobble the food. 'Go easy, boy. You don't look as though you've had a decent meal all your life. Stuffing yourself like that so quickly will only bring on bellyache.'

He was right. Within an hour I was doubled up with colic as the unaccustomed food worked its way through my gut. To my surprise, some of the rowers came to look at me. I had imagined that every oarsman would be chained to their benches, but in fact only a small number, eight in total, were slaves or criminals imprisoned in this way. The rest, more than twenty free men, had elected to do this work. I was to discover that men from various countries became galley rowers by choice. It was considered a skilled, if arduous, job, but the pay and the pickings could be very rewarding: in addition to basic wages the oarsmen received a percentage of the cargo profit and any other booty that might fall their way. On this particular galley, under the command of Captain Cosimo Gastone, the food was nourishing: meat, fish or fowl, with plenty of bread, strong cheeses, and fruit and honey washed down with wine. The oarsmen were exceptionally well-fed as the captain believed they should be in peak condition.

I was to find out in the most brutal way that our very lives depended on the fitness of the rowers.

Chapter Twelve
Saulo

The next day the captain turned me over to the oarsmaster, who was called Panipat. He was a gigantic bear of a man with thickly muscled arms, chest and legs, clad only in a pair of cut-off leather breeches with a whip and a long knife tucked into the waistband. Every inch of his exposed skin was covered in black and blue tattoos, up to and over the surface of his shaved head. Tied around his wrist was a cord from which hung the key that released the chained slaves.

'It's time for you to meet Panipat.' Captain Cosimo poked his cane in my back, prodding me ahead of him along the narrow wooden boardwalk that ran down the centre of the boat.

Panipat was kneeling in the bows talking to the crewman who looked after the cannon positioned there. This was where the small group of chained oarsmen was situated, just behind the prow. The four on one side were Arabs, probably captured in battle and bought by the captain in some slave market. The four on the other side were men from different places who'd been sentenced to the galleys for the severity of their crimes. If we were attacked and our cannon targeted by enemy fire, then they would be first casualties. There was evidence that the whip had been used across their backs and shoulders. I shuddered as I saw them, each one shackled to his bench, for I knew that in time such would be my fate. Unending and for ever.

Captain Cosimo announced our presence. 'If it pleases you, most noble oarsmaster, I have a new galley rat for you.'

Panipat stood up, towering above me. He smiled, a terrifying grin exposing broken and missing teeth. 'Let's have a look at you, little Rata.' He fastened his hands around my throat and swung me up into the air so that my face was barely an inch from his. 'You will obey my every command,' he spat into my face. 'At once and without question. And if you ever give me any trouble, I'll flay every inch of skin from your body. Do you understand?'

The blood thrummed in my brain. I could not even gurgle a reply.

'Answer me!'

He shook me so hard I thought my ears would explode and my eyes pop from my head.

The captain tapped him on the shoulder with his cane. 'The boy cannot answer you as you have your hands around his windpipe.'

Panipat released me to crash onto the deck at his feet, where I croaked, trying to regain my breath.

The captain looked down upon me. 'I think Rata understands you very well,' he observed with some sympathy in his voice.

Panipat explained what he wanted me to do.

At either end of the boardwalk was a barrel of fresh water. I'd to replenish these every evening from a large cask kept below the boardwalk, which was where our cargo was also stowed. I was given a deep wooden ladle with a long handle. During the day I had to fill this ladle and go up and down the boardwalk giving water to the oarsmen as they required it; one side on the way up, the other side on the way down. Most of the freemen had their own water bottles, which I'd also to keep refilled. I myself was allowed a drink each time I made my turn at the stern end of the boat.

We set sail in the early morning. The wind was fresh, so for the first hour or so we were carried along mainly by the sail and I merely walked up and down doing as instructed. The men made bawdy remarks and stuck out elbows to trip me up, but I was used to name-calling and agile on my feet so this didn't bother me very much. Then the sun rose higher, the wind dropped, and we were out on the flat of the water with no shelter in sight. On the raised platform in the stern Captain Cosimo sat under an awning studying his maps and plotting the course. The freemen and even some of the slaves had padded their bench seats with bundles of sacking, and they used strips of it to protect their shoulders and heads from the rays of the noonday sun, for the strip of awning above was not wide enough to cover them adequately. I found that I needed to move faster to keep up with their demands for water. Soon they were shouting insults at me for being too slow.

All the while, Panipat had been squatting on a stool in the stern, just below the command platform, calling out the stroke and directions as the captain, who also acted as pilot, gave instructions for the heading we must take. Now the oarsmaster stood up.

'Ho! Rata!' he shouted to me. 'Give one mouthful to each man as you go up and down. No more than that, or I'll skin you alive!'

The oarsmen began to complain. Panipat now set them a strong, steady stroke, and sweat streamed from their foreheads and forearms. Those slaves and criminals without any cover across their backs suffered most, and on each circuit I made, one older man kept begging me for more water. I shook my head, but finally, in desperation, he clenched his teeth on the wooden rim of the ladle and tried to swallow the whole lot, slopping water onto his face and torso. Panipat leaped up, stamped down the gangway and struck him across the cheek with the butt end of his whip.

'Dog!' he yelled. 'No one on this boat disobeys my orders!' He hit the man again with the flat of his hand, then turned and began to walk back to his place.

Quickly, taking advantage of the fact that Panipat's back was to me, I raised the ladle to my own mouth and gulped down an extra mouthful of water.

Panipat swivelled in an instant.

I didn't see the lash, only felt the sting on my fingers as it curled around my hand and wrested the ladle from my grasp. I stared, dumbfounded, as the ladle spun onto the deck, and then saw, too late, Panipat raise his arm again. A crack – and ah! the vicious bite as the metal tip on the end of the lash sliced across my chest, splitting the thin fabric of my shirt.

'That was but a warning, Rata,' Panipat snarled. 'I could strip your flesh to the bone if I had a mind to.'

Some of the rowers laughed, for to them any diversion was entertainment. Panipat laughed too as he strode back to sit upon his stool. 'Now, Rata, you will drink no more water today until I say you can.'

The day went on. The fierce sun of late summer burned the sky and the sea around us. A light breeze arose and they rigged the sail again. I felt my stomach heave as a bout of sea-sickness gripped me, but I knew not to beg leave to go and vomit over the side. I swallowed the sickness. Bile choked my throat but I carried on with my duties. By mid afternoon I was feverish and staggering with heat and exhaustion. Panipat slowed the stroke to give the men some respite. But

I don't think he would have shown me any mercy had one of the most experienced freemen not intervened. This man was known only by his birthplace, Lomas, an inland village near Málaga. He beckoned for me to come to him and then handed me his water bottle.

'Drink,' he commanded me. 'Else you will collapse and none of us will have any water.'

I glanced fearfully at Panipat, but the oarsmaster turned his head away and pretended not to see.

'Drink,' Lomas repeated. 'I am Panipat's best rower. He knows that so he'll not gainsay me.'

I drank the water and managed to stay on my feet for the rest of the day. By nightfall, when we had still not made port, Panipat ordered the men to rest their oars and went to consult with the captain.

'Sit down here by me, boy,' Lomas told me.

I slumped gratefully down on the gangway next to his rowing station. He peeled back the torn strip of my shirt and, taking a jar from a bag stowed under his bench, unscrewed the lid and held it out.

'Spread some of this salve on your cut,' he said. 'It'll help it heal.'

I thanked him, and then, as I gave him back his jar of ointment, I asked, 'Are we lost?'

'Not completely' – Lomas smiled – 'for it would be hard for even our crazy captain to get totally lost on a closed sea like the Mediterranean, but we should have made landfall an hour ago. It'll be tomorrow before we see Alicante.' He stood up and spat into the sea. 'He was born in Genoa, our captain Cosimo, and the Genoese are supposed to be the best sailors, but this one can hardly find the North Star on a cloudless night.'

'Then, if you are a freeman, why sign on with this boat?' I asked him.

'Captain Cosimo's main skill is his business sense. He employs only four crewmen: the quartermaster, who also looks after the cannon and other weapons, the carpenter-cook, the sail-maker, and the oarsmaster, Panipat. Our captain's a wily trader, making more money than other captains who are better navigators. Although he gambles his own share away before we've even left port, the crew and the freemen rowers make good money on this boat. We take cargoes between ports as far east as the Balearic Islands, and then west to Cádiz on the Atlantic coast of Iberia. Captain Cosimo has an expert nose for what goods are wanted where, and who will pay the most for them. For striking a bargain there's none better. It's a pity he's never going to retire a rich man, but I am able to work two years and then have six months leave to go home and live off my earnings with my wife and son.'

The crewman who was both carpenter and cook had lit coals in a brazier set up inside the firebox in the prow, and began to cook the fresh fish the quartermaster had caught with his harpoon throughout the day. I was surprised by how hungry I felt. Earlier, when I had been retching, I'd thought never to eat food again. Lomas saw me rubbing my belly.

'Ha! You remind me of my own son. Always hungry. You have his colour hair and are about the same size. What age are you?'

'I'm not sure,' I said. 'Sixteen – maybe older.'

Lomas whistled between his teeth. 'Then you've not been fed regularly in your life, have you?'

I said nothing. There was no need to. I knew that I was

undersized and skinny. I could see how thin my arms and legs were.

'Go to the cook. Tell him I sent you, and ask him to give you a piece of fish to eat.'

I stood up. Lomas stretched out his hand to detain me. He pulled me close and spoke quietly in my ear. 'Listen well to what I am going to say to you now, little Rata. You must take care each evening when the men are eating their meal and are allowed to leave their station to see to their toilet. Be sure that you're not alone in any part of the boat at that time. Don't drink any wine. No matter how much the others try to persuade you. Some of these freemen would slit your throat for their own amusement; they're worse criminals than those kept chained in the prow, and more likely to cause you harm than any of the Arab slaves.' He reached below his rowing bench and pushed his bag of belongings to one side. 'You may sleep under there at night.'

Lomas was right. Some of the men did try to encourage me to drink wine, and some looked at me in a way that made me very afraid. At mealtimes I never strayed far from Lomas's rowing bench, and with his protection I was safe – for a while at least. I suffered recurring nightmares, watching my mother starve to death, and living every moment, again and again, of my father's brutal end. My days were occupied obeying the commands of Panipat and keeping lookout for danger to my person. The constant thought bearing me up was the prospect that some day I might avenge my parents.

Meanwhile, one aspect of this new life was better than my old one. I was no longer perpetually hungry. Each day I ate enough to fill my stomach. The weeks passed and we went from autumn to winter. And although the weather became rougher, I acquired a sailor's balance so that my insides no longer heaved at any motion of the boat upon a restless sea. Exposure tanned the surface of my skin, and underneath I could feel hard muscle forming in my arms and legs and across my chest. Working outdoors made me healthier than I'd ever been, and I grew taller – so much so that the captain was eventually forced to find me a larger pair of breeches to wear. I was pleased about all this, yet I knew that each day I developed brought me closer to the time when I would be fit enough to replace one of the older, weaker men and take a seat at the oars in the prow. When that day arrived, Panipat would put a metal cuff around my foot and link the ends together. The chain that kept the slaves in their place on the benches would be attached to this and there I would be, doomed to row for the rest of my life. My fate was sealed, with no hope.

Except . . .

In the waistband of my breeches I still had the knife.

Chapter Thirteen
Zarita

There were horsemen in the yard.

When I heard the clatter of hooves, I rose from where we were finishing our midday meal to go to the window and look out.

'Zarita!' Papa chided me. 'You're not a child any more. You mustn't run away from the table because you are bored and hear some distraction outside.'

He was sitting with his hand over Lorena's. It pained me to see them so entwined, and I would have used any excuse to leave the table where Papa liked us to eat one meal together every day.

Two months ago, when she became my father's wife, Lorena hadn't taken my own mother's place at the opposite end of the table to him. From my earliest days I had sat between my parents and we'd conversed as a threesome and shared our stories and jokes as we ate. After their marriage Lorena had positioned herself at my father's right-hand side, and during the course of the meal she frequently nuzzled against him in the most shameless manner.

Although I was glad Lorena wasn't in Mama's place, she was in the chair that I'd once occupied, and I considered it an affront that she hadn't consulted me before deciding where to sit. At mealtimes I felt left out, for she never included me in any of her conversation and frowned in a disagreeable manner whenever I attempted to join in.

'Horsemen have arrived,' I informed my father. 'One is a monk and the others wear a very strange livery.'

My father gave a tut of irritation that he hadn't succeeded in calling me back to my place. Then he dabbed at his mouth with his napkin and came to the window.

'See . . .' I pointed to where the men were dismounting.

Six horsemen. A monk in a black habit accompanied by five soldiers in tunics with an unusual green cross emblazoned on them.

I heard Papa's intake of breath.

I looked at him curiously. 'Who are they?'

There was a silence and then my father said tightly, 'The soldiers wear the livery of the Holy Inquisition.'

Behind me I heard Lorena gasp aloud. 'I will retire to my room,' she said quickly.

'No, wait,' Papa ordered her. 'I've been told that it's best to be completely open with these people. It will be obvious that they've disturbed us at our meal. Therefore my wife and my daughter would be seated at table. They may join us if they wish to eat.'

There was an imperious knock on the front door. My father bade me sit down and then went himself to open it, intercepting Serafina on the way.

'I will see to these visitors,' he told her. 'I believe them to be representatives of the Inquisition.'

Serafina gave Papa a scared look and made the sign of the cross on her forehead.

'Don't be afraid,' he told her as she scurried back to the kitchen. 'And tell the other servants that they have nothing to fear.'

I'd followed him to the doorway of our dining room, looking out from there into the hallway.

'You should sit back down,' Leonora called out to me. 'I think your father will be annoyed if you are not

56

sitting at table when these men enter the house.'

I flung her a scornful glance over my shoulder. 'As if I would do anything that you advised me!'

Lorena shrugged. 'Very well,' she said, and her voice held a note of amused satisfaction. 'Go your own wilful way, Zarita.' Then she added in a lower tone, 'And suffer the consequences.'

I was determined to stay where I was. And then I thought better of it. The arrival of these men had affected my father in a peculiar way. I wasn't sure how he would react to my disobedience now, and perhaps Lorena had deliberately suggested I should obey him, knowing that I would do the opposite. I considered my stepmother sly enough to engineer a situation to get me into trouble. As I heard Papa open the front door, I fled back to the table and took my place.

Lorena did indeed look disappointed as I sat down again. We heard voices in the hallway and then footsteps approaching. Before the men entered the room, Lorena lifted her shawl, which was draped over the back of her chair, and wrapped it close around her upper body, concealing her cleavage and exposed arms.

'Father Besian, I am pleased to welcome you to my home and to meet my family.' Papa was speaking to the monk who had entered the room ahead of him. And my father, always so in command of himself and others, made a nervous gesture.

Father Besian surveyed us in turn. Lorena nodded her head and lowered her eyes, but when the priest's gaze reached mine, I refused to meekly bow my head as she had done. He looked at me with dark, deep-set eyes. Having been so protected by my mama, I'd only heard vague stories of the trials of the Inquisition via the servants, and couldn't see why we should fear everyone associated with it. It was true that this monk appeared stern, but to me the expression on his face was one of concern.

'I am available for confession while I am here,' he said, 'and I would expect everyone within the household to confess. With honesty and clarity,' he added.

'You must excuse us if we are out of sorts, for this is a house of mourning,' my father told him. 'We still grieve for my wife, who died almost a year ago.'

'I see.' Father Besian thought for a moment and then said, 'It can be that the loss of a loved one causes a person's faith to falter. It benefits the soul to confess these doubts and failings to a priest.'

My own heart fluttered then, for I recalled my sharp words to our local priest, Father Andrés, about the lack of mercy that God had shown when Mama passed away. And like my father and Lorena, a wariness came over me.

Father Besian seemed to sense this. He looked at me again. 'Who is this young woman?' he asked.

'That is my daughter, Zarita,' said Papa.

'And this other lady?' The priest indicated Lorena.

'Lorena.' My father cleared his throat. 'My wife.'

'A second wife?' The priest raised an eyebrow. 'Yet you said it was not yet a twelvemonth since the girl's mother passed away?'

'Zarita is my only child ... a daughter. You will appreciate, Father Besian' – Papa spread his hands, palms upturned – 'a man must have a son to inherit his land and goods.'

I heard Lorena grind her teeth. Was this because my papa was saying that he had married her merely because of her breeding ability? I wondered. An unfamiliar sensation of sympathy for her came to me, but I dismissed it and would not entertain it in my mind.

As quickly as possible Lorena excused herself and left the room. When she reappeared soon after, it was to go to Benediction at the local chapel. I was astounded. Not since May began had Lorena sallied forth late morning or early afternoon. She considered the rays of the summer sun too powerful, and worried they might spoil her complexion. She was dressed in black; not the stylish black of heavy lace and rustling taffeta that she sometimes wore, but plain dark materials, and her face was heavily veiled.

Father Besian looked at her in approval and then addressed me. 'Do you not attend Benediction?' he enquired mildly.

'Zarita works at her studies during the day,' my papa interjected before I could say anything. He gave me a firm look. 'And it would be best that you go and do so now, my daughter.'

It had been so long since Papa had called me 'daughter' that I felt tears well up. He gazed at me steadily, and there was a plea in his eyes that made me get to my feet and obey him.

I went to my room and took out some of the books that Papa had bought for me to read when he'd been more interested in my education. It was difficult to concentrate. The arrival of these men had changed the atmosphere in the household; an unnatural silence had settled everywhere. I went to the window. Usually the servants would sit and chat in a shady spot for an hour or so in the heat of the afternoon: Serafina and the maids preparing vegetables while Garci and the stablelad, Bartolomé, polished horse brasses or engaged in some other leisurely task. Now, the only people around were the soldiers accompanying Father Besian, who were sitting under a tree eating some food. As I watched, Bartolomé, who was Serafina's nephew, came from the stables with a bucket in his hand and a happy smile on his face. He wandered over to the well and began to draw water from the tap. One of the men beckoned to him; immediately he dropped his bucket, spilling the water he'd collected, and trotted over to stand in front of him: Bartolomé was completely without guile and would do anything to please you. Although he was nearly twenty, his mind was as that of a child. My mama had told me that people like Bartolomé are God's most precious beings. They are sent upon this Earth to remind us of how we must never lose our sense of wonderment. I smiled as I saw Bartolomé nodding furiously and waving his arms in the air. I thought, *If these men seek to pry into our affairs, they'll get no sense from him.*

Later my old nurse, Ardelia, brought me my evening meal. 'Your father has asked that you remain in your room until bedtime.'

'Why?' I asked her.

She lowered her voice. 'Don Vicente Alonso thinks it best that you and Lorena are not about while these men are visiting us.' She glanced at the ceiling. 'Father Besian will sleep in the attic above you. He requested the plainest room in the house. The others are in the servants' quarters above the stables.' She gave a wry smile. 'No one there is speaking to them.'

'Apart from Bartolomé,' I said. 'I saw him talking with them earlier.'

'What!' Ardelia looked alarmed. 'I must tell Serafina and Garci.' She hurried from the room.

As I picked at my food, my sense of unease increased.

Why was Ardelia so upset, and why would Papa want me to stay in my room? I didn't mind so much, partly because he'd imposed the same restriction on Lorena, but also because I was glad that I wouldn't have to encounter Father Besian. The thought of confessing to him was beginning to trouble me.

Not long after I retired for the night I heard the creak of floorboards above my head. Father Besian must be preparing for bed. If I had to confess to him, what should I say? I hated Lorena. That was a sin against charity. I'd spoken of it in confession to our priest, Father Andrés, and he'd said it was to do with the great grief I still carried at losing my mother. These bad thoughts were natural feelings but I must try to overcome them. He assured me that they would go away, especially when Lorena produced a baby, as no doubt she would in time. Then I would love that child and would become more accepting of Lorena. I had told Serafina, Garci's wife, that I disliked Lorena very much, and she, with her head bent over the oven, had muttered: 'Not as much as I do.' That had made me laugh, but I knew it wasn't the response my mama would have liked, and I was trying to live as she would have wanted me to. When my spirits were low and these thoughts threatened to overcome me, I would go the convent hospital of my aunt Beatriz and seek balm for my soul.

'Zarita,' she told me, 'you are not your mama. She was a very saintly woman, more holy than I could ever be, and I am a nun. Although this order I have founded is not recognized by any formal papal decree, I have made vows to myself and to God to uphold certain virtues. But know this: I was not the good child of my family. In my youth at court I led a wilder life than was deemed proper for a girl of those times.

My sister, your mama, was the one who had true goodness within her. There are few people who can emulate her.' Aunt Beatriz drew me to her and stroked my hair and reassured me. 'You must be you, Zarita. You can be none other.'

But in addition to this, weighing on my conscience was the other, greater sin, the one I had confessed to no one: the occasion when I had turned my face away from God because He had not spared the life of my mother and my baby brother. I'd buried that deep within me and never spoke of it. A sweat was upon me now. These thoughts came crowding into my mind as the footsteps of Father Besian paced above my head. I'd a strong conviction that if I held anything back from this priest in confession, then he would know. I resolved to avoid confessing to him. Faintly, I heard the chant of prayers as he recited his evening office, and I drifted into restless dreams.

Chapter Fourteen
Zarita

The next morning Lorena and I were quietly eating breakfast in the company of Father Besian when Papa strode into the room.

'I would speak with you!' He addressed the priest sharply. 'In private,' he added.

Father Besian regarded him calmly and said, 'There is nothing that cannot be spoken of in front of your wife and daughter.'

'Did you order these leaflets to be distributed and posted all over my town?' Papa unfolded a piece of paper he had crushed in his hand and handed it to the priest.

Father Besian took the paper from him, laid it on the table and smoothed it out carefully. 'I did,' he said.

I tilted my head to try to read the words that were written on the paper.

'You have no right to call upon the people of this town to inform upon each other in this way.' Papa's voice was tense with anger.

'On the contrary,' Father Besian replied, 'the Chief Inquisitor, Tomás de Torquemada, grants me, as an appointed officer of the Holy Inquisition, the right to do this. It is vital that we root out heresy and discover if any so-called converts from Judaism still hold to their former religious practices. I have discovered that there are both Jews and Muslims living in this town. These are potentially corrupting influences. In my experience, good results are

63

obtained when we call upon the local population to be vigilant and to bear witness for us.'

'There are half a dozen Jewish families confined to the poorest area near the docks and a few Muslim fishermen who tie up their dhows at the furthest jetty. They have never given us any trouble. I am the magistrate of this town: you should have spoken to me before issuing proclamations that might incite unrest.'

Father Besian drank from his cup of warm milk and then set it down before him. 'The only unrest that will follow my announcements will be in the hearts of the unbelievers.'

'What do you propose to do when these informants come forward?' Papa demanded. 'You'll find that there are those who will take the opportunity to avenge an old score or to tell lies about a neighbour against whom they hold a grudge.'

'I will question them very carefully. It will go hard for those who have no genuine reason for their denouncements.'

'You intend to hold an Inquisition in the town?'

'I do.'

'Last night you told me that you were only passing through, and asked me to provide accommodation while you awaited passage on a ship to take you to Almería.'

'I have changed my mind,' Father Besian said.

'And where do you propose to carry out your inquiries and trials?' My father laughed. 'This is not a large town. The gaol is the basement of a one-storeyed building, and my so-called magistrates' court is the small room above.'

Father Besian leaned back in his chair. He looked out of the window at our farm buildings and then about him within the room. He smiled. 'You have a well-appointed house here, Don Alonso. I will use your premises to do this work of God.'

'My house! My home!' Papa reeled back in shock. 'No! That is impossible! I won't allow it.'

'I would remind you, Don Vicente' – the priest's voice became icy – 'that as the local magistrate you are bound under law to assist me in any way I see fit.'

Father Besian stood up, and I was suddenly conscious that he was taller than Papa, and although much thinner, his presence seemed to make my father shrink.

'The Holy Inquisition was set up by Queen Isabella of Castile and King Ferdinand of Aragon as part of their glorious mission to establish the Christian kingdom of Spain. These two monarchs of separate kingdoms within Spanish territory are united, both in marriage and in mind, to bring all other provinces and districts under their command. Even now they fight to take Granada from the Infidel and will replace the flag of the crescent moon with that of the cross on its ramparts. I, as an officer of the Inquisition, have the absolute authority of both Church and State. You should not try to hinder my work in any way. I have often found that those who do so usually have some wrong or ... in-consistency ... within their own family that they are trying to conceal.' The priest stared at my father and then abruptly swivelled to encompass Lorena and myself in his gaze.

The effect of these words on Papa was startling. The colour went from his face as the light does from the sky when a cloud passes across the sun. He staggered and gripped the back of a nearby chair to support himself.

'In addition to posting notices in the town,' Father Besian continued, 'I now tell you that I intend to proclaim the same message to everyone from the pulpit when I preach at mass tomorrow. I expect to see you, your family, and every member of your household in the front pew of the church. An important person like the magistrate should set an example to the rest of the community.'

And so we were there the next day – myself, Papa and Lorena – suitably and soberly dressed. Before the service began we were joined by my aunt Beatriz. A veil was draped from just below her eyes, and the cowl of her habit covered her head and the sides of her face, as was the custom of her Sisters of Compassion whenever they appeared in public. Papa had distanced himself from his sister-in-law when he married Lorena. Although my aunt never made known her feelings about him taking a new wife so soon after her sister's death, I believed this to be the cause of their estrangement. Now he bestowed upon her a look of gratitude for her presence with us this morning.

While Father Besian railed against heretics, Jews, Muslims and all those he claimed threatened the Church and the safety of Spain, we composed ourselves to be quiet and attentive.

'Our monarchs, the virtuous Queen Isabella of Castile, joined in matrimony with the equally righteous King Ferdinand of Aragon, have made it their intention to unite the kingdoms and provinces with a view to making Spain one unified country. This will be one Catholic, unified country. To do this they have waged a holy war, a crusade, against all unbelievers. Even now, they struggle in battle against the Infidel who holds the Kingdom of Granada and who will not yield it to the Christian rule of their majesties. For too long Muslims have sullied Spanish soil and they will be driven out. But there are others in our midst, here within our hearts and homes, whom we must also drive out. These are the ones who can be most deceptive. The ones we must uproot as you would a weed that chokes the good and fruitful plants.'

Father Besian had come to the part in his sermon where he exhorted the congregation to be vigilant, and to inform him and his officers of the Inquisition of any perceived wrongdoing.

'You must report any instance that might be an act of heresy. Even if the one you suspect is a brother, a sister, a parent or a child. Yea,' he thundered, 'be it a daughter who suspects a father, or a mother her own son! I charge you upon pain of mortal sin. You risk the eternal damnation of your immortal soul if you remain silent.'

My aunt took a deep breath. I risked a glance at Papa, and saw his jaw tighten and his face become grim. To one side were our household staff. They sat up in their pew, straight-backed in an attitude of apprehension. All except Bartolomé, who was doing what he always did in church: smiling, playing with his fingers and singing softly to himself. But when the sermon went on much longer than usual, to everyone's consternation he began to make popping noises with his mouth.

Father Besian raised his voice to cover the interruption.

Bartolomé was equal to the challenge. He filled his cheeks with air, and before Serafina could prevent him, smacked both hands against them, causing the loudest farting sound heard in the church for quite some time. A giggle rose in my throat. I pretended to cough. Beside me I felt my aunt's body shaking and realized that she too was suppressing laughter. Father Besian's features suffused with anger. He paused and glared down from the pulpit at Bartolomé, who cheerfully waved up at him. Bartolomé often waved to Father

Andrés as he preached, and Father Andrés would wave back. Bartolomé saw no reason why this priest should be any different from the other. Father Besian cut short his speech and swept down the pulpit stairs.

After the service had ended we went outside in the fresh air, where we breathed more easily. Serafina grabbed Bartolomé by the hand and, followed by the rest of our servants, walked off quickly. I noticed the rest of the towns-people did too; after church services they normally lingered to chat with relatives and friends and catch up with news, but this time they hurried away.

'Who was that idiot who interrupted my sermon?' Father Besian approached us, obviously still outraged by the affront to his dignity.

Papa opened his mouth to reply but my aunt Beatriz interrupted smoothly, 'He is indeed a true idiot, most reverend father. A simple-minded soul. You are so wise to have realized that. There are those, less perceptive, who would have been discomfited by such bad manners.'

Father Besian turned shrewd eyes on my aunt. 'You are . . . ?'

My aunt bowed her head. 'Beatriz de Marzena, of the convent hospital run by the Sisters of Compassion.'

'As a nun, should you not be within your monastery walls?'

'I am sister to Don Vicente Alonso's first wife and, as such, part of his family. He informed me that you wished all his family members to attend your preaching this morning.'

Father Besian surveyed my aunt and then said, 'The Sisters of Compassion? I've travelled through many parts of Spain doing the work of the Holy Inquisition and I've never heard of such an order of nuns.'

'I myself founded the order,' my aunt informed him. 'We

have not yet been formally recognized by our Holy Father the Pope.'

Father Besian gave a sharp intake of breath. 'Indeed?' he said.

It was my papa's turn to interrupt. 'I have business to attend to.' He addressed himself to the priest. 'If you have no need of me at the moment . . .'

Father Besian waved his hand in dismissal. My aunt took the opportunity to step aside. She spoke to my papa: 'Perhaps Zarita could accompany me to the convent and visit for a while?'

Papa nodded – in some relief, I thought.

Within days the town of Las Conchas changed utterly.

The shops and market stalls became much quieter. There were fewer people on the streets, and those that were about looked suspiciously at each other. Strangers, previously welcomed as bringers of commerce, were now shunned. The Arab fishermen left quietly in their dhows and did not return. It was said that the Jews had shuttered their houses and remained inside all night and for most of the hours of daylight. We'd been a sleepy town with a moderately busy harbour. Now we were a closed community where neighbours scarcely greeted each other as they passed in the street. My own home was a place of silence. To my annoyance I was prevented from taking my daily ride. Garci told me that Papa had given instructions that neither Lorena nor I must leave the compound without his permission. To avoid meeting Father Besian I usually went to the convent hospital after mass each morning and spent most of the day there in the company of my aunt and her nuns.

'Apart from any moral consideration about whether one

religion has the right to impose its rules upon another, the actions of this Inquisition are ruining business in our town,' my aunt's deputy in the convent, Sister Maddalena, commented as we sat one day in the parlour making bandages and chatting together.

'Hush' – my aunt glanced towards the door – 'good Sister Maddalena – one never knows who is listening.'

Sister Maddalena, a large and bustling woman who had raised a family of ten children and buried three husbands before deciding to dedicate her life to God, tossed her head. 'Our sisters here would never betray each other, but anyway, I don't care who hears when I speak the truth. People are afraid to go out, to trade, to do anything that might be construed as against the Church. They fear that some busybody will report them.'

I lowered my voice and said, 'Do you believe that one religion has no right to impose its rules upon another? Surely it's our duty as good Christians to evangelize.'

'The king and queen would have it so,' my aunt replied carefully. 'Queen Isabella, in particular, believes that she does the Will of God in her mission to bring all Spain together under the banner of the Cross.'

'And what would gentle Jesus say to her actions in setting up an Inquisition that can use torture when questioning the accused?' Sister Maddalena snorted in derision.

'She thinks it better to suffer on Earth and attain a lasting peace in Heaven.'

Sister Maddalena leaned closer. 'My cousin in Saragossa said that she had six criminals castrated, then hung, drawn and quartered in public in front of the cathedral.'

'She is a monstrous queen,' I said with passion, 'who

could allow so many to be condemned to such a terrible death.'

'Not so monstrous,' my aunt mused. 'She is intelligent and has a kindness in her, especially for her family and friends, but when she sets her mind to do a thing, it will be done. You have to appreciate that when she inherited the throne of Castile from her half-brother, Henry, she took over a ruined kingdom. During his reign Henry had granted favours to wicked and venous men and women. The court was solely a pleasure-seeking institution with scant order or justice dispensed. Bandits roamed the land. There was no rule of law. Isabella changed that, but such was the level of corruption, even amongst the nobles, that she had to be ruthless to do it. She's been criticized for her lack of mercy, but now the peasants can till their land and reap their harvests, and travellers can move about the highways unmolested.'

'You are acquainted with her!' I exclaimed.

My aunt nodded. 'I was. Years ago I spent time at court and I know that her life has not been easy. As a young child she was held in a grim castle, guarded and guided only by an austere and, some say, deranged mother. She was influenced by her confessor, a zealot, and I think this is still the case.'

'And do you believe in this mission of the queen and king?' I asked curiously.

My aunt opened her mouth to reply, but paused and tilted her head in an attitude of listening. She raised her hand and put her finger to her lips. Then, rising swiftly, she went and opened the door.

Father Besian stood there.

'I was about to knock,' he said without hesitation.

My aunt deliberately looked beyond him into the

corridor. 'How rude of the sister who is portress for today not to see that you were conducted personally to my rooms.'

'I dismissed your sister portress,' the priest said, 'and told her that I would find my own way to your parlour. I hope you don't mind?'

'Not at all,' my aunt replied pleasantly. 'Do come in.'

Sister Maddalena stood up. 'I'll bring an infusion of mint to refresh you.'

The priest settled himself in a chair. 'You have spent a comfortable day . . . talking?' he enquired of me.

'My niece and I pray as we work, Father,' my aunt replied.

'Ah, yes, Zarita is the daughter of your sister, isn't she? I can see the likeness between you, especially in the eyes.'

'Zarita resembles her mother, and we were said to be so like as to be twins. But tell me, Father' – my aunt drew her veil across her face – 'how are your investigations progressing?'

Father Besian frowned. 'The Muslims have fled and the Jews are sequestered. As they should be,' he added. 'We have been asked to arbitrate in petty squabbles, but as yet no one has given us any serious information regarding heretical practices.'

'I am glad to hear that.'

'I am not.'

'No?'

'No. It merely means that there are things deeply concealed.'

'Might it not mean that there is nothing amiss here?'

'I have noted lax practices.'

Sister Maddalena returned with the glasses filled with hot water which had been sweetened and infused with leaves of mint.

Father Besian took the glass proffered to him. 'See, here

is an example of which I speak. The tray upon which you serve these drinks is of Arabic origin with writing in their language. Do you know what it means?'

There was a heartbeat of a pause.

'I could not say.'

My aunt had spoken an untruth – if not a direct lie, then certainly a statement made with the intention to deceive the hearer – and I wondered how she would justify it to her confessor. I knew that my aunt had taught herself Arabic in order to read certain texts so that her patients might profit from the superior knowledge she claimed the Moors had of medicine.

'So it could be some blasphemous saying written down within the walls of a monastery and you are ignorant of it.' As my aunt said nothing, the priest held up his glass. 'Also this drink is of Moorish origin.'

My aunt blinked. 'I think you will find that the queen herself drinks an infusion made from mint leaves.'

Father Besian waved his hand. 'It is not for someone like you to know what the queen does or does not do. These are instances of irregularities in this town that cause me disquiet. Your order has no standing within the Church – that in itself could constitute heresy, combined with the lack of respect shown at Holy Mass by the servant of your brother-in-law.'

My aunt got up and went to a cupboard in the corner of the room. From there she took out a box, which she unlocked. She handed Father Besian the scroll it contained. 'This is the deed of the grounds of this convent hospital, the land having been granted to me by Queen Isabella that I might found a hospital and a group of sisters to nurse the needy. The founding of my order was done with her approval. Our petition for recognition, supported by the queen, lies in the Vatican awaiting the attention of the Holy Father.'

Father Besian's face tightened as he read the parchment.

My aunt returned it to the box and closed the lid with a hard snap. 'If this is all you can find wrong in our town,' she said crisply, 'an adult with the mind of a child and a nun drinking a glass of mint tea, I fear that you might make a mockery of the work of the Inquisition.'

The priest's body vibrated with suppressed anger as he stood up to leave. 'I see these transgressions as indications of deeper wrongs. But I am a patient and determined man and will uncover that which people wish to hide.'

There was silence between my aunt and me as Sister Maddalena showed Father Besian out of the convent. I was afraid and I did not understand why.

My aunt came up to me and put her lips close to my ear. 'Ensure that your housekeeper, Serafina, serves pork for dinner tomorrow.'

I smiled in puzzlement. 'My father has no liking for pig meat. It's never served in our house. You know this.'

My aunt did not smile at me in return. Instead she looked very grave and continued in the lowest of voices, 'Listen, Zarita. Do as I tell you in this matter. Tell your father privately that I said that this is what must happen. He will understand and comply.

'Now' – she relaxed her face and took my arm – 'let us walk in the garden for a while and you can put flowers on the grave of the beggar's wife. I know that you like to do this.'

Strolling along the neat pathways of the walled garden soothed me, and I spent some time praying at the graveside I tended. But on my way home my peace was shattered. I was met by Serafina, who came running up to me as I approached our compound. She was weeping and wringing her hands.

'Whatever is the matter?' I asked her.

'They have arrested him! The soldiers of the Inquisition have taken him away to be questioned.'

'Who?' I asked her. 'Who has been taken to be questioned?'

'My nephew,' she cried, and burst out weeping afresh. 'They have arrested Bartolomé.'

Chapter Fifteen
Saulo

'*Pirates!*'

The sail-maker who acted as lookout swung round from his position on the prow of our boat to face the captain. 'Pirates!' he yelled again.

'Could we parley with them?' Captain Cosimo demanded. 'What flag do they fly?'

'None,' came the reply. 'That's how I know she's a brigand. And by the size of her, she has more guns and men than us.'

I stopped with my ladle half in the water barrel and gazed out to where the lookout was pointing. The sail of a larger galley was now visible on a southerly heading.

The captain swore and banged his fist on the table in front of him, causing his jug of water to tumble over and roll down to the lower deck.

I leaped forward, picked it up and refilled it from the barrel. I glanced at Panipat, and the oarsmaster nodded for me to return it to the captain.

A conversation rose amongst the men.

'Have they noticed us?'

'Have they changed direction?'

'Why would they bother? Can't they see we're a trading vessel?'

We could see the other boat more clearly now, a long low craft with double-banked oars. And we also saw that they were altering course to intercept us.

'Perhaps they think we carry gold instead of almond oil and salted fish.'

'They'll be looking for good rowing men to sell as slaves,' I heard Lomas say. He called out to Panipat in a louder voice, 'Get us out of their way, oarsmaster! I want to see my boy again, not be taken for a slave or done to death in a fight we cannot win!'

The rest of the freeman rowers joined in with shouts of agreement:

'Go on, Panipat! Use the whip if you must!'

'Set us a pace and let us row away from here!'

The pirates were lowering their sail to prepare to give chase using their superior oar power.

Captain Cosimo chewed his lip. He studied the map before him. I followed his gaze and saw a wooden disc placed to the left of a large island with the letter M inscribed on it – Mallorca? He glanced up again. 'How is she gunned?'

'Three,' shouted the lookout. 'A full cannon and two culverins, with perhaps another piece in the stern.'

'Outmanned and outgunned,' the captain muttered.

As if to confirm his observation, there was a dull roar as the enemy fired off a warning shot to tell us to heave to.

The ball landed well short, but caused an outcry from the crew. They began to curse the captain for his incompetence in setting a course that had brought us into the path of a predator. They blamed the lookout, saying it was his fault, as if by noticing the pirate galley he was responsible for conjuring up this enemy out of thin air. And when they had vented their initial anger, in fear some turned to prayer, imploring God and other supernatural powers – even the spirits of the sea – to come to their aid.

The captain peered at the map in agitation. 'We need an island – somewhere, anywhere we can run aground.' He raised his magnifying glass to his eye and brought his face down close to the map.

'There,' I said, and pointed to the drawing of a tiny island west of the wooden disc that I guessed represented our boat.

'Well spotted, boy,' he murmured. 'I've found an island!' he said more loudly. Then he called a heading to Panipat.

The crew had crossed dangerous waters before. Our sail was already stowed, the men in position, and Panipat was alert, waiting for the captain's order. The oarsmaster roared out his instructions and our boat turned round. The oarsmen set to, and we sped away across the sea. The men laughed as the gap immediately widened between the two boats.

But the island was further than it had looked on the map, and when I glanced back, the pirate boat was in hot pursuit. The sight of this boat travelling at such a pace behind us, the oars flashing back and forth, fascinated me. I couldn't tear my gaze away. There was no time to give the men water, and anyway, I had enough difficulty in keeping my balance, for our boat had never travelled at this speed before. As I watched, I could see that the pirate ship was closing.

The oarsmen couldn't afford to glance up or break their concentration. The wellbeing of everyone on board depended on their skill and effort now. Panipat, stalking along the wooden boardwalk, was aware of the danger. He cracked his whip above their heads, growling and snarling as he sought to lengthen their strokes, to maximize their energy. The muscles rippled on their torsos. With each backward pull they half stood, and on the return movement bent their knees to almost a sitting position, using the cushion or padding under their haunches to slide their bodies forwards swiftly.

'Pull!' the oarsmaster bawled. 'Pull! Pull! Pull away, you dogs! You misbegotten sons of Adam! You vile carcasses of rotten meat!' Panipat appeared to grow in stature, and flecks of white spit sprayed from his mouth, along with the abuse he poured onto the heads of his men. 'You scum!' he berated them. 'You driftwood! You flea-ridden vermin! You rat-infested corpses of decaying mould! You pieces of useless flotsam! You worthless, good-for-nothing woman-defilers. You blasphemous, rabid snakes that crawl on your bellies and eat the dirt of the Earth! Pull! Pull, I say!'

My mouth hung open in shock. Sweat ran from each man's face and chest and back and legs and arms.

'Pull!' Panipat bellowed. 'Pull! Or I'll kill you where you stand!'

And they pulled: for their oarsmaster, for the captain who kept them well fed and well paid, for the cargo they hoped to profit from, for their pride in their work, for the race to outrun the enemy, they pulled for their very lives.

Our boat shot through the water, swift and true like an arrow in flight.

Yet still the enemy boat gained on us.

'Pull!' Panipat's voice was hoarse. His whip cracked out. 'Pull! Pull!'

The captain was hopping from one foot to the other in a dance of fretful rage, but he knew enough to stay out of Panipat's way and not to interfere.

I saw that the slaves were pulling hard, in time with the rest – which they didn't always do. And it wasn't fear of Panipat that made them do this, I thought, for at this moment he could not single out one man to punish; it must be that they believed their fate would be worse in a pirate ship than if they remained with Captain Cosimo. I saw then that the occupants of our boat had some respect for this man they called the crazy captain, even though they believed his navigation was faulty.

But it appeared they were right in their belief, for still there was no island in sight, and the toll of the hard push began to tell upon them.

Lomas shouted out, 'Where are we going? Don't send us all the way out over the Ocean Sea to the lost lands!'

'An island,' Captain Cosimo shouted back confidently. 'The boy saw an island on the map. We'll take refuge there.'

The horizon remained empty, and suddenly I knew how the captain had felt in times past when the promised port had failed to appear. There *had* been an island on the map, well marked: I had seen it. Was it merely a fancy of the map-maker or an inaccurate sighting by some mariner? If it existed, where was it?

The captain saw my concern and he spoke rapidly. 'The lady sea is deceptive. She's like a woman: when you first meet her she is pleasant and calm, she sparkles with light and she bewitches you; but then she reveals herself as fickle and will not yield up her secrets.' He slammed his hand down upon the table and damned all mapmakers to the eternal fires of Hell.

The pirate boat loosed another shot, and this time the cannonball sang above our head and landed with a splash on the port side.

Our boat slowed by an infinitesimal amount as discouragement entered the minds of the men. And all Panipat's fury could not bring them back to their previous rate. I felt the slackening action under my feet and my breath shortened in fright, for like the rest of the crew I knew that I wouldn't fare so well under the command of a pirate commander.

'Land! Land!' The lookout, crouched down for safety in the prow, had risked raising his head. He yelled and pointed. 'The island! I see it! Praise God and His Holy Mother!'

The men shouted in joy and gave thanks to the saints in Heaven. I could feel tears start to my own eyes and I swept them away with my hand.

We swung a degree south. The oarsmen renewed their efforts. Then they began to call out:

'An island!'

'There is land in sight!'

'Praise be!'

'Is there a beach?'

'Don't steer us onto the rocks, Panipat!'

By now the lookout and the oarsmaster were working together, guiding us through the ring of a semi-submerged reef towards a sandy shore.

My heart continued to thud. I didn't understand how this would make us safe. I could see that the island was un-inhabited – no village or sign of any building, and no citizens to whom we could appeal for help – and the pirate galley was closing fast.

'What can we do?' I asked the captain. 'We cannot fight them ashore any more than we could at sea.'

'We'll run her aground,' he told me. He was now busy rolling his maps and picking up his navigational aids. The carpenter-cook was throwing his tools into a sack while the rest of the crew gathered up the flint box, harpoon and spears, and other vital pieces of equipment. 'You go and fill each man's water bottle as quickly as you can. Go!' the captain shouted in my face as I stared at him stupidly.

I raced to do his bidding. Panipat was already kneeling

beside the chained slaves, using the key on his wrist to unlock their shackles.

I glimpsed an expanse of white sand. And then the boat jarred home and I was pitched forwards.

'Out! Out!' Panipat yelled, and the men jumped out and dragged the boat up the sand as far as they could.

The pirate boat was only a few hundred metres away.

'Every man for himself!' the captain bawled. 'Run! Run!'

He reached for his splendid coat of peacock blue, and I stooped to get it and hand it for him. It was heavy. He would run less well with that on his back. His vanity must be great, I thought, that he should want to keep it when it might cost him his life.

'Here,' he said to me. 'You'll be swifter than I am.' He dropped the maps into a long cylindrical case made of stiffened leather, oiled to be waterproof, and gave it to me to carry. 'Go to cover first,' he told me, 'and then make for the highest point on the island.'

The oarsmen grabbed the possessions they kept under their benches, each sailor having a bag of bits and pieces with their private goods. I had nothing but the map case, but I knew that it was important. And in a childish way I felt pleased that I'd been given charge of it.

We scattered, running away from the ship towards the dense foliage of the island's interior.

'I'll light a fire on the beach when they've gone,' Captain Cosimo called after his men. 'You'll see the smoke and know to come out.'

'Pray that there are no cannibals here,' I heard one man say as we plunged among the trees.

'Or if there are, let's hope they're not hungry.'

Relief at being out of the firing line of the enemy made them joke.

The captain followed me, slashing out in front of him and on each side with his bamboo cane. Where the men ran in any direction to get the most cover of the trees and bushes, the captain told me to make for higher ground. Labouring under the weight of his jacket, the captain toiled upwards until he was some distance from the beach and a good bit higher.

'Let's find out what they're up to.' He took up a position behind a tree and handed me his spyglass. 'What do you see?' he asked me.

I focused on the pirate ship, which had come to rest just outside the reef that protected the bay where we'd run aground. 'They've launched a skiff with some armed men aboard. Will they wreck our boat?' I asked, afraid that we might be marooned and left to die of starvation.

The captain shook his head. 'I don't think so. It's not a religious or political war with that kind of crew. It's commerce; their way of doing business. They steal and sell.' He looked through the eyeglass himself and then handed it back to me. 'I'm hoping they only want our water. Our cargo is of little use to them.' He glanced at the sky. 'Evening's almost upon us. They won't waste the time or effort or ammunition hunting for us in this undergrowth, for we might kill some of them before they capture any of us. If we'd been caught at sea it would've been a different end to the story. They'd have taken the fitter men off for slaves and probably set the boat adrift with the rest of us in it.'

I watched the pirates come ashore and search through our galley. They looked like ordinary seamen, and I said this to the captain. He laughed. 'What did you expect? That they'd be ten feet tall with long black beards, carrying a sword in each hand and a knife between their teeth? Most of us at sea have done some pirating from time to time.' He laughed again as he saw my eyes widen. 'Even ships of the line, flying the flags of their own countries,' he assured me. 'They'll not hesitate to stop and seize goods they fancy on some pretext or other.' He drew his peacock jacket closer around him and stroked the sleeve. 'I may have done it myself on occasion.' And he smiled in a crafty manner.

I looked at him more closely then, and I thought about what had happened today.

As we were forced to wait on the island until the pirates left, and I was no longer constantly on the run supplying thirsty men with water, I had more time to consider various aspects of these events.

I realized that our Captain Cosimo had a secret that he shared with no one. His sight was failing. Now I knew the reason why, although he was a good sailor and a canny man, he sometimes blundered in his navigation. We mainly followed a route from port to port, never straying far from the mainland, because our captain couldn't properly discern distant objects. It was when we had to venture onto the open sea that he found it most difficult. He hadn't seen this small island on his map because the inked mark that indicated its location was tiny and faint. He'd sent me ahead to find the direction of the hill on the island and followed after, striking out before him with his cane, as he did on the boat, to feel his way forward. During the daylight hours while we waited for the pirates to leave, he gave me the spyglass to report to him, for he could probably only see figures as a blur in the distance. And none of this did he wish anyone to know. It must be a recent affliction and he'd not be able to conceal it from his crew for very much longer, but for the present he'd rather be thought an idiot than let it be found out that he was going blind.

I admired him for his courage. And because he never treated me cruelly I decided that I wouldn't betray him. Out of misplaced loyalty I kept his secret and told no one what I knew.

I was too young and inexperienced to appreciate that a half-blind captain would finally and inevitably lead his men to their deaths.

Chapter Sixteen
Saulo

We waited all that night after the pirates left before returning to our boat.

Our wine, most of our water, two lanterns and a cooking pot had disappeared. They'd prised open the lid of the money box nailed to the floor of the captain's sleeping cubicle and taken whatever coins he kept there. Some salted fish was gone, but the rest of the supplies they left, including a barrel of water. They didn't touch the cargo or damage the boat.

This surprised me but the captain said, 'It's not as if we'd be likely to give chase. We're no threat to them, and it would be a bad thing for a sailor to do – to leave another sailor shipwrecked with no water and no means of leaving the island.'

As we made ready to leave, Captain Cosimo called me to stand beside him under the awning where he had his maps spread out on his table.

'There should be a port some miles west of here where we can sell our oil. I don't suppose you can read, boy?'

'I can,' I replied. 'My mother taught me the letters of different alphabets.'

'Did she now?' He raised an eyebrow.

I hadn't thought much about my mother's teaching until I found, as I grew older, that few men knew both western and eastern letters. Most were ignorant of how the words of different languages were formed and sounded. I knew that my mother's parents had opposed her liaison with my father, and they had run off together in defiance of them. Only now did I realize that she must have had a good education herself in order to show me the letters and help me learn to read and write.

'Then spell me that there.' The captain pointed to some writing on the parchment laid out before him.

I had never examined a map closely before and I marvelled at how such a thing could be made, and said as much to the captain. This one showed the coastlines of France, Spain and Portugal, with some of Africa too, and had the place names and ports written at right angles to their position on the land. 'It defies belief that a man can make charts that are completely correct,' I said.

'Aye, exactly,' Captain Cosimo replied gloomily. 'It does indeed defy belief, for they don't have the accuracy they claim. The marine charts should list harbours, coastal features, river mouths and landmarks, and the maps give us the seas and the land. Yet I have run aground on islands where no land should exist, and failed to find many ports where the cartographer has promised me safe haven.'

I looked along the bottom and the top of his map and then at each side. It indicated that there were more lands to the north and the east. I turned the parchment over to look behind it.

'Is that all there is?' I asked.

The captain gave me a strange look. 'At one time the answer to that question would have been yes. But now' – he shrugged – 'there are many stories about what may lie over the Atlantic, to the west beyond the Ocean Sea. One of my own countrymen, a man named Christopher Columbus, hawks his ideas on this to anyone who will listen. That is, any rich and powerful person who will listen. He proposes to find a way westwards to the Orient to gain access to the riches there without the risk of trying to find a sea passage round the bottom end of Africa or paying dues to the Turks to bring the goods through their lands. He seeks funding for an expedition to go and find the route around the back of the map.'

'And will he do it?'

'He must be crazy to think anyone would throw away money on such a venture!'

'You think that it doesn't exist?'

'It's not because it might not exist. The thing that makes the expedition impossible is that the Ocean Sea is too wide to cross. There might be tempests more violent than we can imagine, great whirlpools to drag a ship down, never to be seen again, vast tracks of stagnant water clogged with sea-weed for a thousand miles where the wind does not blow and oars cannot row. There a ship would be becalmed for ever with no fresh water. Men would die of thirst, or go mad and kill each other.'

'Yes, but if you did win through to the other side . . .' My voice tailed off because the captain had lost interest in the conversation and was plotting the course for our next port.

I think that was the moment when it occurred to me that it was possible to voyage not just for trade but for adventure, and it might be something I could do. For I'd begun to fall in love with the sea as her moods and caprices conspired to entrance me. My seasickness was now in the past and I'd grown to look forward to the breath of the wind on my face and the sight of the water so achingly blue under the morning sun. This summer I discovered how warm seawater could be. The only bathing I'd ever done had been in a cold river, and that maybe no more than five or six times in my life. Now I plunged naked from the side of the boat into the sparkling azure water to sport with the men as they splashed and swam, and then lay down on white sand and let the waves creep over my body, lazy and languorous with heat.

I loved watching the prow of our galley parting the waves as we followed our course. With the arrival of autumn the days were brought to a close by a sky displaying the most wondrous colours of sunset – rose and yellow, violet, lavender, indigo, crimson. And when the piercing brightness of the stars appeared in the darkling blue of the great vault of the heavens over our heads, I fell asleep with my lullaby the lap-lap-lapping of water against the sides of the vessel.

Our cargoes were small and mostly raw trade: ore and grain, nuts and oil, gum mastic, alum, saffron and salt. Ships that carried precious metals, furs or jewels were larger and travelled with escorts. We went in and out of the ports on the northern coastline of the Mediterranean Sea, and out into the Atlantic to reach the busy Spanish port of Cádiz, where bigger ships brought in goods from the northern lands, such as wool from England and animal skins from Iceland. We avoided sailing close to North Africa for fear of the many pirates known to be operating along the Barbary Coast, and because of the war waged by Queen Isabella and King Ferdinand against the Muslim peoples. They now wanted the Kingdom of Granada in the south of Spain, which for hundreds of years had been ruled by the Moors. Lomas thought they would eventually banish the Muslims and the Jews completely, even though Jews had served them well in high government office in the past.

As the weather cooled and the daylight hours shortened, the captain consulted with me more and more when reading his maps. In addition to being able to decipher letters, I had an aptitude for arithmetic and had quickly picked up how to interpret the charts, using the almanac and other aids.

Throughout winter and into the spring of the following year I learned the names of the constellations and how to calculate our position using the ascendancy of the North Star on the horizon. When Panipat growled his displeasure about me doing easier tasks, Captain Cosimo laughed off his objections. The oarsmaster glared at me suspiciously and was even more annoyed when, one day, after docking at a port south of Cádiz, the captain stated that he was taking me ashore with him while he negotiated his business.

Panipat put a leg iron round my ankle and fastened a light-weight chain to it. He gave the end of the chain to the captain, who wrapped it around his wrist. Although the chain was thin and quite unobtrusive, I felt humiliated – I was being treated no better than a wild animal. But I knew not to protest. Panipat eyed me as we made to leave the boat. He struck his whip stock violently into the palm of his hand, as if to remind me what my fate would be if I tried to escape.

Captain Cosimo twirled his stick and used it to thrust me ahead of him. Accompanied by two crewmen, we went down the gangplank, along the quayside and through the arched gate into the town. We visited the merchants' agent, where the captain made his deal and filled his purse. He gave the crewmen their wages and money for provisions, and we followed the twisted lanes and alleys leading to the market-place and the cacophony of sound from tethered livestock and squawking birds of dazzling plumage. Piles of spices and remedies for every ailment from toothache to baldness were sold by wizened street vendors, clashing cymbals and bang-ing drums as they tried to attract customers using the common language of signs and mime to advertise their wares. Captain Cosimo left the quartermaster and the carpenter-cook to haggle over the price of food and replacements for our stolen lamps and cooking pot, and pulled me towards a quieter corner of the souk. Here were the carpet and cloth sellers, the weavers, the tailors, and, almost certainly, the back rooms where a man could roll dice and so lose the money he carried.

We went into a building and the captain unwrapped the chain from his wrist and tied me to a rail on the ground floor. He patted my head. 'I treat you well, don't I, boy?' he demanded.

'Yes, Captain Cosimo,' I replied.

'So you'll not run off?'

I shook my head.

'If you did,' the captain sighed, 'Panipat would make it his business to find you, and he would punish you so severely that you'd wish for death. Whereas if you stay on my boat we might work together, for I think I could teach you proper seafaring skills; in time there might be some reward in it for you.'

He saw my expression change when he said this. For in truth I'd intended to run as soon as he turned his back. But now this was a different proposition. 'I'd not become a slave rower?' I asked him.

'That would be a waste of your talents. Would you learn under my instruction? You might be able to calculate the course by yourself, although I'd always call the headings. What say you?'

I suspect he knew that if he made many more mistakes he'd no longer by able to deceive the crew about his failing eyesight. Now he hoped to mask his navigation faults by using me as the scapegoat for anything that went wrong. 'I'd like to do that, yes,' I agreed.

'Good lad. We may have some trouble from Panipat, who has not taken to you as I have. But I'll watch out for you. And you will do the same for me.' He patted my head again. 'Rest here for a bit. I'll be back soon.'

When Captain Cosimo returned, he looked well pleased. It must have been the effect of alcohol, for when we got back to the boat and he took out his purse it was obviously much lighter than it had been earlier. He seemed unperturbed at losing his own profits. After distributing shares to the oarsmen and the rest of the crew, he was left with only a few coins to lock away in his money box.

We sailed out of that port in good humour, with a new cargo and fresh provisions. A few miles out we heaved to, for every month or so the slaves were unchained to wash and swim in the sea, where there was no chance of them escaping. None of them ever tried to swim off. Panipat, watching over them with a deadly pointed harpoon lying across his lap, was enough to deter even the most foolhardy. In any case, when the cook began to prepare a hot meal, the smell of the sizzling food and the prospect of a full belly with a mug or two of wine brought them clambering back aboard.

This was the time when the crew, both slaves and freemen, talked of the sea. And though they were in awe of its power, they had affection for this provider of their sustenance.

'Better than the woman I was married to,' said one.

'Which woman would marry you?' jibed another.

The first man only laughed. 'I've seen yours, and I know why you signed on for seven years. If that was what I was going home to, I'd have aimed for double that term.'

Some of the oarsmen would tell stories of their former lives. The four Arab slaves, who were placed together on the starboard side of the boat, murmured quietly amongst themselves, but of the other four slaves, two admitted to being thieves, and one to having committed a murder. Jean-Luc, a Frenchman, had been a soldier and had killed his wife in a drunken rage; Sebastien, a very tall thin man, was a priest. 'I was taken by the Inquisition,' he told us, 'for preaching heresy. I escaped. It was either spending my life on a galley or burning at the stake. I chose this. Some days when our crazy captain has us lost, I think I might have been better off toasting in the flames than slowly roasting here in the sun.'

They asked me about my former life but I hadn't much to tell – except that we had always lived in fear. I think my father believed that we were being pursued by my mother's family, intent on killing him for taking her away from them without permission. I don't know why they had forbidden the match. Both my parents seemed educated and well spoken, neither one inferior to the other. Perhaps it was a difference in religion. They never discussed it, but we had constantly moved home. My father had a good knowledge of horses, and in my early youth he was able to find employment and began to teach me his work training them. But ever since I could recall, my mother had been sickly. And as I grew up, she became more and more ill, until most of our money went on her medicine. Not long after we arrived in Las Conchas a new sickness came upon her and she took to her bed. She was no longer fit to travel far, and neither my father nor I could find work. Our savings were soon gone and with no family to turn to for help, we became beggars. It was a sorry tale and I didn't choose to share all of it, for when I thought of my mother and father, the hurt of losing them fed the canker of poison that was the vow of vengeance within me. I only told my companions that misfortune had robbed me of my parents.

Full of wine and drowsy, the men made jokes and laughed, and as I sat with them, I felt a part of their company. In the absence of my parents I was glad to be on this boat. I experienced a surge of loyalty for our crazy captain and thought that in future I would indeed try to watch out for him.

That day was to come sooner than I expected.

The day when I left my boyhood behind and killed a man.

Chapter Seventeen
Zarita

'You have ordered the arrest of my servant, Bartolomé.'

I could clearly hear Papa's voice even though his study door was closed. Father Besian's reply was lower but audible. 'He has been disrespectful to the point of blasphemy.'

'Bartolomé is not aware that his actions can be interpreted in that way.'

I gave Serafina a little push towards the kitchen. 'You attend to your duties. I will go and add my voice to Papa's pleas.'

'I have the right to arrest anyone I think may be a heretic or who may be conspiring against Holy Mother Church.'

Father Besian and my father were standing facing each other as I entered the room. They were so intent on their argument that they took no note of my presence.

'The boy you have arrested is a simpleton and has no idea what a heretic is.'

'Yesterday my men asked him if he had ever entertained wicked thoughts against priests or the Church and he replied that he had.'

'Bartolomé would agree with anything anyone said,' Papa, never a patient man, snapped in return. 'It's in his nature to do so. He has no thoughts to call his own and seeks to please everyone he meets.'

'Furthermore,' the priest continued, 'when asked if he had ever plotted to attack the priest during mass, he said that he did sometimes entertain these thoughts when he attended the holy service.'

My father laughed harshly. 'The sermons of certain priests might warrant such a reaction.'

'I caution you to be mindful of what you say.' There was an edge to the priest's voice.

'I told you, the boy is a simpleton! He can barely dress himself unaided. He could no more conspire against the Church than he could count from one to one hundred. Surely you can see that?'

'Even in the simplest person the evil one seeks to find a place.'

'He's only a boy!' Papa exploded in exasperation.

'Almost twenty years of age makes him a man, but I will bear in mind all you have said when he is put to the question.'

'Put to the question!' My father looked appalled. 'You surely don't intend to question the boy by trial?'

'If I am dissatisfied with his initial answers, yes.'

'But you know what his initial answers will be, so why proceed—' Papa broke off as if he was beginning to work out the import of what he had just heard. He looked more closely at the priest. 'What game do you play here that you use the boy as your pawn?'

Father Besian hesitated. Then he said, 'It may be that our examination of this first person accused of wrongdoing will prompt the townsfolk to lead us to others.'

There was something happening within the room that I didn't understand, but I was too young, foolish and head-strong to be prudent and wait and listen. I burst out, 'There are no others!' I cried out. 'The people of this town are good souls. You must release Bartolomé at once!'

Both men swung round to face me. The colour leeched from my father's face. 'Zarita! You shouldn't be here.'

'On the contrary,' said Father Besian. 'This is exactly where your daughter should be. She is old enough to appreciate right from wrong, and must learn what will and will not be tolerated by Church and State.' He turned back to my father. 'I give you this instruction now. No one may leave this town without first applying to me for permission. That order includes every member of your staff and family. Anyone who tries to do so will be arrested and held by the officers of the Inquisition.'

Chapter Eighteen
Zarita

The next morning I was awoken by a scream.

I came fully awake in an instant, thinking it was a bad dream where I was reaching out across a stormy sea to my mother, only to watch the boat she was in capsize and sink.

Another scream.

This time I knew it wasn't part of my nightmare.

The scream came from the direction of our barn at the far end of the paddock. I sat up. My eyes opened wide as I heard another high-pitched cry, then another, and another, and after that a long moaning noise. It sounded like an animal in its death throes. I sprang from my bed, threw on a long wrap and went out of my room onto the upper landing.

Below me in the lower hall Lorena was arguing with Papa.

'I want to go to my father's house!'

'Father Besian has given instructions in the name of the Inquisition,' Papa told her. 'No one must leave the town without his express permission.'

'We're not really part of the town.' Lorena waved her arms in the air. 'This house is almost outside the town. The grounds are part of the countryside. We cannot be included in the order governing the township.'

'Father Besian has indicated that he holds the occupants of this house under the jurisdiction of the Inquisition.'

'As magistrate, surely you have more power, more rights, than the ordinary people!'

I began to descend the stairs.

Lorena voice became shrill. 'I must get away from here!'

'I'm sorry.' Papa spoke to her more gently. 'You cannot leave.'

'I will say I am pregnant.'

'Would that you were,' Papa replied with a tinge of bitterness in his voice.

Lorena's mouth twisted down, but he didn't notice.

'You can say that I fainted and we feared for the life of the child, so I went into the hills to my father's house where it's cooler.'

'No,' Papa said. 'It will not do.'

Lorena struck out with her fists against his chest. He stepped back under the onslaught and tried to grasp her hands. She pushed away from him and rushed to mount the stairs, screeching for her maid as she did so. She almost knocked me over in her haste.

Papa looked up after her and saw me standing there.

'Zarita! Perhaps you should go to the convent for today and stay there with your aunt Beatriz. It might be . . . safer.'

'I don't know about that,' I replied. 'Father Besian doesn't approve of my aunt's community of sisters.' I looked towards the outside door. 'I heard screaming, as though one of the horses were suffering. Is there something wrong?'

Papa bent his head to avoid my gaze. 'I must go back to the barn and see what's happening. Stay here until I return.' And he left me there and hurried from the house.

I went to the dining room. Breakfast was not yet set out so I made my way to the kitchen. It was early, but not so early that the staff shouldn't be astir and preparing food. There was no one there.

The kitchen door was ajar. I walked over and looked out. Serafina and Ardelia stood by the vegetable garden, looking towards the barn. They were holding onto each other in a fearful manner.

'What's going on?' I called to them. 'Is one of the horses ill?'

As they didn't reply, I continued, 'Where's Garci? Is he with my father?'

They turned their faces to me. Serafina's eyes were red and her cheeks were blotched. Ardelia too was crying. Another scream sounded out.

'Bartolomé!' Serafina fell to her knees, stretching her hands to Heaven and crying out, 'Blessed Mary, intercede for him!'

The truth slammed into me so violently that I doubled up with the force. I gasped and put my hands to my stomach.

The sounds I'd assumed came from an animal in pain were uttered by the boy, Bartolomé.

I straightened up, gathered my wrap about me and ran out of the house, past the stable block and down through the paddock towards the barn. Behind me I heard Ardelia calling me to come back.

The door was wide open. A rope had been put over the beam and two soldiers held one end. The other end was attached to Bartolomé's wrists, which were tied behind him, and he was being hoisted up into the air. Outside the barn was a brazier of glowing coals. A poker, its tip white-hot, rested on the metal struts. The boy's shirt was open and there were scorch marks on his skin. Father Besian, Papa, Garci and the other soldiers stood in a group by the door.

I took all of this in within an instant, and then I was in the barn screaming at the top my voice, 'Release him! Let him down from there! Now!'

Father Besian nodded. The soldiers holding the rope let go. Bartolomé crashed onto the floor of the barn.

'Zarita!'

I ignored my father's shout and ran to where poor Bartolomé lay on the ground. I tore at his bonds with my fingernails but I couldn't loosen them. He was sobbing like an inconsolable baby. I lifted his head and cradled it on my lap. My wrap was open: the onlookers could plainly see me in my night shift.

'Zarita!' My papa was shocked beyond speaking.

I looked up at him in scorn. 'You might be able to stand and watch this injustice but I cannot!'

'Cover yourself, child.' He started forward.

Father Besian laid his hand upon his arm. 'I will take my men from here and leave you with your daughter and your servants.'

I saw his face when he said this, and there was a gleam of satisfaction in his eyes.

Garci came and took Bartolomé away from me. 'I'll take care of him,' he said.

Papa pulled me to my feet. He took off his jacket, wrapped it around me and hurried me back to the house.

I expected his anger: I had made a spectacle of myself, behaved in a disgraceful manner. But it was as though the spirit had gone from him. He stood by the kitchen door watching Garci clean Bartolomé's wounds at the water trough, helped by Ardelia and Serafina. He spoke only one sentence:

'Now the flood gates will open.'

I could get no more out of my father, so I dressed and went to see my aunt to tell her what was happening.

She was furious. I'd never before seen Aunt Beatriz lose control of her emotions.

'Does this insane man think God's purpose is served by torturing a witless boy!'

I recalled what my papa had been saying to Father Besian when I'd entered his study the previous evening. 'Papa said that Father Besian is using Bartolomé as his pawn.'

'Ah!' My aunt paused in her rant. 'Ah. I see that cunning priest's intention. So far the townspeople have stood firm against him. He means to slide a wedge of fear between their closed ranks.'

The questioning under torture of Bartolomé was like a tidal wave cascading through our streets. The reaction was immediate, and began within my own home.

'I have heard,' Lorena said at dinner that very night, 'that there is a Jewish doctor in the town who attends the slum dwellers.' She paused to glance at Father Besian. 'He might have information that would be of use to you.' Her hand wavered as she raised her wine glass to her lips.

My heart fluttered. Did she mean the doctor who had helped the beggar's wife? Papa opened his mouth as if to speak but said nothing.

Father Besian looked at Lorena in approval. 'Thank you, my dear,' he said. 'Unfortunately, Jews who have never con-verted are tolerated in Spain. Although . . . that may change. In any case I am aware of this so-called doctor. Someone has already spoken of him to me.'

Father Besian knew about the Jewish doctor! Anxiety caused my stomach to heave. Who had told him? Could it have been Garci, trading information in an attempt to protect Bartolomé? Garci and his wife, Serafina, had no children of their own and had taken the boy in when Serafina's sister died. They loved him as the son they never had, and perhaps Garci would not remain silent if he could help him in any way.

But what effect would this have on me? Thoughts frantically chased one after the other in my mind. I didn't want Father Besian pursuing the doctor who had attended the beggar's wife. He would find out that I had asked for his help. I could be suspected as a heretic for consorting with Jews! Maybe there was another guilty person he could occupy himself with? I stumbled over my words as I spoke. 'There's a place near the dockside where it's said that women of low character consort.'

'Why, thank you, Zarita.' The priest smiled and nodded. I smiled in return, relief flooding through me.

Lorena flashed me a look of dislike. My father's shoulders sagged, and he bent his head to his plate of food.

The next day the denouncements started in earnest.

Pieces of paper, some with only a name roughly written upon them, were slid under the gates of our compound or nailed to the wood outside. Others were tied to rocks and thrown over the wall. These were brought to Father Besian, who studied them. He had the manner of a cat crouching outside a mouse hole. 'At last,' he purred. 'The truth pushes its way up through the mire.'

Then the arrests began.

Our barn was used for general interrogations while the more serious wrong-doers were taken to the town gaol. I was no longer allowed anywhere near the paddock. I missed talking to the horses, grooming and stroking their coats and plaiting their manes. Garci turned them into some meadows to graze. I heard him tell my father that they were disturbed by the goings-on in the barn.

We never again heard such screams as had come from Bartolomé that morning. The barn door was kept shut, and Father Besian used the period when the household was at mass for his most rigorous questioning of his suspects. My aunt had been correct. It had been a deliberate ploy to allow Bartolomé's screams to wake everyone that first morning in order to strike terror into our hearts and make us more malleable. Father Besian had known that the story would run through the town like a fever: all he had to do was sit back and wait for the expected results.

The trials came to an end. Half a dozen or so people had been found guilty of a number of transgressions. An old man who'd converted to Christianity a while ago had, as his years progressed, returned to the rites of his Jewish religion. There was to be a series of public punishments. Those guilty of minor offences would confess in church on Sunday and be given prayers to say or works of charity to perform. More serious sinners, like Bartolomé, were to be publicly scourged. The man found guilty of heresy was to be burned alive.

It was after nine one evening when we heard this news. Father Besian was at the town gaol. Despite the lateness of the hour Papa went to speak to him.

I waited up until Papa returned. When he came into the house, I poured him some wine – not the heavy, sickly type that we had been consuming since Lorena had taken charge of our kitchen staff, but a glass from a bottle of plain country wine that we'd drunk when Mama was alive.

Papa took the glass from my hand and sipped from it. Then he set it down upon the sideboard.

'You've not been able to obtain a pardon for this man?' I said.

'Not a complete pardon, no.' He sat down heavily in a nearby chair.

I went and knelt before him. My face was on a level with his own. His eyes were open, but he wasn't looking at me. He was staring beyond me to some inner private place where I had no access.

'Would money help?' I asked him. 'You can have everything I own. The necklace Mama left me. Anything.'

He smiled and touched my face as if seeing me properly for the first time in almost a year. 'Sweet Zarita,' he said. 'Kind, like your mama; but impulsive, too impulsive for your own good.'

'Will they not grant this old man mercy?' I asked.

He waited for a moment before replying. 'I have obtained for him' – he rubbed his forehead with his hand – 'a mercy of sorts.'

'They will not burn him then?'

'They will burn him,' my father replied grimly. 'It's just that he'll not be alive when they do it.'

Chapter Nineteen
Saulo

We were three days out of Barbate when disaster overtook us.

The captain and I were following a heading south along the Atlantic coast of Andalucía, with the intention of eventually swinging eastwards to take us back into the Mediterranean, when a violent storm came roaring in from the open sea and drove us entirely off course. Winter had passed, and for the last few weeks we'd witnessed enormous chattering flocks of migrating birds sweeping across the straits from Africa, heralding spring for the lands of Europe. The winter had been mild, so the shock of this sudden severe weather coming in April was all the greater. Driving hail battered the boat and great breaking waves pounded out of the west, threatening to engulf us.

Above the booming thunder the captain managed to scream in my ear, 'Imagine the full fury of this in the Atlantic Ocean! Would any but a lunatic sail out there with the man Columbus to face such a storm?'

'Yes!' I shouted back as the waves whipped my face, and my head and my heart sang in exhilaration at this struggle with the elements of nature. 'Yes, I would!'

We lowered the sail and stowed away our precious goods, then clung on and rode out the worst of it. Eventually it began to pass over. Sunlight lanced out of grey skies and the wash became a steady swell. Panipat and the oarsmen went on bailing while the quartermaster checked the cargo and the carpenter-cook and the sail-maker examined the mast, which had taken a beating and needed repair. Occupied by clearing up, and with dense clouds still tumbling and growling off to starboard, none of us noticed the white square of a sail appear on the horizon.

No lookout had been posted. Every man was busy, including the captain. He'd even taken off his peacock jacket in order to crouch down in the prow and check that the flint box was dry. The men were wringing out their possessions. Beside me in the bilges, Lomas was checking that the contents of his bag were safe. Suddenly I raised my head and saw the ship coming alongside no more than a hundred metres away.

My voice strangled in my throat. I could only grab Lomas by the arm and croak a warning.

He followed my gaze and yelled at the top of his voice, 'Muster! Muster!'

The men scrambled to their places and I jumped onto the boardwalk.

There was a bang. The other ship had fired a cannon shot. It went clear across our decks. Lomas grabbed my ankle so that I fell flat on my face.

'Get down,' he yelled, 'lest you want your head blown off!'

She was a tall three-masted privateer, with cannon on each side. And she was flying the flag of the crescent moon.

A shout of joy came from one of the Muslim slaves, and he called out to his companions. They raised their hands, pointing at the flag, smiling and waving.

I saw flame leap out again from the mouth of a cannon mounted on the ship's foredeck. The ball went over and splatted into the water beside us.

'She's too high in the water!' the man in front of Lomas shouted. 'Her cannon won't harm us.'

'I wouldn't be too sure of that,' someone else replied as the next ball skimmed the deck, whapped against our mast, causing it to wobble, and then took off the awning draped above the captain's table.

'No talk!' Panipat shouted in fury. 'Use your energy to pull!'

But there wasn't an island in sight and the Turks now saw that we had chained Muslim slaves who were crying out to them for rescue. They closed on us, intending to kill the Spanish crew.

'For the love of God, release us or we'll drown if our galley is holed!' one of the slaves pleaded to Panipat.

'And have you jump overboard?' he swore at them in reply. 'Not this time, you dogs. Get on, you curs! Get on!' He lashed out with his whip.

The oars groaned as the men bent and pulled. Muscles stood out like ropes on their backs. The captain stamped his feet in frustration. We were far off course, and without knowing our location he couldn't give Panipat an accurate heading. The Turks had us within their grasp and there was nowhere to go.

'O Lord, deliver us!' the quartermaster prayed as he handed out spears to the crew.

One of our freeman rowers spoke to me: 'If you know what's good for you, boy, you'll make a run for it. When we're boarded, seize your chance to jump and swim. Cling to anything that floats and try to get away. Better to drown than be captured by the Infidel. These heathens will use you for sport before they slit your belly open and toss you to the fish.'

I touched the waistband of my breeches where my knife was hidden.

The privateer was now so close we could see men lined up with grappling hooks, ready to throw down to pull us in. They were shouting to the Arab slaves, who replied in their own language.

'Tell them how good a captain I've been!' Captain Cosimo begged our chained Arab men. 'I've always fed you and treated you fairly.'

The slaves laughed in his face and defiantly rested on their oars, disobeying Panipat's instructions.

'Let us parley!' Captain Cosimo hailed the ship in the dozen or so languages in which he could say these words. 'Name your terms of surrender!'

The answer came in a rush of descending arrows. There would be no discussion. They intended to take whatever we had.

A grappling hook with a line attached came hurtling across the water and thudded into the side of the boat. It failed to find a hold and fell back into the sea. The next one trailed across the deck and caught the side. Our galley shuddered, and a loud *huzzah* sounded from the enemy. I didn't need to be told what to do. I ran forward, wrested the hook free and threw it back into the water. Arrows struck the deck all around me, one glancing against my arm. I jumped back among the oarsmen for safety. They cheered me as I crouched at their feet.

Then a contrary wind caught the sails of the other ship and she drifted away from us. Our men cheered even louder and bent over their oars. We began to make headway.

The gap between the two vessels widened. But the Turks were without doubt among the best seamen we had encountered. They altered their angle of approach to bring their prow to bear on our side.

'Turn us!' Captain Cosimo screamed at Panipat. 'Turn us! We must not let them ram us on our broadside!'

Our men stood up and sculled hard. Our boat spun like a piece of cork in a river.

'We can't outgun them,' Captain Cosimo shouted in glee, 'but we might outmanoeuvre them!'

It seemed as though he was right. We were losing them. They'd no oarsmen to give them power to change direction. They relied solely on the wind, and luck was with us – but for how long?

Blindly the free oarsmen obeyed the stroke command, and there was more open water between the vessels.

The captain had a rough heading and he shouted out to Panipat. Was it possible that we might get away?

The freemen and the port-side slaves settled into a fast rhythm. The boat went on, moving with the flow of the sea.

But the Arab oarsmen were slacking – there was no doubt about it. Whereas eight months ago I wouldn't have sensed the movement of the boat through the water, now I was experienced enough to feel the sluggishness jar through my very bones.

Panipat became as one demented. He ran up to the prow and began to beat the Arab slaves mercilessly. They bent their backs and took the blows but pulled not one iota harder. Finally he took his long knife from his belt and put it behind the ear of the nearest slave. 'Pull, you son of Satan,' he screeched, 'or I'll skewer your skull and take your place myself!'

The Arabs began to pull harder.

Our vessel was swift and light and had a skilled oars-master and crew. Now that we'd put distance between ourselves and the larger ship, the captain hoped to be gone.

But the bigger vessel had tacked and the Turks were bringing it round again.

We could still get away. Why did the captain not alter course?

Panipat glanced out across the waves and then back to Captain Cosimo. 'Change our bearing!' he shouted.

The gap was closing again. Fast.

And then I realized that, at that distance, Captain Cosimo could not see the enemy ship tacking to turn against us.

I crawled along the boardwalk to the command platform and grabbed the captain's arm. 'She's coming about!' I shouted. 'She's coming about!'

Captain Cosimo blinked and stared at me. A mind-numbing pause. Then, within half a minute, he took in what I was telling him.

He was thirty seconds too late.

A shadow loomed over our heads as the privateer, prow out-thrust, bore down on us.

With a crunch of splintering wood she rammed us amidships.

Chapter Twenty
Saulo

Men were flung all ways. Panipat was hurled into the air. Huge though he was, the force of the collision tossed him head over heels like a child's doll. He slammed back down onto the deck, stunned. A dozen of the freemen were caught under the hull of the enemy ship. They disappeared in a welter of broken planks, ripping, grinding noises and horrendous cries. At the stern end those who had survived the impact began to bail furiously as water swirled in about their feet.

We weren't broken in half, just impaled upon the front of the Turkish ship, like a fish caught by spear. And, whether by luck or deliberate act, the Turks had breached us towards the stern end, so that it was the freemen who suffered most and the Arab and other slaves who remained unharmed above sea level in the prow.

Panipat got to his feet and began to rally the men. The quartermaster was already at our cannon, with Captain Cosimo beside him, striking a spark for the fuse from the flint box. It was to be a fight to the death.

Our gun fired off. David against Goliath. A bang and a whistling noise. The acrid smell of gunpowder. The cannon-ball struck the foresail of the bigger ship and tore a huge rent in the fabric.

'Take that!' Our crazy captain shook his fists above his head. 'Ram my boat, would you? Now you'll pay for it!'

A stream of foul insults came from the quartermaster, directed towards the enemy. The rest of our crew and oarsmen joined in, creating a din to rival the cries and orders coming from our attackers. The quartermaster picked up another ball, preparing to reload our cannon. A volley of small cannon shot rattled out from the ship above us, and the quartermaster fell across the cannon, blood streaming from his face.

One of the Arab oarsmen began to whoop and shout.

In a fury Panipat seized his knife and stabbed him through the neck. Blood spurted out splattering over those beside him who began a caterwauling lament. From the Turkish ship arrows showered down around Panipat. One caught him in his leg. He snapped it off and threw it aside disdainfully, still standing upright among the chaos and uproar.

I had been jolted across the width of the boat. Now I half rose and hunkered forward to the prow to help the captain. Together we levered the dead quartermaster off the cannon.

'We'll aim for the sailors this time,' I said as I lowered the barrel.

'Yes,' the captain snarled. 'Try to blast some of those murderers out of the water.'

We fired another shot. With a thunderous clap, flame spouted from the mouth of the gun. The cannonball cut a swathe through the men standing at the rail of the Turkish ship.

'We got them!' I shouted. 'We got them!'

The captain laughed in delight. 'Let's send them another message, the same as the last!'

But the effect of our success on the larger ship was to bring more armed men to the rails just above us. I saw them gathering and quickly grabbed another cannonball. Just as they were about to fire, I thrust it down the open end of the barrel.

'The metal will burn you,' the captain warned me. 'Be careful, boy—'

The skin of my hands singed on the red-hot metal. I yelped in pain and jumped back.

In that instant the Turks let off another round of small cannon shot. I stared in horror as, just in front of me, Captain Cosimo crumpled to the deck. The front of his shirt was pierced in several places. Blood ran freely from these holes.

The sound of the battle suddenly seemed to come to my ears from far away. I got down on my knees beside our fallen captain, hardly aware of the cannonball whizzing past my own head.

I tore off my shirt to try to staunch the blood flowing from the captain's wounds. The deck was slippery beneath me, red with his blood flowing from his body as fast as an outgoing tide. My captain was dying. I knew it, and so did he.

'My jacket,' he mumbled, blood seeping from between his teeth. 'Give me my jacket.'

I reached out and drew over his peacock jacket. Awkwardly I lifted it and laid it upon him. He gave a sigh as he stroked it, the pallor of his face turning from tan to wax in less than a minute. And he died there, before me, with what appeared to be a look of satisfaction on his face.

I rocked back on my heels. He was gone. Our brave, foolish, proud, crazy Captain Cosimo was no more. I was bereft. Apart from the debt I owed him for all he'd taught me in the months I'd been on his boat, I knew that I had lost a friend as well as a mentor. My face was wet.

A shout brought me to my senses. Lomas was gesticulating at me. 'Get you to cover, boy! Hide yourself!'

There was no time to grieve for Captain Cosimo. The enemy were recharging their guns while arrows, spears, and rocks thudded onto our deck. Although they gathered up what they could and threw it back, many of our men fell under this onslaught. The sail-maker went over the side with a spear in his belly. The Turks' strategy was plain: they would massacre us from the safety of their decks and then come aboard and release the slaves. I rolled myself into a ball and cowered as far under the protection of the gun platform as I was able.

Then a different noise resounded through the boat. Given the circumstances it was the strangest sound I'd ever heard. The remainder of our men were cheering and whistling.

I peered out and saw a ship swiftly approaching us.

A ship of the line, a troop ship, flying a flag bearing the crests of Castile and Aragon.

With another similar ship coming up behind.

I too began to shout for joy – but had enough sense to do so without emerging from my hiding place.

The first Spanish ship came up, guns firing, on the Turks' stern. The enemy sailors ran to the other end of their ship to defend themselves. The second Spanish ship sailed round to our starboard side and tried to edge closer. They threw netting down over their sides so that our survivors could clamber up. The hull still held, and though the few men left there floundered in the water, they managed to get out.

The Turkish ship now tried to disengage from us to win free of the fray.

'Make them stay until our men get off!' Panipat called to the Spanish sailors above us. 'She's holding us together. If she pulls away we'll sink in seconds!' He bellowed out to the remainder of our men. 'Abandon ship! Abandon ship!'

I was at the top of the netting when I heard the voices of the slaves.

'Help us!' they begged. 'Don't leave us to die!'

'We are drowning! We are drowning!'

Below me, as the Turkish ship tried to pull away from us, it was causing the prow of our galley to settle. The sea was making ready to claim her.

I looked to our rescuers.

The Spaniards were too busy with the fight to see or care what was happening below them. No one would come to the aid of the chained men.

'Mercy! Mercy!' The pleas of the slaves were both desperate and pitiful.

The shoulders of one of the Arab slaves, a short stocky fellow, were already under water.

I hesitated; the prow dipped again.

The man's neck and face submerged. His voice gurgled as the water seeped into his mouth.

The rest shouted louder. The dying cries of the drowning men proved too much for me. I slid back down the netting to meet Panipat on his way up.

'Give me the key,' I said.

Panipat shook his head. 'They can drown like rats on a sinking ship. It was they who brought us to this state. We would've got clear had they not rowed sluggishly and refused to obey my orders.'

It was partly true. If the Arab oarsmen hadn't worked against us then we might have pulled away earlier; but in the main, it was bad luck and Captain Cosimo with his poor eyesight that had led us to disaster.

'They don't deserve to drown,' I began. 'If the captain—'

Panipat drew back his fist and sent me sprawling with a punch in the mouth. 'They will die where they sit,' he declared. 'Every one of them.'

A yowling came from the throats of the chained men. The two remaining Arab slaves were tearing frantically at their shackles as the water rose up. One had contorted his body and was trying to bite through his own ankle. Of the four slaves on the port side, three were up to their necks in water, and although the last one, the tallest man, Sebastien, tried to support them, the weight of the shackles and chains was dragging them down. The boat settled again, and one of them went under. It was Jean-Luc. I saw bubbles breaking from his mouth and the terrified look on the faces of the remaining three.

I turned to Panipat. 'Give me the key!'

'You will never have it,' Panipat declared. 'Never!'

And saying this, he snatched the key from the cord at his wrist. Then he opened his mouth wide and put the key inside.

Chapter Twenty-one
Zarita

Bartolomé was led out in procession with the other prisoners.

There was a gasp as they appeared. The one to be burned wore a long conical hat and a tabard depicting images of devils and flames in lurid colours of orange, scarlet and red.

We'd heard of such things happening elsewhere in Spain. Being a port meant that traders came and went through Las Conchas – sailors, merchants, packmen, muleteers and the like. The stories they told in the dockside taverns spread via the marketplace and became part of the social currency of the town. But while we'd repeated these stories and wondered about the truth of them, I'd assumed they were mostly wild exaggerations.

The reality was worse; more abominable than all those dramatic accounts gathered together.

The minor transgressors were to be punished first. They were to be flogged, apart from the youngest, a boy of about eleven or twelve – who, it was decided, would be beaten with a stick. He'd confessed to stealing fruit from a farmer by climbing over his wall and plundering his orchard.

In the crowd a woman moaned. 'He's so young to be punished in this way.'

An old woman with a sour face commented, 'Sin must be punished – better in this world than in the next. He took that which wasn't his. That makes him a thief. It's against the law of man and of God.'

'Isn't it what boys do when they are that age?' a man remarked.

'Hush, hush.' A young woman tried to silence him. 'Don't speak out like that.'

Garci turned and glared at her. 'May your mother's milk curdle in your breasts,' he said, 'that you should deny the normal nature of a child.'

Under his fierce gaze she shrank away. I looked at Garci and gave my head a shake. He shouldn't be so hard on her. Two children clutched at her dress, both of them boys. She wasn't denying the truth of Garci's words. She was simply in dread of any attention being drawn to this part of the crowd where she was trying to shield her sons among her skirts.

Now my father appeared, looking older and more care-worn than I had seen him since the day of my mother's death. And I began to comprehend the gravity of his situation. As the local magistrate, he was responsible for carrying out any recommended sentence imposed by the tribunal of the Inquisition on these poor unfortunates. The officers of the Inquisition had no jurisdiction over our corporeal bodies. The guilty must be handed over to state officials to carry out sentence. It had been Papa's responsibility to have the town square cleared, to summon the townspeople as ordered by Father Besian and to arrange for an area to be sectioned off with the appropriate equipment to perform these grisly deeds.

The boy to be beaten.

The other sinners, including Bartolomé, to be scourged.

The heretic to be burned.

A raised dais had been erected, and on this sat my father and the officers of the tribunal. As his family and household members, we had been accorded a place of importance with an unimpeded view, and we stood at the front of the crowd to one side. When we arrived, Lorena beckoned to Ramón Salazar and he came to stand beside us.

The boy was brought forward and tied to a post and his shirt was removed.

It was at least brief.

He was struck rapidly across the back six times, one blow for each piece of fruit he'd stolen. The boy's howls set off every child in the crowd, already sensing the tension in the watching adults.

Garci, who was a devout man, said in my ear, 'It is not the work of God that is being carried out here today.'

Now it was Bartolomé's turn to be led to the punishment block. It required two men to drag him there, for although he was weak of mind, he had done manual labour all his life and was physically very strong. His normal beatific smile had been replaced by an expression of confusion and fear. His eyes were starting from his head and he glanced around desperately, letting out squeals and making frightened mewling noises.

I was too scared to turn my head away. Father Besian had made it clear that the townspeople were there to bear witness. Anyone who did not attend – unless seriously ill – anyone who looked away when punishment was being administered would be suspected of being a sympathizer. Ardelia and Serafina clung to each other, while Garci tried to encircle the three of us with his arms.

At the last moment, just before he reached the post, Bartolomé caught sight of us in the crowd. His face changed in recognition. He struggled and tried to break free and called out Serafina's name pathetically.

'Auntie Serafina! Help me! Help me please!'

He was grabbed roughly and hustled to his place of

punishment. There he was scourged with a metal-tipped whip until his skin split apart and his back bled.

I closed my eyes as they led forward two women found guilty of prostitution. Had it been my denouncement, my repeating to Father Besian the rumours I'd heard of immoral acts taking place in certain houses near the docks that had caused this? Their hair was cut off and their dresses pulled down so that they were stripped to the waist before being laid on the scourging block. Their screams echoed in my head.

Finally the sins of the heretic were read out. His neighbours had verified that he was a *converso*, an old Jew who, years ago, had converted to Christianity. He'd been spied upon and it had been proven that he was secretly practising his Jewish faith, and under questioning he'd admitted this. He shambled along as he walked to the stake. I thought at first that it was because his legs were fettered, but then I saw it was because he'd been tortured. His limbs no longer obeyed his will. They bound him to the stake and then heaped kindling about his feet.

I heard Lorena whisper to Ramón, 'Is it true that sometimes they dampen the wood so that it causes them to roast more slowly?' She said this in such a pretend piteous voice that it made me want to gag.

'I've heard it shortens the ordeal as the victims are overcome by the smoke before they burn,' Ramón said in a comforting way. He bent his head to her ear to reply. She used this to insinuate herself nearer to him.

'Oh, it's too terrible to watch.' She ran her tongue over her lips. She was clearly horrified, yet at the same time excited in a disturbing way. She pressed herself even closer and appeared to semi-swoon. Ramón put his arm out to steady her.

A flint was struck to light a long brand, one end soaked in pitch. This flaming torch was set to the pile of wood. There was a crackling as the kindling caught, and then slowly the flames spread through the remainder of the wood. The crowd sighed as one, swayed, and moved back. The flames rose higher, bright red fire eating at the edge of the old man's garments. He began to cry out – first to Father Besian for mercy and then to God. His voice became a stretched screaming babble.

A vision came to me as though it were I amidst the fire. I could feel heat on the soles of my own feet. The flames all about me . . .

I twist my body to avoid them and a moan escapes my lips. The hot searing redness glows among the bundles of sticks. Around me bright spots of fire . . . like eyes piercing and tearing my body in the intense heat. Then a flame, a true flame, leaps up. It has the hem of my dress. It is a grey dress of rough cloth that I wear. This flame runs up my outer skirts like an animal intent on devouring me. Across my breast.

I am transfixed. It is surging over my head. Already the hot singeing smell of burning hair is in my nostrils, the pungent odour of scorching clothes, and a nauseating smell of flesh being devoured by fire.

I cannot move. The smoke rises. My vision is impeded.

I cannot see. I cannot breathe. I try to put my hand to my throat.

I am unable to stir. My arms are fastened by my sides. My breath is coming in short gasps. I make a little miaou of grief . . .

Father Besian turned his head slowly, as if loath to remove his sight from the spectacle of the man being roasted alive. His eyes bore down on me, drilling into my brain through to the back of my skull.

I swayed and would have fallen had not Garci tightened his arm around me.

Father Besian's gaze came upon me and went past. His head stopped, his eyes swivelled back to my face.

Papa too moved his head to see what the disturbance was. A frown furrowed his brow, and he gave me a look of such intensity that I did not recognize.

Father Besian's eyes flickered over me once more, and were gone. He made a gesture with his right hand. This was to show mercy. The executioner went behind the stake and quickly throttled the man. The cries of the heretic were cut off.

But the suffocating smoke rose up and enveloped me.

Chapter Twenty-two
Saulo

A wail went up from the drowning men as Panipat closed his mouth to swallow the key.

My hand went to the waistband of my breeches and the knife was in my grasp. I sprang at him.

Throwing my whole weight behind the blow, I stabbed the oarsmaster in the eyeball. He screamed and flung up his hands to protect himself. My fingers tore at his mouth. He tried to clamp it shut but I put my hand over his nose and squeezed as hard as I could until he opened his mouth, screaming curses at me.

I had the key! I had the key!

I turned towards the prow. In one moving mass the remaining slaves strained against their chains as they tried to surge forward. The boat rocked violently.

I stepped back. I saw that if I went close to them they would pull me to pieces.

'I have the shackle key!' I shouted above the tumult. 'But I will only unlock the man who sits still!' I held the key high above my head. 'If anyone rushes me or tries to get this key I'll throw it overboard!'

They stopped then.

'Sit down!' I shouted. 'Sit down!'

This they would not do. But they bent their knees a little to show that they were paying attention. Muttering and moving restlessly, they watched me.

I approached them warily. In keeping my attention fixed on them I forgot about Panipat behind me. I didn't see him reach for the long harpoon we used to catch fish.

It was one of the slaves, Sebastien, who shouted a warning and pointed behind me.

I turned. Panipat towered over me. His arm was already drawn back and now he launched the harpoon like a javelin straight into my face. I jerked my head sideways and the vicious tip of the point sliced open my cheek before thudding into the wood of the mast behind me. Ducking down, I ran at Panipat to head-butt him in the groin.

He laughed at my feebleness, and grasping a good handful of my hair, he yanked my head up and back. My throat was exposed. He laughed again as he reached for the long knife he kept tucked in his belt.

But I hadn't been so stupid as to run at Panipat thinking to overcome him with brute strength. I had already pulled his long knife from his belt. I slashed at him wildly and managed to cut open his arm.

He grunted and began to swing me further away from him that he might aim a blow. I held the long knife out in front of me and pointed it at him. Above our heads, we heard a straining shuddering and the sound of breaking wood. The impact of the harpoon, embedding itself in the mast of our boat, had been the last assault it could take. With an explosive crack it split in two and came down upon us both.

Panipat staggered back. The key went scuttering along the deck.

A great moan of despair came from the mouths of the slaves. Two more on the port side went under, and now the last one was in peril. It was Sebastien. The water lapped around his neck.

Panipat sat down heavily. Blood was pouring from his chest. His long knife was buried deep in his ribs, close to his heart. Driven forward by the force of the falling mast upon me I had killed the oarsmaster with his own knife. In a daze I crawled along the deck and picked up the key. I lowered myself into the forward rowing space on the port side. No bubbles came from the place where the other two had gone under. The water was now so high that I had to plunge my head underneath the surface to see the place where the key fitted.

The dead face of Jean-Luc, eyes wide open, bumped against my own. I screamed and stood up, spluttering water. The remaining slave, Sebastien, stared at me, all hope gone. He leaned back wearily into the water, as if longing for respite and the peace of death. I took an enormous gulp of air and plunged back underneath. I turned the key in the lock of Sebastien's ankle-cuff. When he felt the weight drop away from him, he kicked it free and rose up, water streaming from his hair, tears coursing down his cheeks.

He hugged me, and then we both turned without hesitation to the two Arabs who might be rescued on the other side. Hands clawing in the air, they were sinking quickly. Sebastien came under the water beside me and bore them up as I fumbled the key into the locks. As soon as their chains were loosened, we laid them on the boardwalk and pummelled their backs and chests until they spewed water from their lungs.

We half dragged them past the body of Panipat and hauled them with us up the netting. These two, who had called on the Turks to rescue them, now copied Sebastien: he was shouting as loudly as he could, 'By the rules of combat at sea I am a free man!

'I declare for Spain!'

'For Spain! For Spain!'

'Long live Queen Isabella of Castile!'

'Long live King Ferdinand!'

And, as I clambered aboard, I too declared myself a Spanish freeman.

Chapter Twenty-three
Zarita

Lorena was smirking in a way I didn't understand.

'Zarita . . .' Papa spoke to me gently – so gently, in fact, that I raised my head to look at him. It seemed an age since he'd addressed me in such a tender way. Our household was still recovering after the departure of Father Besian and his officers of the Inquisition a few weeks earlier.

'This gentleman has come to call at our house.' Papa was introducing me to a man I'd never seen before, Don Piero Alvarez. 'Perhaps you would like to stroll in the garden together?'

Don Piero inclined his head to me. 'That would be most pleasant,' he said.

I smiled my assent.

Don Piero was very nervous. He wiped his brow with his hand and offered me his arm. He was of my father's age and I assumed him to be a business acquaintance, for I had never heard his name mentioned as a friend of the family.

Lorena was standing next to the long windows that led into the garden. She placed her hand on Don Piero's sleeve as we passed. She looked up into his face and laughed, and made some trite remark while twirling a lock of her hair in her fingers.

He didn't respond as most men did, by gazing at her with interest. Instead he moved a step away and bowed formally to her.

I found myself warming to this older man. *At last*, I thought, *a man wise enough to see through her silly ways and foolish talk.*

'Perhaps you would like to show Don Piero your mama's garden,' Papa suggested. 'You may walk there with him. I have some papers to look over and sign but I'll be within call at all times.'

I glanced at him. Such a strange thing to say! It wasn't as though I was being escorted by some young man like Ramón Salazar. In my ignorance and stupidity I didn't see what was being contrived without my knowledge.

Lorena ran the tip of her tongue around her lips and laughed again, a knowing laugh.

My father frowned at her and she cast her eyes down, but as she did so she gave me an odd look. Her eyes usually betrayed her dislike, but this time they flashed triumphantly.

I showed Don Piero the rose bushes that Mama had cultivated. Now that summer was here they were blooming. He admired their colour and beauty. Inhaling their heavy scent brought her presence back to me in sweet aching sadness. It was almost August: soon it would be a whole year since Mama's death. To my surprise I found I was able to chat with this stranger about my mother the way I might have done had I an older uncle or even a grandparent to converse with. Don Piero was kind and courteous and listened attentively. Eventually he said, 'May we rest for a short while, Zarita?'

I looked back at the house. How long did my father expect me to entertain this man? We sat down on a bench in the shade of an overhanging bush.

'Tell me more of your mama,' Don Piero urged me. He laid his hand over mine. 'I can sense a great loss in your life.'

'Yes,' I agreed. Tears gathered behind my eyes. At home I didn't have many opportunities to talk about my feelings for Mama. Papa had closed himself off from me and Ramón too was distant when I broached the subject. It was a relief to find someone who seemed to understand that need within me.

'You are lonely.' He nodded and took my hand in his. 'I understand that, for I too am lonely.'

'Your wife, she passed away,' I murmured in reply. I recalled Papa saying as he'd introduced us that Don Piero's wife had died around the same time as Mama.

'We were very happy together,' he said. 'We enjoyed great companionship, and she gave me four good sons.'

'Ah, yes,' I said, my voice tinged with resentment. 'The sons a woman is obliged to bear.'

'Is it a thing you fear, Zarita?'

'What?' I asked him, startled.

'Childbirth.'

'I haven't really thought about it,' I said. What a peculiar turn the conversation had taken! I was unsure whether this topic was quite seemly for us to be discussing.

'It was just that I wondered why you do not look to marry.' Don Piero hesitated. 'Most young girls of your age would be at least formally engaged. You are a great beauty and I am sure you are a good girl.' He said these last words very earnestly. 'I truly do. I'm not saying this to flatter you.'

'I believe you.' I laughed uncomfortably.

'And if it is the other matter that gives you anxiety, then, be assured, I would not trouble you like that.'

I had no idea what Don Piero was taking about, but as I'd found him very sympathetic I didn't want to be rude. I gave him a quick smile and tried to see if Papa was beckoning from the window. Surely by now he would have concluded his business and we could return to the house?

I disengaged myself from Don Piero's grasp and began to get up from the garden bench.

'No, stay,' he begged. 'There's something more I want to say to you.'

I sat back down, and Don Piero went on quickly, stammering as he spoke, 'Your father and I have discussed this. We came to an understanding. I would be very kind. I imagine us sitting together in the quiet of the evening, chatting. I could tell you stories of my life, and you would speak of household matters. We might travel. I have a yearning to see other lands before I die. They say that the islands of Greece are marvellous, with many ancient ruins. I'm sure you would be pleased to see these things and together we—'

I turned to face him. Had he taken leave of his senses as old people do, and begun to ramble, voicing thoughts only loosely connected with the realities of the world?

'Sir,' I began, 'I've no idea of what you are speaking. How could I possibly travel with you? It would not be proper for a man of your years and a young girl.'

'But I promise you' – there was a pleading note in Don Piero's voice – 'it is companionship I seek. I would not bother you in any intimate way.'

Realization came crashing into my mind, and with it the full import of Lorena's smirks. She meant to be rid of me by marrying me off to this old man!

I gasped in outrage. 'Sir!' I leaped up, forgetting my decorum and manners. 'I must, I must—' I set off towards the house and ran indoors.

My father was seated at his desk. He held a pen in his hand. Was he about to sign my life away? It must have been that schemer, Lorena, who had worked this persuasion on him. She was standing just behind him, her hands at the top of his back, massaging the muscles of his shoulders and neck.

It was something I had done when Papa suffered a tension headache. The sight of this served to inflame me further.

'How dare you!' I stalked across the room.

'Why, Zarita,' Lorena asked, looking up at me and opening her eyes very wide, 'whatever is the matter?'

And at the sight of her upturned face with its look of pretend innocence, I drew back my hand and slapped her hard across her cheek.

Lorena squealed in real pain and fright.

And I had my own gratifying moment of triumph and surge of elation.

Confused and bewildered, Don Piero was looking on in dismay from the open garden doors. He glanced at my father. 'You assured me that she was not so unruly . . .' His voice tailed off. His look of disgust did more to bring me to my senses than either my father's anger or Lorena's sobbing.

I knew that I had lost something – my dignity, my pride – I didn't know exactly what name to call it. By allowing Lorena to drive me to the point where I was no longer in control of my actions, I'd diminished myself. Yes, she'd provoked me to this scene, but I had allowed her to do it.

Don Piero left, and Papa called me for a chilly interview in his study.

'Zarita, when you were alone with Don Piero, did he do you any harm?'

'No, Papa.'

'Did he make an improper suggestion to you?'

'He did not.'

'Did he in any way behave incorrectly?'

I shook my head.

'What did he say that upset you so much?' When I didn't reply, Papa raised his voice to me. 'Zarita, how did Don Piero conduct himself in your presence?'

'He was very kind and decent,' I admitted.

'Did you like him?'

'I did like him, but—'

'There is no "but". You have been afforded more than many other girls of families in similar circumstances, Zarita. You have been allowed time to meet and talk with a man I consider suitable as a husband for you. You say yourself that he made a favourable impression you. Very many women do not even see the intended groom before their wedding.'

'Papa, you cannot mean this. Ramón Salazar and I—'

'It might be best to forget Ramón Salazar.'

'No!'

'Listen to me, Zarita!' Papa almost shouted at me. 'I am trying to be considerate of your feelings.' He took me by the shoulders. 'Can I not impart a speck of wisdom into your head? I will not live for ever. What do you think will happen to you when I die?'

I was bewildered by his question. 'I will remain here,' I replied. 'What else would I do?'

'This is not your house. It will not be your house when I die. It will belong to Lorena.'

Lorena!

'What!' I saw the truth in his eyes. Lorena would own the house and the land. If I had to rely on her good graces, she would have me out on the street in only my shift. I would be cleaning the stables, downtrodden and humiliated.

'I will not marry that old man,' I said stubbornly. 'You cannot make me.'

My father sighed. 'It isn't for you to decide what you may

or may not do, but in any case I described you to Don Piero as kind and gentle. I doubt if he'll be willing to contract a marriage to such a wild-tempered girl.' He looked at me as if he'd never known me. 'I told him that you were an obedient daughter who would do anything to please her papa and obey his wishes.'

I held my head up high and faced my father. 'Not any more, Papa,' I replied. 'Not any more.'

Now Lorena ruled over me.

Her position was secured. She'd learned that she would be in complete command of the house when Papa was gone, so she began to take control now. With the imminent threat of the Inquisition removed – it was on record that our town had been inspected – there was less likelihood of them returning. Lorena's behaviour became worse. When Papa was not at home she was less modest and more flagrant in her entertainments.

She brought friends of her own age into the house, men and women, and gossiped with them for hours on end. On occasion I was forced to sit in their company and listen to their idle speculations. Some of them professed a wide knowledge of worldly affairs. I smiled to myself when they talked like this and said nothing. There was more wisdom spoken in the enclosed community of my aunt's nuns than by these self-regarding sophisticates.

One day their conversation turned to the topic of exploration, and the news that the queen and king were considering financing an expedition by an unknown mariner to see if there were lands to the west across the Ocean Sea.

'They say that people live on islands out there who are not true human beings – men who are only half human,' one woman commented.

'Then why should our taxes go to pay for such an expedition?' another asked. 'We won't be able to take these people as slaves. The men will be no use for anything if they are only half human.'

'That depends on which half,' Lorena said with a bawdy chuckle. Her companions joined in, laughing uproariously.

At first I was silent as I didn't understand the joke. But as comprehension dawned, my face blushed and that sent them into another round of laughter at my expense.

'Zarita needs to be married.' Lorena made a gesture in my direction. 'She is over sixteen years old and still doesn't know which end of a flute plays the best tune.'

'Hush,' said one of her friends. 'She lost the mama who would have told her what she needed to know. And anyway' – she lowered her voice – 'one can see that she is only a simple village girl without any skills.'

My face burned even redder, but now it was with anger.

I snapped my fan closed and got up and left the room. How Lorena despised me! But then she had a right to, for I was a person to be looked down upon. I had blundered in trying to help Bartolomé and only succeeded in antagonizing Father Besian. I had insulted Don Piero, offending an honourable and kindly man by being unable to turn down an offer of marriage in a graceful manner. And worst of all, my cries, the stupid selfish screaming of a petulant child, had caused a man to hang.

I went up to my bedroom, pulled off my dress and bodice, untied my hair and lay down on the bed in my petticoats. Tomorrow was the anniversary of my mother's death. Yet another occasion when I'd behaved badly: rather than considering her needs, I had thought only of my own. I should have sat down beside her and held her hand. Instead

I'd flung myself upon her bed, crying out for her not to leave me. Throbbing, blinding pain bound my temples in an iron grip; a migraine of such intensity that I could not raise my head. Ardelia came and stroked my brow. She wrung out a cotton cloth in cold water and laid it across my temples.

I felt tears oozing from under my eyelids.

'Ah, cry, sweetheart,' she said. 'Cry, my darling. Cry for your mama and lost baby brother who would have prevented this had either or both of them lived. Cry for your childhood, now gone for ever. And cry for your papa, for I fear he is lost too.'

Ardelia sang me old nursery rhymes and songs and tried to soothe me. But I cried and cried for hours; through that night and the following night, and the one after that, and on and on, until I was weak and then feverish, and didn't know what day or hour it was.

The doctor was summoned, a fat useless man who knew nothing of illnesses of the body or of the mind.

'She is malingering.' A waspish voice hovered above my head.

Lorena.

'Perhaps . . .' The doctor sounded unsure. 'One never knows. She is hot and flushed and there was a case of Plague on one of the offshore islands not fifty miles away. Remember we are a port. Disease can come here, brought by the ships.'

'She must be quarantined then.' Lorena's voice was much firmer now. 'I will make arrangements for her to be sent away.'

The words echoed in my head.

'Sent away.'

Away, away, away . . .

Chapter Twenty-four
Saulo

Only seven of our freemen rowers and one of the crew made it to safety. Of the oarsmen, two succumbed to their wounds the next day. One of those who died was Lomas.

I went to see him. The Spanish doctor on board the ship had administered an opiate to dull his pain but there was nothing else that could be done for him. He was lucid as he spoke his last words to me.

'Take my goods.' He indicated the bag of possessions that he'd gathered up when scrambling clear of our sinking galley. 'The money I have is for my wife and my son. Will you go and give it to them?'

When I promised that I would do this, Lomas told me his family name and the location of the town where they lived. 'Tell them' – his voice wavered, whether from his condition or emotion I couldn't say – 'tell them, all I did, I did for them.'

I sat by him for an hour after he'd expired, feeling a deep loss resonating in me. Lomas had treated me as a father might a son, and his passing brought back memories of my parents. I rubbed my throat to ease the choking sensation I always felt when I thought of my father. I recalled the events in the magistrate's compound and how Don Vicente Alonso had hit my father in the mouth. And I thought of my reaction when Panipat had done this to me – my knife was in my fist in an instant and I'd plunged it into his eye. How much worse was the fate I planned for the magistrate and his family! I intended to keep the promise I'd made to Lomas to seek out his wife and son, for I knew that I would return to Spain to deal with my own personal business of revenge.

When the cannon of the two Spanish ships had pounded the Turks into submission, they boarded the privateer to capture the men and raid their valuables and cargo before turning her adrift. Our galley was lying partially submerged, still caught up under the prow of the Turkish vessel. I went with the last man of our crew, the carpenter-cook, to collect anything of worth.

The body of Panipat lay where he'd fallen, half sitting with the shaft of his own knife protruding from his chest. I pulled it out and quickly stuck it in my own belt lest the carpenter-cook should see and comment on how the oars-master had died. We tied weights to the dead bodies before pushing them over the side to their graves in the sea. I had to prise Captain Cosimo's stiff fingers from his jacket. I thought perhaps I should wrap him in it, for it was almost heavy enough to pull him under, but the carpenter-cook said quickly, 'You take the jacket, boy. That's legitimate spoils of war. I'll have the rest of the captain's stuff.'

I saw him go into the captain's cubicle, break open the money box and help himself to the few coins inside.

He winked at me and laid his finger along the side of his nose. 'We'll both keep quiet as to what we're about.'

I took this to mean that if I said nothing about him taking the money then he'd tell no one that I had originally been bought as a slave for a barrel of cheap wine. He collected his tools and cooking utensils and left. I lifted the map case and navigational aids. Burdened with these and the peacock jacket, I struggled back up the netting.

A tall man with blond hair stood at the ship's rail. He leaned over the side to help me and eyed the navigational aids and the map case with interest. 'I'm a mariner and explorer,' he said. 'I'd be interested in assessing your salvage. If they're of any use to me I might be able to offer you a good price for them.'

'I don't know,' I replied. 'Our captain was training me to be a navigator and . . . and—' To my embarrassment my voice cracked with emotion as I thought of Captain Cosimo, now lying dead at the bottom of the sea.

'Ah.' The tall man gave me an intelligent look. 'You have a connection to these things that is worth more than their market value?'

I nodded.

'What is your name?' he enquired gently.

'Saulo,' I mumbled.

'And your captain perished defending his men and his boat?'

Again I nodded, not sure that my voice was capable of an answer.

In a gesture of sympathy he placed his hand on my arm. 'Saulo, I tell you, the bonds of loyalty that are forged between men of the sea are very intense.'

He waited until I composed myself and then said, 'Let me at least look at your maps. When you've had that wound on your cheek attended to and rested after your ordeal, come and find me. My name is Christopher Columbus.'

The Spanish ships were on route to Gran Canaria in the Canary Islands, territories situated outside the Mediterranean in the Ocean Sea, and recently brought under the rule of Castile. It was the intention of the conquering nation to plant sugarcane as the land there was deemed suitable for this crop. These ships carried plants and all manner of other things – furniture, foodstuffs, arms, garrison supplies, soldiers and colonists – for Spain wanted a land base off the coast of Africa to equal that set up by the Portuguese elsewhere.

Having thoroughly looted the Turkish vessel, the Spanish were now continuing on their journey. Christopher Columbus was standing on deck talking with the commander of the soldiers when I went to speak with him the next day. This was the man that Captain Cosimo had mentioned – the mariner and explorer who believed that there was a way around the back of maps.

'My galley captain was from Genoa,' I told Columbus. 'He mentioned your name, saying you were an explorer and a skilful mariner. But then, he said the Genoese were the best sailors.'

Columbus nodded. 'Genoa is a tiny state with no room for expansion. We have always looked to the sea for our livelihood, for trade and to travel and colonize. We are expert merchants and navigators.' He said this last sentence with no trace of arrogance in his voice. It was as if he were stating a fact with which no honest person would disagree. 'Your captain was unlucky to get caught by the Turkish ship.'

'Not so much bad luck,' I replied. And I told him of the captain's afflicted sight and how it had cost him his life.

'A captain has hard decisions to make but he shouldn't risk the lives of his crew unnecessarily.'

'Isn't that what you will do if you try to sail to the other side of the Ocean Sea?'

'No,' said Columbus, 'for I have toiled for years research-ing and planning every detail. There will the danger of the unknown, but what is a life worth without some adventure in it? And the sea beckons to me to sail out upon her breast and explore her mysteries.'

His sentiments chimed with my own, and I think he recognized that. We spent the rest of the voyage in each other's company, and he told of his past expeditions and his dream of finding new countries. He asked me about myself, and I found myself telling him some of my life story. I left out the part about the manner of my father's death and my desire to hunt down his killer.

Columbus looked at my maps and gave me a few coins in exchange for permission to take notes from some of them. But in the main they were of little use to him. Captain Cosimo's maps were of the type known as portolan maps, Columbus explained, which show only the view of land as seen from the sea, with mountains and other features marked so that a captain sailing in inshore waters might work out his location. Some of the maps Columbus had were of a different kind, as if viewed from above. They showed the seas of the known world, its countries, cities and towns. The person who'd made them must pretend to be a great bird or a god who can hover high in the sky above the seas and the Earth and observe all that is below.

Columbus had spent time in Portugal, trying without success to persuade the authorities there to invest in his expedition. Now he was pursuing sponsorship with Queen Isabella and King Ferdinand and had more solid hopes of their support. He had been told that his application would be considered by a committee of learned men at the Spanish court. At present he was on a trip to explore the possibility of using the Spanish port at Las Palmas in Gran Canaria as a final stop before sailing west. He'd already sailed south along the African coast in the company of the Portuguese, hoping to reach the end of the continent and find a way round to reach India and the Far East. But so far all who'd done so had not reached the end of land to the south.

'Africa is infinitely larger than any cartographer has projected so far,' Columbus told me.

'Is it worth exploring in itself?' I asked him.

He told me stories of his journey along the west coast of the huge continent, where the colours of the waves flash the iridescent blue of a kingfisher and there are waterfalls so high that they look as though they fall from the door of Heaven. I was both excited and afraid to hear of lands where magical horned beasts roamed and it was rumoured that men ate other men for food. Natives would run onto the beach when they saw a ship passing to wave spears in the air and chant in previously unheard languages. Sometimes they put out in long boats to trade foodstuffs and fresh water. There Columbus had eaten fruit and plants unseen in Europe. My own senses awakened as he spoke. He was a magnificent storyteller. He'd read the diaries of Marco Polo and other explorers and recounted their tales of finding hoards of gemstones, pearls and amber, mingling these with his own experiences. In the evenings I sat on deck with the sails spread full-bellied above me, listening to him and watching his animated face, eyes shining in the light from the ship's lantern; and I ached to go off exploring.

But Columbus's main interest lay to the west, where the rolling ocean stretched to infinity. Beyond it lay the furthest ends of the Earth, and who knew what was waiting to be discovered in those extremities? I'd heard they were peopled by demons who'd escaped the realms of the underworld by using their enormous hooked claws to climb up into our world. They roamed these faraway waters in the company of grotesque sea creatures and fish of gigantic proportions with jagged teeth and stinging tentacles. These were capable of squirting poison into a man's eyes, so that his face and body turned black within minutes and he died screaming in agony. Most of the crew believed that it was madness to venture too far in that direction. Despite their taunts and warnings, Christopher Columbus was determined to navigate his way through these perils.

When questioned or challenged, he would tilt his head, and with an expression that was a mixture of zeal and determination, declare: 'The world is round. I can – no, I *will* find the way to the east by sailing west.'

Chapter Twenty-five
Zarita

Papa came to visit me in the convent hospital.

My aunt had insisted on taking me there when I became ill with a fever the doctor could not name. She'd wanted to nurse me personally and dismissed his suspicions that I might have the Plague; I was exhausted and required rest, she declared. She tended me like a sick baby, spooning food into my mouth and listening quietly to my emotional outpourings.

'You are suffering delayed grief for the loss of your mother,' she told me plainly. 'To lose a mother at any time in your life is a dreadful blow, but as you were on the cusp of womanhood it has affected you very deeply. And' – Aunt Beatriz struggled to express herself without sounding critical of another person – 'your father's decision to remarry so quickly has made it extremely difficult for you to find an outlet for this emotion.' She shivered. 'Added to which there was the disturbance of our recent visitors.'

I assumed that she meant Father Besian. 'Bartolomé is no longer the happy boy I once knew,' I said sadly. 'I doubt if he will ever recover.'

'With God's good grace he will.' Aunt Beatriz kissed my forehead. 'And so will you.'

Now, a few weeks later, I was well enough to be taken to sit with my aunt in her parlour when Papa came and stood before me.

'I hear that you are almost well again, Zarita,' he said. 'However, I do not think that you can return to my house.' He spoke stiffly, not meeting my gaze.

'Papa!' I reached for his hand as I tried to rise from my chair but he moved away from me.

'It's better this way,' he went on. He addressed himself to my aunt. 'I will endow the convent with money. You may name an amount.'

My aunt tried to meet his eye but he looked away from her too. 'When I accept a novice here it is not a question of money,' she said. 'To become a nun a woman should have a true vocation. She must know her own mind. Zarita is very young.'

'Tsk!' Papa made a sound of annoyance. 'Many girls are married and are indeed mothers by her age. I have indulged my daughter in her waywardness, but now is the time to settle things and—'

'What are you speaking of?' I looked from one to the other in bewilderment. 'Is it my future you discuss?'

'I want you to be safe and secure,' Papa said firmly. 'I understand that you might have an aversion to marriage, and this is the only place where I can be assured that you will be taken care of.'

'No!' I cried out, for I didn't want to be walled up inside a convent, even though my aunt and her helpers seemed happy here. The thought of being unable to go freely wherever and whenever I chose, to be denied the joy of walking under the moon at night instead of retiring early to bed – of riding my horse, of singing and dancing when I pleased – horrified me. 'I have no aversion to marriage,' I told Papa.

I was thinking that I could wed Ramón: if that happened, then I'd have my own household and some finances to manage. Even a small amount of money would allow me a measure of independence. Papa would have to give me a sizeable dowry. Although of aristocratic lineage, Ramón's family, like that of Lorena and many of the nobles, had no funds. This was why Lorena had come questing after an older man with money. She had position and a place in society by dint of her father's name, but couldn't afford new dresses or jewellery without access to my papa's money. If Papa himself could marry, then he could easily afford to pay for my wedding.

'Let me be married.'

'To whom will you be married, Zarita?' Papa asked me coldly.

'Why, to Ramón Salazar,' I said. 'We have an understanding.' I paused as I realized that over the last months Ramón had avoided discussing any plans for our future together.

'Ramón Salazar—' Papa began.

My aunt touched my father's sleeve. 'Be gentle, good brother, Don Vicente. Zarita has no inkling of recent events.'

'Of what do I have no knowledge?' I asked them. 'What are you saying?'

Impatiently Papa brushed my aunt's hand away. 'That's exactly what I mean. The girl should be a woman now and yet she behaves like a child. And it is my fault – yes, I admit that. I made a pet of her.' He turned and looked at me, heartache and regret showing on his face. 'I listened to your mama and I spoiled you, and for that I am sorry. It means I protected you too much, and now you are ignorant of the ways of the world.'

'Tell me what I should know,' I said, my breath now coming more rapidly.

Papa spoke brutally. 'The family of Ramón Salazar want nothing more to do with you.'

'That can't be true,' I replied. 'Ramón looked at me

in a certain way. He still speaks to me . . . frequently.'

It was my turn to falter, for now that it was said out loud I saw that I had to admit to noticing that Ramón had cooled in his attitude to me. 'I see in his eyes . . .' I began.

'What you see in his eyes is desire, the way any man would desire a woman as beautiful as you are.' My papa spoke more softly. 'But even if he did hold some affection for you, his family will not permit the marriage now.'

'Why not? They didn't object before.'

'We agreed on an end to any negotiation,' Papa hesitated and then went on, 'and I was not unhappy about this. They cited economies and inconvenience. Ramón has gone to the court to be with his uncle, who is in charge of troops taking part in the siege outside Granada, which is where the queen and king hope to finally crush the Moors.'

'Why would Ramón leave without bidding me farewell? He sent no letter. Why would his family change their mind when it was them who so eagerly sought my hand for their son?'

'You are despoiled, child.' Again Papa could not face me as he spoke. 'The assault of the beggar in the church makes you a less attractive prospect. That's why I tried to arrange something else. Don Piero said he would welcome a companion. He knew of the assault on your person but believed you were an innocent victim.'

'But I was!' I gasped. I recalled Don Piero insisting earnestly that he believed I was a good person. I hadn't picked up the inference that there was any doubt about that. 'It isn't right that a woman's reputation can be brought down by the actions of another. In any case, the beggar barely touched me!'

Papa shook his head. 'You mustn't try to change the story

now that it stands in the way of something you want. The damage is done.'

'There was no damage done to me,' I said desperately. 'I tried to explain this to you at the time, but you wouldn't listen. You were so grief-stricken at losing Mama and the baby—'

Papa held up his hand. 'Stop!' he ordered me. 'The particulars are of no consequence, Zarita. You suffered an assault upon your person. It has changed your personality. It's made you say and do things you wouldn't have done before – make threats and strike out at people. The situation is now so serious that you cannot be allowed to roam free as you once did. It's for your own safety that you must be contained somewhere.' Then he added, 'And for the safety of others.'

'This cannot be!' I said.

'It can and it is,' Papa said grimly. 'I've made a decision and I will not be moved on it. You cannot marry. You cannot come home. Don't you see? There is nothing else for it, Zarita. You must be shut up in the convent.'

Chapter Twenty-six
Saulo

We sailed past the island in the bay of Las Palmas and tied up at the dockside. This new settlement of Castile was a loose arrangement of streets and alleys, with a small church, an army barracks, some official-looking buildings and market stalls surrounded by more substantial houses and trading units.

Christopher Columbus had letters of introduction to the governor of the island, and on presenting these he was given an apartment. He offered me hospitality until such time as the ships were ready to leave and we might gain passage back to Spain.

'A renowned cartographer and cosmographer has made his home here and I intend to seek him out. I suspect the sea is in your blood, Saulo, so you might want to come with me when I visit him. It would benefit you to acquire more knowledge of the stars and shipping lore.'

The first thing I had to sort out was how to acquire some Spanish identity papers. This proved remarkably easy. Christopher Columbus vouchsafed that I'd been on a ship flying the Spanish flag, and that it had been wrecked by an act of enemy aggression and my possessions lost. The governor ordered new documents drawn up for me, and because I had some goods belonging to the freeman rower who'd befriended me, I could pass myself off as a member of his family. Thus I became Saulo de Lomas. When the governor's clerk paused at the section marked 'occupation', Columbus leaned forward and said, 'Write down *Master Mariner*.'

As I gathered up my papers and left the offices, Columbus slapped my back and said cheerfully, 'With me as your patron, Saulo, a master mariner is what you will be.'

And so I spent the next seven months or so under the tutelage of Christopher Columbus. He taught me the rudiments of Latin and Greek and Arabic that I might better understand ancient and modern texts on celestial information. I read extensively: both through the books in the governor's library but also Columbus's collections – a huge variety of materials relating to exploration and the sea. He'd studied the works of the English traveller Sir John Mandeville, who wrote of the existence of monsters, and also the less fanciful tales of Marco Polo. He had a multitude of charts and maps, garnered mainly during his time spent in Portugal. He showed me letters of encouragement from respected professors and mapmakers in different countries, such as the famous Florentine doctor, Toscanelli. These bolstered his self-belief and enthusiasm. I began to realize that Christopher Columbus was not the madman or dreamer that Captain Cosimo and others thought him. He had a vision, but his ideas for its practical application were grounded in accrued facts and learned skills.

When we'd been on board the Spanish ship, Columbus had made notes on the currents of both water and air, perfecting his calculations about the gyre of winds that blow westwards on the latitude of the Canary Islands and return eastwards to Europe above the Azores. Now he hired a dhow, and we spent the summer and autumn sailing offshore around the northern waters of Gran Canaria, testing the tides and wind velocity. He showed how it was possible to know the position of your ship upon the ocean by measuring the height in degrees of the Sun by day and the North Star at night.

'We use a quadrant, but the ancient Arabs learned to navigate using a *kamal* – a piece of wood and a length of knotted string.'

It wasn't Columbus's first visit to the Canaries. He told me he'd already travelled as far west as had ever been charted, to the Azores and Cape Verde islands. The inhabitants there had shown him seed pods that they'd collected from their beaches. Columbus was convinced they were from plants not known to the western world. The islanders described to him the facial features of bodies washed ashore: the men were not similar to any race on this side of the Ocean Sea.

As our friendship developed, he trusted me enough to let me look at the secret maps he intended to use for crossing the Ocean Sea. These were unlike anything I'd ever seen. The known world and the projected world were combined, with both land and sea drawn upon a grid-like pattern with lines of longitude and latitude. He referred to latitude as the 'altura', and had notebooks with lists of these reckonings made for the ports in all discovered territories.

'If we go far enough south, the North Star will disappear below the horizon, so it becomes essential to find your position by using the Sun. Then it's necessary to make adjustments to accommodate the Sun's varying position in the sky during the changing seasons.'

As if a sea mist was rolling back, I saw that in this way one didn't need to hug the coastline to navigate accurately. It could also be done with a reasonable level of certainty in open uncharted waters. Even without the best navigational instruments, an aptitude in using dead reckoning would mean that you could return to a previous position with some degree of accuracy.

Columbus was watching my face as I made this discovery.

'The Portuguese have known about this for years,' he said. 'And now, not only do I have this functional knowledge . . .' He tapped his head. 'Inside here I have the learning of the ancients and the wisdom of the best minds of our day!'

Late one night he took me to visit the cartographer he'd already conferred with. The man was an Arab, and his shop was in a back street near the docks. As we entered, Columbus murmured a greeting in Arabic and the old man replied equally quietly. They made a sign to each other as I wandered among the shelves and peered at ancient parchments, old scrolls and leather-bound books with hinged and locked corded bindings. The shopkeeper went outside and looked up and down the street, then shuttered the window, re-entered the shop, and closed and locked the door.

'Come this way,' he said. Drawing aside a heavy curtain threaded with red and green, he ushered us through to his private room.

The Arab opened a chest and lifted out an object wrapped in a velvet cloth. When he removed the covering, it was revealed to be a large ball made of wood with the outline of the lands and seas of the known world painted on it. Columbus took it in his hands and examined it carefully.

'Look, Saulo,' he said, his voice reverberating in excitement. 'The first depiction ever made of the world as a globe!'

I followed the direction of his finger as it traced a line from the Canary Islands, where we now were, all the way across the Atlantic to where the Arab cartographer had begun to sketch the unknown dreamed-of coastline of far Cathay.

'Yes,' Columbus breathed. 'This is exactly what I want. With this I will convince the King and Queen of Spain and their many advisers that my plan is feasible.'

Chapter Twenty-seven
Saulo

We revisited the Arab's shop, usually in the hours of darkness. Listening to the conversations he had with Columbus I learned more about the waves and the winds and the storms at sea than any book could teach me.

Thus the time passed and my knowledge increased, until one day in early December we got word that the Spanish ships were making ready to return to Spain.

'I must hurry to finish the details on this map-in-the-round,' said the Arab cartographer when Columbus gave him this news.

'You have all my information and my further projections,' Columbus said.

'Yes . . .' The Arab hesitated.

Christopher Columbus looked at him closely. 'You don't believe my figures are correct?'

'There are discrepancies. The circumference of the Earth has been estimated at varying amounts. Yours is a conservative figure.'

'I use more than one source. Where is the problem?'

'The Atlantic – the Ocean Sea as you call it . . . To reach the far eastern side of Asia, the water between this island of Gran Canaria and the shores of Cathay needs to be much wider.'

'There is evidence in the Bible that states the land is in proportion to the seas.' Columbus spoke with conviction.

The old man said nothing.

'And my older sources go back to Egyptian times.'

The Arab grunted. 'Ah, yes, Ptolemy.'

From the books I'd read I now knew that Ptolemy had not been accurate in all his suppositions.

'Ptolemy, and others,' Columbus replied. 'I am correct in this. I know I am.'

I caught the glance of the Arab and his eyes slid away from mine. He was too intelligent to pursue an argument with a man whose mind was so unequivocally made up. But I had glimpsed the stubbornness of Columbus; a flaw in his character that caused him on occasion to disregard the opinions of others or those who disagreed with him.

Despite his misgivings as to the accuracy of the markings, the Arab cartographer fulfilled his commission and the map-in-the-round painted upon the wooden ball was finished and varnished in time for us to take it with us when we set sail for Spain.

Columbus stood at the ship's rail looking back at Las Palmas as we headed for the open sea. 'When I return, it will be as leader of an expedition such as the world has never known!' he said.

I said goodbye to the slave Sebastien, who'd decided not to return to Spain. He liked the hot dry climate of the Canaries and had joined an order of mendicant monks who were establishing a community to assist the native peoples.

It was good to be at sea again. I had a sense of home-coming and was able to observe a larger crew and a professional pilot at work and witness the practical application of the theoretical knowledge I'd learned over the last months. I soon realized that book-learning differs from actuality, and mentioned this to Columbus.

He nodded. 'Without experience a man has no true expertise.'

'And yet,' I said, 'you have no experience of the waters where you intend to sail.'

On the day the coast of Spain came into sight we were standing on deck together.

'Saulo,' said Columbus, 'you are young and fit. You know adequate navigation to be a good sailor. If I am recruiting crew in the near future, would you be available?'

My heart quickened and my brain whirled. What kind of adventure would that be? To cross the Ocean Sea! I imagined myself on the deck of such a ship as might make that journey, setting off to find a land where no man had set foot. 'Captain Cosimo told me that others have tried what you intend but have failed and turned back,' I told him.

'They sailed west from northern waters, deliberately going against the wind, for they feared if they did not, then they would have no wind to blow them home. I intend to set off from further south than from where those westerlies blow. Castile now has a port in the Canary Islands which is far enough south for me to pick up the prevailing winds that blow from east to west. You yourself saw the truth of this. So that is how I will make the outward journey. When I've discovered the route west to the East and reached landfall, then I will sail in a northerly direction along the coast of the Orient and pick up the westerlies to bring me home.'

'These winds that blow across the ocean . . .' I asked him. 'What if they fail? What if you are becalmed?'

He looked at me in delight. 'So you have given it thought. You *are* intrigued by the prospect of discovering new sailing routes.'

And he talked animatedly about the astrolabe he'd

purchased from the Arab mapmaker, but I noticed he hadn't answered my question.

'This extra knowledge of mine will quell all doubts and set aside any objections put forward by the royal advisers. I have been seeking patronage for many years,' Columbus went on, 'but I'm very confident this time. The queen and king are now in the last stages of the siege of Granada. By Christmas the city will fall. In the new year of fourteen ninety-two they will ride in triumph through the streets of Granada to the palace of the Alhambra. And when they've done this they will be in a mood to listen to me. I recognize in them something of myself. Ferdinand gained the throne of Aragon and Isabella that of Castile after huge upheaval and long struggles. They were successful because they believed in themselves. I too believe in my destiny.'

'And do you think they'll support your plans?'

Columbus patted his tunic. Inside he had the latest letter from one of his most ardent supporters, a Father Juan Perez of the La Rábida monastery, where Columbus's young son was being educated. 'Father Perez writes to tell me that Queen Isabella herself wishes to speak to me! The royal treasurer has sent him an advance of money to pay for fine clothes so that I will be able to appear properly dressed at court. Therefore I know that they now look on me with favour.'

Later, as I prepared for sleep, I thought of the only clothes I possessed: second-hand garments that Lomas had given me when I'd outgrown those I'd worn as a boy, and some others paid for by Columbus – rough sandals, a pair of hose and a tunic – and . . . the splendid but not very useful jacket that had once belonged to Captain Cosimo. I pulled it out of Lomas's bag and picked idly at the embroidery on the peacock jacket. I would sell it as soon as I got ashore and use the money to find my way back to Las Conchas. It was too heavy and cumbersome for me to wear. I moved to toss it to one side.

Then I paused and held it up. I'd noticed a curious thing. There was a weighting within the jacket that wasn't accounted for by either the padding or the embroidery. I took Panipat's long knife from my waistband to rip open the lining.

And discovered the second secret of Captain Cosimo.

I saw why there was never much money in the galley cash box, despite the captain's astute trading skills; why he never let the jacket out of his sight; and why, even though it was so heavy, he'd brought it with him when we ran aground on the deserted island fleeing in peril of our life.

When he'd left me in the marketplace the day he'd collected his profit from the cargo, Captain Cosimo hadn't gone off to gamble secretly. Instead he'd paid one of the tailors of the souk to stitch his coins into the jacket lining – something he must have done in every port where we traded. My canny captain hadn't squandered his money. He'd been saving it against the day when he would no longer be able to sail his boat to make a living.

I shoved my fingers through the hole I'd made with my knife. Florins, lions, reals, ducats, doubloons – all manner of silver and gold coins were tucked into the seams, along the hem and around the waist.

I had a fortune in my hands.

Christopher Columbus spoke to me again as the ship docked in the deepwater port of Cádiz and we made ready to disembark.

'I would dearly love to join an exploration such as yours,' I told him, 'but I have business to see to. Family matters that I must . . . put right.'

For although I had no hope of finding my mother alive, I knew that I had to return to Las Conchas and search for her. But, be she alive or dead, I still needed to go there, for I intended to come face to face with the magistrate who had executed my father.

'I too have family I need to attend to,' Columbus replied. 'I must go to Palos to see my son. After I've spoken to him I will travel to the court outside Granada for my audience with the queen. If you change your mind, Saulo, that's where you'll find me.'

I watched him walk away across the quayside, a man who believed that his destiny had been writ, yet had to struggle to see it come true. I contemplated the prospect of sailing off to explore the world. And I hoped that one day I might indeed board ship with Christopher Columbus.

But first I had a mission to accomplish.

Lomas had charged me with ensuring that his family received his wages. His dying declaration was one of love. 'All I did, I did for them.'

I thought of my own family. It had shamed my father to beg but he'd done it; for the same reason Lomas had indentured himself to row in the galley – in order to provide for his family. And just as Lomas's family was owed money, my father was owed justice.

So I would find Lomas's family and give them his savings. But it would be while I was on my way to seek out Don Vicente Alonso de Carbazón. I would return to Las Conchas and go to the magistrate's house to burn it to the ground – and fulfil my vow of vengeance.

PART THREE
PRISONER OF
THE INQUISITION

1491–1492

Chapter Twenty-eight
Zarita

Sister Maddalena laid the cutting shears close to my ear.

The grating sound of metal on metal.

My hair, the shining locks of burnished black that Mama had brushed each evening and my papa had plaited before I went riding with him each morning, tumbled onto the cold tiled floor.

Tears trickled down my cheeks. People had always admired my hair. Many said it was what made me distinctive. From when I was the tiniest child Ardelia, my nurse, had told me the story of the princess who'd been rescued from a tower by a prince using her hair as a rope to climb up to reach her. Ardelia declared that one day a rich and handsome prince would ride up to our house, fall deeply in love with me, and I would become his bride – all because of the length and lustre of my beautiful hair.

Sister Maddalena fetched a broom and gave it to me to sweep up. 'A woman's hair can be her bondage,' she said briskly. 'Think on it, Sister Zarita de Marzena.'

In my aunt's order of nuns a woman could keep her given name. I would still be Zarita, and I'd decided to adopt Mama's family name rather than use Papa's name any more, as, in my view, my father had abandoned me. Not long after the terrible day when he'd told me what was to become of me, we'd learned that Lorena was expecting a child. I realized that Papa would soon be taken up with his new family and then there would no longer be a place for me in his house. I was left with no option but to enter the convent.

My aunt was very quiet on this matter. She wouldn't speak against Papa. I wasn't sure if this was to do with one of the vows of her order: to be charitable in all things. Surely she wasn't supporting Papa's point of view? Once, when I'd been railing against him, she'd murmured, 'Sometimes people do what they think is for the best, and their intentions are misinterpreted.'

I'd put my hands over my ears. 'I won't listen to any justification of his actions. As he has cast me off, thus will I do to him.'

And so it was as Zarita de Marzena that I began my new life as a novice in the convent of the Sisters of Compassion.

Summer cooled into autumn, and autumn became winter, but to my surprise the greyness of the skies was not reflected in my spirits. There was a happiness present in the enclosed community of women that I hadn't expected. The nuns took joy from their work and prayer. They laughed when they ate and sewed together, and delighted in both playing and singing music for Evensong each night.

Removed from the tension of my home and the constant bickering with Lorena, I found calmness seeping into my mind and I began to acquire a peace and perspective that had been absent in my life. My aunt ensured that her nuns continued their education, and encouraged discussions on history, philosophy, politics and science. Many of the texts she used were from scrolls by Jewish scholars and books she'd translated from the Arabic language. Through letters from relatives and friends the enclosed community was kept well informed of events in the outside world.

And so we learned of the culmination of the inquiry by the Inquisition into the case of the holy child of La Guardia.

In November 1491 an *auto-da-fé* was held where three people of Jewish origin, accused of capturing, torturing and crucifying a Christian boy child, were burned to death.

'Despite no family reporting a child missing during the time the boy was supposed to have disappeared.' Sister Maddalena shook her head. 'And despite no body being found; stories were told and denouncements made. It's likely that the officers of the Inquisition employed the same tactics as they used here to get people to betray one another.'

It was December before this news reached us. I was with my aunt and Sister Maddalena in the sewing room, engaged in embroidering a new altar cloth for our chapel in preparation for Christmas.

'This is what happens when fear and suspicion are let loose,' my aunt Beatriz observed. 'It requires a great deal of self-discipline to rein in one's emotions and act in a thoughtful way.'

I began to cry.

The two nuns looked at me and then at each other. Neither of them rose to place their arm around my shoulder or to pat my hand. 'Sister Zarita,' my aunt said calmly, 'tell us why you are distressed.'

'I'm a foolish girl,' I sobbed. 'I did as those you speak of did. I was one of the betrayers of this town when it was inspected by the Inquisition. When I heard the screams of Bartolomé on the morning they began to question him; when I saw what they had done to him; when' – I gulped, tears and tension causing my throat to block and my voice to tremble – 'when I knew that they planned more atrocities for him, I would have said anything, *anything*, to make them stop.' I shuddered. 'They had prepared red-hot pokers and pincers, and . . . and . . .' The memory of that day in the barn rose up in my mind as a vision and I couldn't continue.

My aunt said in a matter-of-fact tone, 'It's only to be expected that you would react in a certain way upon seeing another human being that you love suffering torture.'

'An innocent human being,' Sister Maddalena interjected.

'Yes, indeed, Sister Maddalena,' my aunt went on. 'An innocent human being in great pain. Naturally one would take steps to try to prevent it continuing. I wouldn't blame myself too much over that incident.'

I swallowed my tears and tried to compose myself. If I was to recognize my guilt, then I must do it properly and not in an emotional outburst under the guise of concern for the welfare of another. 'I don't even have that excuse. When I spoke out it was because someone else had named the doctor who lives in the Jewish quarter of the town.'

'Then you named someone to protect another,' Sister Maddalena said loyally.

'No,' I said. 'When I spoke out to avert Father Besian's attention from the doctor, it was only partly to protect *him* . . . It was mainly to protect myself.' There, I had said it. I had owned up to my cowardice. I hung my head in shame for my actions, but nonetheless felt an enormous relief wash through me. 'I thought that if Father Besian quizzed the doctor, then he might say that I'd consulted him and then they would question me.'

'You consulted the Jewish doctor, Zarita!' Sister Maddalena exclaimed.

I nodded. 'I went to the Jewish doctor's house to enquire if he knew of a sick woman in the area. It was he who brought me to the beggar's wife and told me she was dying.'

Sister Maddalena glanced at my aunt. 'We didn't realize

things had happened in quite that way. When you came to us with the dying woman we thought you'd sought her out yourself and realized that she needed hospital care.'

'Who else knows about this?' my aunt said sharply.

'No one, only us. And Garci,' I added.

'You are sure?'

'Yes, why do you ask?'

'In a small town everyone can learn each other's business. Or' – she reflected for a moment – 'members of a household can find out things about each other.'

I looked from one to the other in anxiety. 'Have I brought trouble to your door? I had no idea—'

My aunt smiled reassuringly. 'Let's not dwell on this matter. Father Besian is gone away, we hope never to return. We are little fish compared to the huge catch they hope to make when they finally take Granada.'

There was a silence in the room and then Sister Maddalena asked, 'Whom did you denounce?'

'I spoke against the women who seduce the sailors at the docks. And I feel responsible that two of them were taken to be stripped and scourged. Although they are bad women,' I observed.

'Are they?' my aunt said quietly. 'Would it surprise you to know that we treat some of them within these walls, discreetly and free of charge?'

'No,' I said. 'For in the months I've been here I know you practise true mercy and compassion to everyone without question.'

'And would it shock you to learn that they have clients other than the sailors and packmen who pass through the docks?'

I stared at my aunt. 'I don't know what you mean.'

165

'I mean that respectable men of this town visit these places in the hours of darkness. Men of all classes and affluence. They use and abuse these women. If a pregnancy occurs, they usually abandon them, sometimes even exhorting them to kill the baby, and try to have the women punished if they don't do this.'

'Yet,' I demurred, 'don't they bring this treatment on themselves by their wanton behaviour? Why would any decent woman resort to living in such a manner?'

My aunt leaned forward and looked into my face. 'How would you live, Zarita, cast out by your father, if you didn't have a kindly aunt to take you in?'

I put my head in my hands. 'I am so weak,' I whispered.

'You are young,' said Sister Maddalena. 'The getting of wisdom is not easy.'

'I should not have denounced them. I am guilty of a sin against charity.'

'We are all guilty in some way or other,' my aunt replied. 'I too have regrets over how I acted at the time of our Inquisition. I shouldn't have spoken to the priest, Father Besian, in the manner I did. I almost taunted him. I said that he would be ridiculed if he used a nun drinking mint and a simple-minded boy as examples of heresy. Also, it was pride that led me to show him the script from Queen Isabella granting me the land and her approval for my order. I could have acted more humbly and remained silent when he chastized me. But I didn't. I do believe that our interview annoyed him to such a degree that when he saw he could not catch me out, he decided that he would abuse poor Bartolomé instead. Remember, I had spoken up for Bartolomé earlier outside the church after the service.'

I shivered. I too had tried to intercede for Bartolomé.

'It is not wise to cross so vengeful a man,' my aunt said. 'Father Besian is the type to bear a grudge, to wait and wait until he can be revenged on the person he thinks has offended him.'

Chapter Twenty-nine
Saulo

It was revenge I wanted more than anything else.

More than the gold I'd discovered in Captain Cosimo's jacket, more than to travel with Christopher Columbus to discover new lands, I sought to fulfil the vow I'd made to kill the magistrate. The nightmares that had abated somewhat during my time in the Canary Islands tormented me regularly on my return to Spain.

But the Spain I came back to in 1491 seemed different from the one I'd been forced to leave nearly eighteen months previously. As I travelled east from Cádiz to find the family of the oarsman, Lomas, I saw a people affected by the workings of the Inquisition. In the sea ports where Captain Cosimo had traded, the merchants had often been Jews, but now, inland, there was evidence that many Jewish businesses had closed up. Villagers and innkeepers were wary of strangers. Or had it always been thus and I'd simply been too young and protected by my parents to fully understand what was going on in the wider world?

When I stopped to eat, I noticed that landlords made a great show of informing customers that pork was offered on their menu. Presumably this was to let it be known that they had no connection or sympathy with non-Christian customs, as pork is forbidden to those of certain other faiths. Folk were guarded and suspicious in their remarks, and the talk was mainly of the case of the holy child of La Guardia. Some time before, a young boy of that town had disappeared and eventually, under questioning, a Jew confessed to crucifying the child. A few weeks ago, in November, he, along with two others, had been burned at the stake.

When I commented that anyone might confess to anything depending on the method of interrogation used by the questioner, I soon found myself sitting alone at the dining table. Minutes later the innkeeper came and told me that no room was available for me to rest there that night.

I moved on as quickly as I could, and eventually, north of Málaga, came to the hilltop town where Lomas's wife and son and mother lived. I added some money from the peacock jacket to what Lomas had given me for them, but refused an offer of a meal and a bed for the night. Their grief was too much for me to bear, bringing as it did memories of the loss of my own father. I set out again, heading east, my soul burning afresh with the desire for vengeance.

When I reached the outskirts of Las Conchas and saw the streets near the dockside again, violent emotions began to rage within me.

I'd purchased a good horse and dark clothes so that I could travel easily and unnoticed, and I arrived in the town in mid-December as evening fell. I went immediately to the house where my father had paid rent on our squalid room. There was another family living there so I found the landlord and asked for information about his previous tenants. For fear of some informer I didn't declare that I was any kin to the people I was enquiring about, but I was confident that no one would recognize me. I had grown; my skin was darker, my hair lighter. No longer an undernourished child, I guessed my age was over seventeen, and I was muscular where I'd been thin. I looked and spoke differently. Tall and broad shouldered, I had acquired the confidence that comes with wealth and life experience.

And I was bold, for I had murder in mind.

The landlord assessed my clothes, my bulk and my manner. He replied, telling me the man of that house had been executed, the boy sold as a slave, and the woman had died, and no doubt now lay in a pauper's grave. He looked at me slyly, and said, 'There was rent due.'

I put my hand to my belt, where I carried the long knife I'd pulled from Panipat's body.

'But no matter,' the landlord said hurriedly, backing away. 'No matter.'

Now, under the cover of dark, I stood outside the compound of the magistrate's house in Las Conchas.

I went to the exact spot on the wall where, almost a year and a half ago, I'd climbed up to try to reach my father. The foothold was still there – the place where my frantic bare feet had dug out a hole in the plaster to scrabble my way to the top of the wall. Stronger and taller, I was astride the wall in seconds. As I'd anticipated, there were dogs in the yard. I lobbed the poisoned meat I'd brought with me towards them. There were some yelps and the sound of jaws tearing at the flesh, followed by snuffles and silence. Ten more minutes elapsed before I dropped down from the wall and crept towards the house, a shadow moving in the night.

I waited in the darkness.

Had I found my mother alive, I might have delayed my actions against these people. Although I knew it was a vain hope to imagine that she might still live, hearing my mother's death confirmed had inflamed my anger so that I trembled with anticipation of what I was about to do.

I stood under the tree where they'd hanged my father. I felt the surface of its trunk under my fingers. It had scraped against my legs as I'd bounced and swung about when they hoisted me up. A dreadful image of my father's face appeared before my eyes. The look of dumbfounded terror; the sound of choking. I pressed my fists over my ears.

I took my knife and scraped away a ring of bark right around the tree. Then, from a pouch at my belt, I took a substance I'd bought from the same alchemist who'd sold me the dog poison, and I rubbed this on the exposed flesh of the tree.

From the staff quarters above the stable block at the side of the house I could hear a murmur of voices. Despite the lateness of the hour some of the servants were awake. Their outside doors were closed over against the winter weather, and unless I was very unlucky, it was too cold for anyone to open a shutter to look out. I crept past the building and on towards the barn at the end of the paddock.

It was empty. I found the oil lanterns and poured their contents onto the floor. Before striking a flint to set the fire, I took water from the trough and dampened the straw in places to delay the flames taking hold. I didn't want the blaze here attracting the attention of the occupants of the house before I had broken in to deal with them. I'd planned exactly what I was going to do.

There was light showing from a window on the ground floor. I flattened myself against the wall next to this window, tilted my head and looked in.

Don Vicente Alonso sat at his desk in his study. There were papers before him but he wasn't reading them. Instead he stared off into space. His hair and beard were more grey than I remembered and his face had deeper lines around the eyes and mouth.

I went round to the back door. It was of solid oak.

I couldn't hope to split the panelling. Nor did I want to break a window as I might lose my advantage of surprise.

Tentatively I put my hand on the handle and turned it. The door opened with hardly a sound. Fate was with me. They must be so confident of the protection afforded by the guard dogs that they didn't bother to secure the outside door each evening. I slipped into the house and saw that there was a bolt on the inside of the back door. It was most likely Don Vicente's responsibility to bolt it when his household staff retired to their quarters over the stables. He probably left this task until he himself was going to bed. I smiled grimly as I pushed the bolt across to bar the door. It was a mistake he would pay for with his life.

Quiet as a cat, I walked along the hall and opened the study door.

'Good evening, Don Vicente Alonso de Carbazón, magistrate of Las Conchas.'

He leaped up with a cry of fright. I crossed the room and put my long knife to his neck.

'Where is your family, Don Vicente Alonso?'

He gaped at me, but his natural defences instinctively made him answer. 'I have no family. Get out of my house.'

'You have at least a daughter. That I know for sure. And to have a daughter, a man like you would almost certainly have a wife.'

'Who are you?' he demanded imperiously. 'What are you doing here? Why have you broken into my home?'

I gave a mocking laugh. 'It's too late for you to ask questions,' I said. 'You should have asked questions a year ago last August. Then you might have discovered the truth and not rushed to order the hanging of an innocent man.'

He started back. 'You must be the son of that beggar. I should have hanged you alongside your father – you brigand, you thief, you cur, you – you—'

With my free hand I cuffed him across his mouth to silence him.

'You will tell me where your family is, else I will remove your eyeballs, one by one.'

'I will not,' he said in defiance.

'Very well,' I replied. 'I will blind you and then I will go through the house looking for them.'

When the don heard me say that, he hesitated. Then he spoke haughtily. 'My daughter is at court. Safely away from filth like you.'

'And your wife?'

'No,' he said. 'No. There is no wife. My wife died . . . was dying, that day . . .' He collected himself. 'The incident of which you speak took place on the day – indeed, in the very seconds when my wife was passing from this world to the next.'

I narrowed my eyes and studied his face. He'd spoken with confidence when he'd said that his daughter was not here, but he'd faltered at the mention of a wife. His eyes flicked to the ceiling.

'Could it be that you took another wife?' I speculated. And as soon as I'd said the words I knew I'd hit the mark. I pricked the skin of his throat with my knife.

'Call on her,' I told him.

'She is not here.'

Somewhere upstairs a floorboard creaked.

'We both know that your wife is within the house. Now call on her to come.'

'No,' he replied. 'I will not.'

'I will kill you.'

'You mean to kill me anyway. Do your worst. I will not obey you.'

His obstinacy frightened me, making me reckless. 'So be it,' I said. 'We will burn her alive.' I took the candelabra and set it to the curtains. Then I lifted an ornate glass lamp and smashed it on the floor. The oil ran along the tiles; the flames flowed rapidly after. They began to curl around the wooden table legs.

'Let us wait,' I said, pretending to be unconcerned, 'until she begins to roast in her bed upstairs.'

Don Vicente became agitated. 'I concede that I have a wife. But let us talk about this situation. I also have money. A great deal of money. How much do you want?'

'You think you will pay for what you did to me with money!' I spat the words at him.

He wiped my spittle from his face. 'I will give you anything – anything. Name it.'

The room was becoming hot and filling with smoke. The fire had already leaped to the top of the curtains and was now moving across the ceiling.

'You took away from me everything I ever owned or wanted,' I said.

'You can have everything of mine. Everything.' He was panting and waving his hands desperately in the air. 'All of this.'

'I want your life,' I told him, 'and the life of everyone you hold dear. I will wipe out your breed and your seed.' I quoted the words he had used when giving the order for me to be hanged alongside my father.

Now he was afraid. And I rejoiced at the expression in his eyes and on his face.

'Mercy!' he begged. He held out his hands to me in supplication and appeared to stumble. 'Mercy!'

I leaned forward. Perhaps I *would* be merciful, but for now I would savour this exquisite moment of revenge.

However, this magistrate was clever and cunning and was playing a ruse to catch me off guard. He ducked under my elbow and ran for the door, shouting as he went, 'Lorena! Barricade yourself in your room and call for help. Lorena! Lorena! Open the window and call for help!'

He appeared to trip as he reached the bottom of the stairs, and fell, clutching at his chest. I caught up with him and kicked him as he had done my father.

He didn't stir.

I prodded him with my boot and told him to get up.

Still he did not move.

I bent down cautiously and turned him onto his back.

With eyes wide open he stared up at me.

He was dead.

Don Vicente Alonso, the magistrate, was dead.

His face was suffused with redness. He must have had a heart attack.

At the top of the stairs a woman appeared. She screamed when she saw me. She screamed again, pointing beyond me. I turned. The hall was ablaze. Behind and around me a roaring fire was devouring everything in its path.

The woman shrieked, 'Help! Help! Save me! Save me!'

The flames were scorching us both. I went to the front door and wrenched it open.

Behind me came the woman. I turned. Her hair hung free on her shoulders. She had thrown a house coat around her nightclothes, but it gaped open and I could see that she was heavy with child.

His seed, I thought. *I should destroy his child as he'd said he would destroy my father's. I should raise my knife and murder her where she stands.* There was red blood behind my eyes, and in my mouth the taste of vengeance. Yet I did not move.

The woman stopped and stared at me. I was blocking her exit from the house. Then she began to flail her arms like an insane person and I saw that the fire had got hold of her, and her hair and clothes were aflame. She rushed at me frenziedly.

I stepped aside and let her pass.

She ran away behind the house in the direction of the barn.

'No!' I shouted after her. 'Not that way!'

Suddenly there was an almighty bang and the roof of the barn blew off. Pieces of wood hurtled high above my head and came crashing down beside me. There must have been gunpowder or some kind of explosive stored inside. The pregnant woman couldn't have survived. The realization of her horrendous fate caused my knees to buckle.

There was a lull. Cinders and ash blew through the air. A babble of noise came from the rooms above the stable block on the far side of the house. I raced for the wall and leaped to the top. I didn't stop to look back.

The magistrate, Don Vicente Alonso, was dead. His former wife was dead. His present wife and unborn child were dead.

I should have been glad, rejoicing that my enemies were gone. But the overriding feeling that surged through my mind and body was one of horror and self-disgust.

Chapter Thirty
Zarita

The house was roofless.

Wind blew through the open beams and goats trotted off at my approach. A figure came from the stable block. Even though it was only a few months since I'd seen him, I almost didn't recognize Garci, my father's farm manager. He was a changed man, his dark hair now almost white, his brow furrowed.

He looked at me in my garb of convent grey with the close-fitting coif and wimple. 'Zarita,' he said sadly, 'they have cut off your beautiful hair.'

I recalled what Sister Maddalena had told me regarding a woman's hair, and I thought how much time it saved me not having to comb or dress long hair every day. Also . . . there were few mirrors in a convent.

I replied truthfully, 'I did mind very much to begin with, but now I hardly think of it at all.'

Serafina and Ardelia, both looking wretched, stood at the door of the servants' quarters. Behind them I caught sight of Bartolomé in a corner, mumbling to himself and rocking backwards and forwards. My heart contracted. This once perpetually happy boy had not smiled since the day of his arrest by the Inquisition.

Garci watched me as my gaze travelled around the compound. I frowned as I looked at the tree growing before our front door. Its bark had split apart and there was some kind of rot forming upon it. It would be dead before spring-time. Garci looked from me to the tree and back again. We were both remembering the day my father hanged the beggar. The day my beloved mama died. I gazed at the tree with its mutilated trunk and I shivered.

I turned to look at the house. 'Do we know who did this?' I asked Garci.

He shrugged. 'Who can say? There's so much strife nowadays between Christians, Jews and Moors that criminals take advantage of the conflict and form outlaw bands who thieve and murder with no allegiance to any cause.'

'Have other farmhouses or estates been attacked recently?'

'Not that we've heard.'

'Then they picked my father in particular.'

Garci was not a stupid man. 'I wondered about that,' he said. 'For it would make better sense to choose a more remote estate to rob. This house is close to the town. There are other, richer pickings located further away from where help might come.'

'Was it perhaps an act of vengeance?'

'Anyone that your father sentenced might bear a grudge,' Garci replied. 'Although I don't think they intended to blow up the barn. In case orders ever came from the government instructing him to raise a militia, your father kept gunpowder and some arms stored in an old cellar under the barn. But apart from your father and myself, no one knew of that. The heat from the fire must have caused it to ignite. The explosion rocked the town – people came with buckets of water. We managed to douse the flames in the house, but not before a great deal of damage was done.'

I went towards the house. 'Show me,' I said, 'where you found my papa's body.'

As Garci took me inside the building, an overwhelming

sadness came over me. So many happy days of my youth had been spent here. And now my mama and papa and our beautiful house were all gone.

Garci pointed to the foot of the staircase. 'Your father lay there.'

Through my tears I asked Garci how he thought Papa had died.

'It would have been very quick,' he assured me. 'He'd not been beaten, nor stabbed, nor run through with a sword. The doctor examined him and concluded that he'd had a heart attack. Your papa told no one, but I knew he'd been having chest pains off and on for over a year.' Garci paused, and then added, 'Since your mama died.'

So Papa had suffered grief just as I had. His death seemed to bring me closer to him. Yet he had married again so quickly. As that thought came to me, I asked Garci, 'There was only one body found?'

'Yes.'

'So . . . what of Lorena?'

'We think she got out of the house and went towards the barn. Ardelia is sure she heard someone running past her window, screaming, just before the barn blew up. Lorena must have been caught in the explosion, and such was the intensity, nothing of her would remain.'

I cringed inside when I thought of Lorena's end. She'd died horribly, in absolute terror. Though I'd disliked her, I wouldn't have wished such a fate upon her, nor upon the innocent child who would have died as she perished.

'Was her baby not due to be born soon?'

'Within weeks, yes.'

She must be dead. What other alternative was there? A gang of robbers wouldn't kidnap a heavily pregnant woman.

'Tell me the circumstances in the house before these men arrived.'

'Your stepmother, Lorena, had retired for the night. She was increasingly tired. These last few days she'd been unwell and restless. Although the birthing date is weeks away, Ardelia said that she thought the baby was stirring, getting ready to be born. Lorena had gone to bed. Your father was sitting in his study reading through some papers. Recently he'd been spending a lot of time sorting out financial documents. The lamps and candles were lit. I brought him a glass of wine and bade him goodnight, leaving him to lock up the house from the inside as he always did. I walked the perimeter as usual. All was quiet, nothing amiss. I let the dogs into the yard, ate my own meal with Serafina, and we went to bed. Most everyone else was sleeping. Ardelia and Lorena's maid, who share a room, were awake, gossiping together, but then they too fell asleep. The first noise we heard was the explosion, although Ardelia thinks she awoke moments earlier when she heard Lorena screaming.'

I walked through the hall and what remained of the kitchen and dining room. This was not the work of some random band of marauders. None of the paintings or silk hangings had been taken; neither had the plate or any house-hold valuables been touched.

In the study I stood by the charred remains of the desk and I thought of my papa. I imagined him confronted by these men. He would not have submitted easily to their demands or threats.

Proud and disdainful, Papa would have done everything he could to protect Lorena and his unborn child. I glanced upward. Had she heard the disturbance and come down to see what was happening? Had Papa managed to shout a warning to her? He was an honourable man. He would have done that. Even if he'd died in the attempt.

I walked slowly back to the foot of the stairs. This was where he had fallen. He must have run here and died trying to protect his family. And Lorena, hearing him call out, would have come to the top landing. I imagined her looking down at these robbers. My father shouting to her, ordering her to barricade herself in her room.

I made to mount the stairs.

Behind me Garci said, 'The steps are unsafe.'

'I want to reach the upper floor,' I told him.

He fetched a ladder and helped me clamber up. The floorboards cracked under our feet.

'You must not go to the upstairs sitting room,' he advised me.

That room had been my mother's sitting room, the one that Lorena had taken over to entertain her guests at those foolish little parties she'd hosted.

The main bedroom was to the right and the floorboards were more sound there. The fire hadn't reached here: the only damage had been done by smoke. The door was ajar, the bed-clothes in disarray. Lorena hadn't shut herself in. I examined the door panelling. There was no axe mark, no dent in the wood. On the dressing table lay an open box of jewellery. I ran my fingers through the soot-blackened beads.

Set against human life, how trivial and worthless these things were.

I gazed around me, thinking. If she hadn't hidden in here, had Lorena tried to escape via the window? The casement was shut and locked. I sighed and leaned against the glass. Garci was right: she must have run out in the direction of the barn and perished in the explosion.

I looked outside. The view from this room was towards the paddock, the barn and the forest. Behind the road that lay beyond our back gate were the trees, both deciduous and evergreen. I recalled the walks Mama and I had taken there; the stories she'd told me of wolves and goblins. She'd warned me not to wander across the road to play on my own and never to go there at night. But Lorena hadn't heard those tales. If my father had called out to warn her that they were under attack, perhaps she'd contrived to evade these men. If she'd managed to escape the house, then the forest wouldn't appear a place of dread, it would be a place of refuge.

I turned and walked quickly from the room. 'Saddle me a horse, Garci,' I said. 'I am going into the forest.'

Chapter Thirty-one
Zarita

We found Lorena very easily.

She was half lying against a tree trunk not far into the forest. Her nightgown was blackened and torn, her hair and one side of her face burned. I dismounted, and Garci held the reins while I went forward and knelt beside her. Lorena shrank away from me. Evening shadows were settling in the undergrowth. With the light behind me I suppose I looked like a menacing man approaching her.

'Don't fear, Lorena,' I told her. 'It is I, Zarita. Garci is here too. We have come to help you.'

'The men,' she said. 'There are men in the house.'

'They've gone,' I assured her. I knelt down. 'Where are you hurt?'

'I came into the forest,' she rambled feverishly. 'I tried to hide. Is he dead, your father? It's not my fault. He shouted to warn me. I begged for mercy. I thought the man was going to kill me but he let me go. I didn't go far into the forest. I was afraid.'

'It's all right now,' I said. 'They've gone.'

Lorena groaned as she tried to rise, and fell back.

I put my arm under her shoulder. 'Is your ankle broken? Your leg?'

'The baby' – she pointed to her stomach – 'it's earlier than it should be but I think the baby is coming.'

Garci ran back to find a cart while I tried to help Lorena sit up. She dug her nails into my arm and got herself halfway there, but then twisted round to kneel on all fours. She

183

gasped. 'There is something wrong. I've had these contractions for hours and the child does not move to begin its passage out of my body.'

'My mama was in labour for two days and a night,' I said.

'I don't want to hear about your mama!' she said spitefully. 'Tell me what is left of the house. Anything to take my mind off this pain.'

'The house is . . . damaged.'

'And my husband? Is he dead?'

'My papa is . . .' I hesitated. The promise I'd made as a novice to show charity in all things came into my mind and I tried to speak gently. 'I am sorry to tell you that your husband is dead.'

'I know,' she said. 'I saw him fall. He tried to warn me.'

Ah, so I had been right! Papa's last act had been a noble one.

'And I ran downstairs to him.' Lorena began to cry in a piteous manner.

'You were brave,' I soothed her.

'He called on me to barricade myself in my room.'

'Yes, yes,' I said. 'Papa was trying to protect you and his unborn child.'

Lorena gave me a bitter smile. She looked as though she were about to say something, but just then Garci returned with Ardelia and Serafina. We manhandled Lorena into the cart and transported her, moaning, as fast as we could to the convent hospital.

Sister Maddalena took charge, pushing both my aunt and me from the room. 'Make some infusion of raspberry,' she said. 'It helps a birth. Go on. To the kitchen with both of you. I'll put a salve on her burns and prepare her for her childbed.'

Within minutes Maddalena joined us in the convent kitchen, her face serious. 'The baby is lying across her belly,' she said. 'Also Lorena has begun to bleed heavily. It requires more skill than I have to deliver this child safely.'

'Let us send for a doctor,' I suggested.

'We treat Plague victims and the dockside women who acquire various diseases through association with infected clients,' Sister Maddalena informed me. 'The town doctor will not come here.'

'What can we do?'

'I don't know,' my aunt replied.

'Then who *does* know?' I asked.

'No one.' Sister Maddalena blessed herself. 'If it is God's will—'

'It is *not* God's will that a mother and a child should die!' I shouted. 'I cannot and will not believe that.'

'Hush, Zarita.' My aunt laid her hand on my arm. 'What you say sounds like blasphemy.'

I shook off her hand. 'It cannot be the first time that this kind of thing has occurred. There must be someone who knows something more than we do about the complications of childbirth.'

The vivid recollections of Mama's death were searing through me like labour pains of my own. Every time Lorena cried out, I heard again my own mother doing the same as she birthed the son who'd died. Even though it was nearly eighteen months ago, I vividly remembered how raw fear had fastened a hold on my mind. It was part of the reason I'd sent a message to Ramón to come and escort me to the church to light a candle. Cowardice had propelled me away from the house. When I thought of the events of that day, I regretted what I'd done. Had Mama asked for me as she lay dying, and I hadn't been there?

I pressed my fingers to my temples. This mode of thinking was useless. I knew from past experience that it brought my mind down in a spiral of self-pity and defeated my spirit. I scolded myself – my time in the convent among the constant selfless acts of the sisters had helped me mature. I could not countenance internal self-absorption. I would not allow myself to think in this way.

'Someone must have skills that we do not have,' I declared.

Apart from the fat town doctor, what other doctors did I know? Only the one.

I ran to get my outdoor cloak from its hook in the hall, calling over my shoulder as I went, 'I'll be back as soon as I can. And I will bring a doctor with me.'

Chapter Thirty-two
Saulo

I didn't look back to watch the burning house of the magistrate, Don Vicente Alonso.

When I reached the main highway I rode away from Las Conchas, all that night and most of the next day. Eventually complete exhaustion forced me to find an inn. I paid for a room and fell fully-clothed onto the bed, where I slept until I came to with a fierce headache and pangs in my stomach.

It was dark outside. I had no idea where I was or whether the hour was early or late. I'd dreamed that I was at sea, up to my neck in water on a sinking ship . . .

The bloated faces of drowned sailors drift past me. One of them is Jean-Luc; his mouth is open, crying for succour. But I can hear nothing. Above my head, the mast shatters as if hit by cannon shot. My father is hanging there, his eyes popping from his head. Slowly, silently, the mast bends towards me. I try to move out of its way, but my legs will not obey my will. I am paralysed as death descends upon me. I give out a moan of terror and throw up my hands to ward off the blow. My eyes open and I sit up in bed, shaking and sobbing.

The next days were spent in a similar manner. I had no idea where I was going or what I was doing. During the day I rode until I almost tumbled from my saddle. Then I slept the sleep of the doomed, dreaming terrifying nightmares without end. The pain in my belly increased so much that I needed to consult a doctor in one of the towns where I rested.

He said he could find nothing wrong with me except that I looked as though I needed a good night's sleep. For an extra coin he offered to provide a sleeping draught. I shook my head and made to leave his rooms. As he saw me out of his house, he looked at me closely again and asked, 'When did you last eat?'

I went back to the inn and forced myself to swallow the first food I'd tasted in five days. After twenty-four hours of agonizing belly cramps, I began to recover.

When I thought of what I'd done, a lowering feeling of shame began to creep through me. I thrust it aside and replaced it with another, encouraging anger to be the superior emotion boiling to the surface. I had been cheated, I told myself. Don Vicente and his wife had died by accident, not specifically at my hand.

But there was still the daughter. The magistrate had said she was at the royal court.

I asked the location of Granada and found that I'd ridden well out of my way. The next morning I arose and proceeded more slowly towards the place where Queen Isabella and King Ferdinand were at present holding court.

A hard cold weight had replaced the burning hatred inside my body. I carried it within me like a boulder used by farmers to weigh down the bag when drowning litter runts.

Nothing moved it or diminished it in any way: not drinking myself into an insensible state, nor nights spent with women, nor gambling, nor any other so-called pleasures that men deem sport or amusement to pass their time. There were plenty of such diversions available. As I got nearer to Granada, the villages and towns were full of every type of camp follower and army supplier.

One morning, in a town less than three hours' ride from

Granada, I looked properly in the slice of reflective glass hanging on my bedroom door, and the face of a ruffian looked back at me. If I was to continue with my mission, I would have to do something about my appearance. I shaved and bathed, and after prising some coins from the peacock jacket that I kept rolled up in my saddlebag, I went in search of more elaborate clothes to wear. The tailor I found assured me that he personally designed the costumes worn by the most prestigious nobles in all Spain, including the royal personages – the crown prince, the infantas, and Queen Isabella and King Ferdinand.

'Although taller than his majesty, you do have the look of a man from Aragon,' he said as he took my measurements.

It was a question rather than a statement, but I was not rising like a fish to feed on his bait.

'Do I?' I replied.

He stood back to survey me. 'Or maybe you hail from Catalonia? How are things going in that country now?'

This tailor didn't only want to know my origins, he wanted my politics too. I'd picked up enough knowledge on my way here to know that the Catalans were not kindly disposed to living under King Ferdinand and his Aragon government.

'I wouldn't know,' I retorted. 'I'm recently returned from sea.'

'A mariner!' the man exclaimed. 'Like the famous Christopher Columbus, even now in attendance on the queen and king?'

I grunted. 'I know him, yes.'

The tailor prattled on about how sewing special outfits for mariners was also part of his repertoire, all the while probing me for personal information. I wondered if he was one of the spies that were said to cluster around places of government or merely a casual informant like many other people. It was only when the subject of money came up, when he refused to cut any cloth unless I put down a deposit, that I realized most of his quizzing was designed to discover whether I had the means to pay him. What a delight it was to idly take out a gold coin, spin it on his shop counter, and say casually that I would take two – no, make that three – complete suits of clothing in a variety of patterns, a heavy winter cloak; and yes, I did agree that if I hoped to present myself at court then I would need his most luxurious fur capelet to sit around my neck.

In the end I found him very useful, for in his attempts to garner information he imparted to me a great deal about the workings of the court. He advised me on the most suitable clothes for court functions, the way one should act on specific occasions, how to effect an introduction, when it was considered acceptable to speak out and when to remain silent, and many other tips on manners and modes of behaviour.

While my clothes were being sewn I enquired exactly where the court was and how I might gain access to it. The words of the magistrate, Don Vicente Alonso, were in my mind. When I'd asked for the whereabouts of his daughter, he'd said she was safe. Protected. Within the court. Where the likes of me could never reach her.

My mouth twisted as I reflected how my fortunes had changed. I, Saulo, son of a sick mother and a destitute beggar, had contacts in royal circles. I thought of the mariner, Christopher Columbus, self-styled admiral of the Ocean Sea. He was now my friend. He admired the skills I possessed and would make me welcome. Under his patronage I would obtain free entry, right into the innermost circle of the royal court, to the feet of the queen and king.

No matter how well guarded she was, I would reach the magistrate's daughter. I had to destroy her. I blamed her for the hard stone of resentment still lying within me. It existed because of her. She'd been the start of all my woes. My father had most likely asked her for only one coin. If she'd given it to him, then he, and possibly my mother, would be alive today. It was her fault they were not.

So I would seek her out.

And I would kill her.

Chapter Thirty-three
Zarita

'First you must wash your hands and arms.'

Sister Maddalena snorted and glared at the Jewish doctor. 'We know the rules of hygiene very well here.'

The doctor looked around the room with its spotless floor and bed linen. He inclined his head. 'I appreciate that and I compliment you on it. Nevertheless I insist that you wash once more. I may have brought infection in from outside. Therefore you must roll back your sleeves to the elbow and wash all exposed skin.'

My aunt hesitated. It wasn't right for a man, and worse, a non-Christian man, to see the exposed flesh of a professed nun.

'Oh, do it!' I said crossly. Lorena's howls were agitating me beyond reason. I pushed up my sleeves as far as they would go and washed my hands and arms thoroughly. My aunt and Sister Maddalena followed my example.

'Now I must examine the patient.' The Jewish doctor approached the bed and spoke gently to Lorena, asking her to tell him her name and assuring her that he would do everything in his power to help her. His quiet authority seemed to calm her. If she realized he was a Jew, she gave no sign.

My aunt put her hands beneath the bedcover and raised up Lorena's nightgown. Then she folded down the top sheet to expose only her stomach. The doctor prodded with his fingers and Lorena grimaced. The doctor's face showed no indication of what he felt. When he'd finished, he stood back. 'There is an irregularity,' he said. 'I must make a further examination.'

There was silence in the room.

Lorena chewed on her lip. Even my liberal-minded aunt flinched.

'The birth canal,' the doctor said distinctly, so that there could be no mistaking his intention. 'I must probe the passage itself to determine if there is a blockage preventing the baby from being expelled.'

'That would be improper,' my aunt whispered.

'Let him do it!' Lorena shouted. 'It is I, not you, enduring the pain!'

She kicked her legs up, tossing the sheet aside so that her buttocks and her private parts were exposed. 'Let him look at whatever he wants!' She shrieked in hysterical laughter. 'More than one man has done so before him! It's why I am in this condition now!'

What could she mean? Everyone in the room avoided each other's eyes.

My aunt glanced towards the door. 'You don't know what you're saying,' she said, trying to hush Lorena's ranting.

Sister Maddalena took away the blood-soaked towels from under Lorena's hips and replaced them with fresh ones.

'You must hold her legs bent up and back,' the doctor instructed the two nuns.

Sister Maddalena and my aunt exchanged looks. It was Maddalena who stepped forward first to obey his instructions.

The doctor watched Lorena's face as he probed her with his fingers. Then he addressed himself to her. 'Your baby is lying crosswise to the opening of your womb. In that position the child cannot be born. It may be possible to turn it, but this is not without risk. You are bleeding from some unknown internal place and I doubt that I'm capable of halting the haemorrhage.'

Lorena's face had taken on a pink flush and her eyes glittered as if she were in a fever. As she did not reply to the doctor, my aunt asked, 'What is the alternative?'

'We may cut open her belly and try to rescue the child. She will almost certainly die and possibly the child too.'

'And if we do nothing?'

'Her suffering increases so much that she might go mad. Eventually she dies in agony and then the child too dies.'

'Go ahead!' Lorena spoke in a rush, as if she'd been listening but only just come to a decision. 'Do it. Turn the child and let me be rid of it from my body.'

The Jewish doctor faced me. 'In this state the woman cannot give her permission. If any fatal consequence comes of this action then it would be deemed that I had assaulted her in the most vile manner. That I had taken advantage of a woman while her mind was unsound. I need someone who has wardship of her, or who is her kin, to confirm that I am allowed to do this.'

'I am her – her . . .' My tongue stumbled on the words. 'I am her stepdaughter. I give you the permission you need.'

Sister Maddalena hurried to write out a document for me to sign while the doctor again washed his hands and returned to the bed. He pummelled at Lorena's belly. This time he was not gentle and took no notice of her shrieks as he struggled to turn the child so it would lie head down in the birth canal. Without ceasing his efforts he kept manipulating the baby towards the course he desired. Sweat ran down his face, glistening on his eyebrows and beard.

Lorena was roaring. Her contractions now followed each

other without respite. I wiped her brow as she thrashed in the bed and my aunt and Sister Maddalena coaxed the child from her womb. Lorena gave an almighty scream as the head crowned, and then another cry was heard in the room.

The heart-stopping, insistent, desperate cry of the newborn.

'A boy,' my aunt announced, holding up a blood-red, raw, squirming baby.

My heart and head spun with relief and joy.

The doctor took him and pronounced him healthy. He then looked again at the intimate parts of Lorena's body. He drew me and my aunt aside. 'She will not live long,' he told us. 'It's as I thought. There is a bleeding that I cannot stop.'

'Is there anything we can do?'

'You might want to summon one of your priests to guide her soul into the afterlife that has been prepared by your God for his followers.'

As the Jewish doctor packed away his instruments in a worn leather bag, it struck me how weary he looked. I thought of how it must reduce a doctor to know that some-one he has treated will, despite his best efforts, die.

'My belly aches,' Lorena said in a weary voice. 'I can feel blood seeping between my legs. Is there nothing that can be done to stop it?'

I glanced at the doctor.

'Is there?' Lorena persisted.

'No,' he told her plainly.

'Then I am doomed.' Tears coursed down her cheeks.

'Let her see the child,' the doctor advised us. 'It will give her fortitude and hope. If not for herself personally, then she'll draw strength for her ordeal to come, knowing that she leaves part of herself in this world.'

But Lorena turned her face away when the child was brought to her. 'No,' she said bitterly. 'I'll not look upon him. I'll not let him see me. He will know another as his mother, not I.'

Beatriz put the baby in the crib Maddalena had prepared. I went to sit by Lorena's bed.

She looked at me. 'They say that when you are dying you speak the truth. I am near death, so I will confess to you the wrongs I have done. It may be my one chance to enter into Heaven. For if it is left to the virtue of the life I have lived, of my mind and my body' – she laughed, and a sudden flash of the old Lorena, of her rash gaiety, shone through the pallor on her face – 'then I am both doomed *and* damned.'

'We will summon a priest,' I said.

'Oh, no!' Lorena pursed her lips. 'No. For I would give the priest you brought such nightmares and put such wild thoughts into his head that he wouldn't be able to cope. Then he would have to confess to another, and he in turn to yet a third, and so it would go on, and think what a fuss and consternation there would be.'

At one time that kind of commotion would have suited Lorena very well, I thought to myself; she who loved so much to have men gazing after her and thinking all sorts about her.

My aunt addressed herself to Sister Maddalena. 'Please escort the good doctor to our front door and then fetch a priest to hear this woman's confession.'

Sister Maddalena nodded and went out with the doctor while my aunt Beatriz gave Lorena the potion he'd left. He'd told us that it might cause confusion in her mind but would give her a painless passage from this world to the next.

Lorena opened her eyes wide to stare at me. 'Why did you help me?' she demanded. 'Why, when I treated you so badly, Zarita, did you care enough to try to save my life and that of my child?'

I could not truly express why I'd done so. Living the life of a nun meant translating the love of God into charitable action rather than merely reciting words. But it was more than that. 'You were my father's wife,' I said. 'And the baby is kin to me.'

'The baby isn't any kin of yours.'

'Of course he is,' I said. 'Try to rest.'

'I say again, Zarita, that none of your family's blood runs within that child.'

I assumed that the opiate was starting to take effect. As the doctor had forewarned us, Lorena was losing her mental faculties. I made to place a cloth on her brow but she pushed my hand away.

'Listen to me, Zarita! Your father was anxious for a son and we didn't seem able to make one together. I tried every folk remedy and potion, but none worked. Then I began to think that he was tiring of me and my attractions, so I decided to lie with another younger man whose seed might bear fruit in my womb.'

My aunt looked at Lorena in alarm. 'You are wandering in your thoughts, Lorena. Better to be quiet now.'

'I'm not so confused that I don't know the true father of my own son!' Lorena exclaimed. 'His name is Ramón Salazar.'

Chapter Thirty-four
Zarita

'What!'

'The child you worked so hard to save was not sired by your father, Zarita,' Lorena said emphatically. 'Believe me, I know. I managed to make your father believe that it was his, but it wasn't. The child was conceived by my reckless plan to provide him with a son so that my own position would be secure.'

'Your child's father is Ramón Salazar?' My voice croaked in stunned disbelief.

'He is. Ramón has such an empty face with no distinguishing features that I thought the child would have mainly my looks. But I shouldn't have done it. I ask you to forgive me.'

I looked to my aunt Beatriz for guidance. But she was equally taken aback. I fumbled for words as I tried to absorb what I'd just heard.

'This is not a sin that it's in my power to forgive,' I told Lorena. 'The wrong you did there was to my father, and I am glad that he's not here to discover that truth.'

'But the son he wanted was partly for your sake!' Lorena cried out. 'Oh yes, your father longed for a son to carry his name, but it was also for your welfare. He thought you too young and headstrong to manage your own affairs. He worried that when he died, a devious man might come along and master you and have command of all your possessions. He wanted to father a son on me so that the boy would grow up to protect his older sister!'

'Papa still had concern for my welfare?'

'He loved you very much, your father, but men are such gulls when they desire a woman. It's easy to twist their minds and their hearts. I used my position in your father's affections and I turned him against you. I told him that you hated me insanely and lied to others about me. I reported that you'd taken some of my things; that you'd stolen my personal possessions, and contrived to leave these in your room so that he could find them there.'

I gasped. 'My father said nothing of this to me.'

'Of course he wouldn't. He made me promise never to speak of it to anyone else. But it forced him to agree with me at last that you should be sent away, for I said you might do the new baby harm. After he saw you slap my face on the day Don Piero called to propose to you, I convinced him that you had a wildness in you. I said you'd made threats, that you hinted of bad things you might do if ever there was a new child in the house.'

No wonder Papa believed me half mad and wanted to put me safely away.

'It was *I* who was insane.' Lorena's breathing was heavier, yet she seemed to gather reserves of strength from within to carry on making her last confession. 'I was madly jealous of his love for you. For myself, I cannot say that I loved your father. I married him to get out of my own father's home, where there was no spare money for parties or pretty clothes. I wanted to have some fun and command my own household, and with you there it was impossible. Even when he'd banished you to the convent, he went on loving you. He spoke of you often; of how you used to read to each other at night.'

My heart was comforted. At last I understood now why

Lorena wanted me gone and I felt true and sincere sympathy for her position.

'I need your forgiveness,' said Lorena in distress. 'I beg for it. Please say that you forgive me that I may suffer less torment in the afterlife.'

'I do. I do.' I knelt by her bed and took her hand in mine. 'I readily forgive you, Lorena. The fault was not only yours. I should have been more welcoming. I see now that I didn't care for my father's happiness. I resented you for taking the black mourning curtains from the windows. But it was the right thing to do – to let some light into the house after four months of grief. I forgive you.'

'But I have done a greater misdeed.' Lorena's eyes were dulling, her eyelids drooping down.

'It's all right,' I assured her. 'Be at peace.'

'No, you must pay attention, Zarita. I was so envious of you. I did everything I could to be like you. I listened to his stories. I tried to read his books – his dull, dull books. But he loved you, always you. So I thought that if I could get rid of you, then I would be able to control the house and him.'

'You had your way in that, Lorena. Papa sent me away.'

'Yes, but as soon as you were gone he missed you. He told me how you used to ride out together each day.'

Papa had loved me.

I remembered the early mornings of my childhood – going to the stables as the sun was rising and a bluish pale moon hung in the sky. Papa was by my side as we cantered past the forest to the green valley, hearing the call of wild creatures, seeing the hovering kestrel and hawk. A fast gallop through the meadows of sweet green grass and then a trot home, with him telling me tales of his own childhood. I felt

200

a great pang of loss and wished that our last times together had been more pleasant.

'Your papa actually *pined* for you.' Lorena's speech was slurred, but in her desire to unburden her soul she forced herself to continue. 'I felt rejected. And the servants who'd disliked me from the beginning now hated me. Oh, they wouldn't have gone so far as to poison me, but they resented my being in your mother's rooms. They gave me sullen looks and performed each task I asked them as slowly as possible. I blamed all this on you. And then I think your papa began to turn from me and become watchful. His health was giving him worries. He started to sort his papers and make arrangements for the disposal of his estate. I discovered that he'd taken a large amount of money and hidden it away somewhere. It was for you, in case anything happened to him. He was having recurring pains in his chest and believed his heart was weakening. I think he thought he might be close to death. And I knew his next step would be to disinherit me and perhaps even the child if he found out it wasn't his. So I made plans to rid myself of you.' She raised her head up from her pillow. 'I decided that I would kill you!'

'This is mere fancy,' I said firmly. 'We quarrelled, that's true, but no real malice was intended.'

'It was on my part,' Lorena said hoarsely. 'You must escape. Zarita, you must escape!'

'It is safe here,' I told her.

'Nowhere is safe from them.' Her eyes darted around in panic. 'Nowhere. You must leave Spain.'

Leave Spain! She was delirious. I took the cloth, wrung it out in cold water and bathed her forehead. Her skin looked like my mama's had the day she'd died. She was slipping away very quickly now. I spoke to my aunt: 'Where is the priest?'

'I'll go and find out.' She hurried from the room.

'Are we alone?' Lorena whispered.

'Yes.' I had to lean close to her mouth to hear.

'I have betrayed you, Zarita, in the most . . . most wicked way.'

'Anything you have done, I forgive.'

'The letter . . .' Now she really was drifting, her mind clouding as her spirit began to disassociate itself from her body, ready for its flight to the next world. 'There's no escape. The letter . . . The letter . . .'

The door opened and my aunt entered with the priest. He set out the bowls of holy oils on the bedside table and opened his prayer book.

'Zarita,' Lorena said faintly, 'you will burn . . . the letter . . .'

I nodded. 'Yes, I will burn the letter.' I had no idea what letter she meant, but I agreed with what she was saying in order to placate her in her last moments. 'All your papers will be burned.' This had already happened. I thought of the charred remains in the family home.

'Too late,' she murmured. 'It is gone.'

If the letter was gone, then why did she want me to burn it?

Within a minute, Lorena too was gone. Her breathing rattled and then ceased. My aunt waited before drawing up the sheet to cover her face.

'What ailed her at the end?' The priest looked at me searchingly.

'She was rambling,' I said. 'Everything was mixed up in her head.' It was not for me to make a confession on behalf of another.

'I will pray for her troubled soul,' the priest said, and then added thoughtfully, 'It was as if she carried a great guilt and did not want to face her Maker with it still on her conscience; something specific . . . something yet to be discovered.'

Chapter Thirty-five
Saulo

About a week after Christmas I rode through the outskirts of the royal encampment at Santa Fe.

The court was making ready for the official royal entry into Granada as the city's ruler, Sultan Boabdil, had agreed to surrender the city on the second of January. Queen Isabella and King Ferdinand had given orders that following this there would be a glorious triumphal procession to signify that the *Reconquista* was complete. The Moors were vanquished and the country was united under Spanish rule.

Outside the walls the nobility and clergy were gathering in tents and temporary accommodation. Wooden storage units and supplies and equipment clustered around this new village that Queen Isabella had ordered built out of the solid rock in order that the army could continue the siege through the winter. It took me most of the day to find news of Christopher Columbus. No one I spoke to knew where he was; many didn't recognize his name. Perhaps he wasn't as well known at court as he'd claimed. Then it occurred to me to seek out the court astronomer, and sure enough, Columbus was lodged there and I found him seated in this man's quarters, deep in conversation with a group of important-looking men.

'Saulo!' He greeted me eagerly. 'The business that you had to attend to has obviously brought you profit.' He indicated my new clothes. I didn't reply. He was not to know of my unfinished business, or of the deed I was here to perform. He waved to me to stand beside his chair while he continued his conversation with these men, who were advisers to the queen and king.

'I can do this, I promise you,' Columbus was assuring them. 'If you give me the funding then this coming year, fourteen ninety-two, will be the one when I prove that my calculations are correct. I will find the passage west before any other man.'

'To finance such an expedition would cost a great deal of money.'

This comment came from a man dressed in the garb of a notary. It was known that the monarchs guarded their purses against the ruinous cost of the war.

'True, but the rewards would far outweigh the costs. And we strive to succeed not only for wealth. Queen Isabella vowed that all Spain would be Christian. This would be her opportunity to evangelize previously unknown territory.'

'A bountiful harvest of souls for God,' one of the monks agreed. He wore the habit of the Franciscans, the order which had befriended Columbus.

For a moment I thought of embarking on this dangerous and ambitious expedition. To slough off my cares for an adventure in a new place. What islands we might discover on the way! What fabulous peoples to meet, what exotic tastes to sample, what sights to see: animals and plants that no European had ever set eyes on before. For me it was not so much the glory that might come with these discoveries; rather it was the excitement of exploration that enchanted me, as I saw it did Columbus. His stance altered when he talked of his plans and dreams. His eyes glistened as he described what might be, the endless possibilities of new lands, the wonderment of knowing all God's creation. He saw it as a duty to get to know the furthest extremities of our universe. This was why the Franciscans were drawn to his side, for they followed the rule of the man of Assisi who'd marvelled at and respected every living thing. I understood that, for Christopher Columbus, it was almost as if finding the new route to bring spices out of the East, away from the control of the Ottoman Empire, were a secondary purpose. Something he'd thought of to please his backers and coax them to invest in his project.

'The prestige alone would be immense,' Columbus continued. 'To be the first country to have ventured so far; to be the nation that proves that the world is round . . .'

'Round . . .? How . . .?' another of his listeners asked. 'Circular? A disc? A dome?'

'A globe,' said Columbus. He plunged his hand into a bag lying at his feet, and with a theatrical flourish brought out the large wooden ball on which was painted the known countries of the Earth. 'Like this!'

'Ahh!' His audience gave a satisfyingly appreciative gasp. They moved closer to study it.

'If you can go round west to east *and* east to west, there must still be a flat surface at the top and bottom,' one of the priests observed.

'I don't believe so,' Columbus said gravely. 'I believe the world to be round in its entirety – completely, like a ball.'

The priest leaned forward and asked, 'Then where is the location of Heaven and Hell?'

There ensued a lively debate among the clergy present as to whether the ideas of Christopher Columbus could be accommodated in theological terms. I saw that, although there were doubters, he had managed over the years to gather a group of loyal and intelligent supporters. But this particular priest was not to be silenced. He picked up the wooden ball and examined it. 'What did you call this?'

'A globe, Father Besian,' replied Christopher Columbus. 'It represents the world on which we live.'

'A globe,' Father Besian repeated. He indicated the manner in which the countries curved around its surface. 'If we live upon a curved surface, then how,' he demanded triumphantly, 'does one not fall off?'

The court astronomer spoke up. 'We believe a force exists that keeps us bound to Earth.'

'The will of the Almighty,' Father Besian intoned.

There was a silence. And then the Franciscan friar smiled at Father Besian. 'What else could it be?'

When the court advisers had left, Columbus went over to the table by the window, where one of his maps was laid out. He placed the tips of his index and middle finger on Spain. Then he walked them across the flat surface until they reached the end of the table where the parchment met the wooden board. Columbus made one more step with his forefinger extended so that it hung in mid air, and then allowed his hand to drop over the side of the table.

'Do you believe that is the fate that awaits me, Saulo?'

I stared at the floor and then my eyes returned to the map. 'No, I do not,' I replied. 'I think there will be great peril in getting there, and even more in getting home. But . . . just think – suppose a man went out westwards and did not return across the Ocean Sea, but came sailing home from the East.'

'Exactly!' Columbus voice resonated with excitement. 'To voyage round the whole world, and return bringing gifts! From the East! Like the Magi, bearing gold and frankincense!

Mysterious, exotic and wonderful! Laden down with silver, spices and silks from Cathay!'

'That is a land I'd like to see.'

'Then you must come with me, Saulo.' He seized my hands in his own. 'Come with me! Be part of the adventure!'

Chapter Thirty-six
Zarita

'I think you should make a visit to the royal court.'

It was the day after Christmas. A wet nurse had been secured for Lorena's baby, and it had been one of the pleasures of my life to give the care of the boy child into the hands of Garci, Serafina and Ardelia. He would live with them in the staff quarters until the estate was settled and the house rebuilt. As far as they knew, this was my father's son and they welcomed him with joy. And I found too that the baby had insinuated himself into my heart, which to my surprise had not shattered when I'd learned that Ramón had betrayed me in the arms of Lorena. Garci restored my old cradle, and Serafina and Ardelia made baby clothes. The sheets and blankets were freshly laundered and I brought him to them on Christmas Day. As he was tucked in, the little boy gurgled and blew a bubble from his lips.

I'd turned to leave and saw Bartolomé standing watching. 'Why don't you come and say hello?' I prompted him.

He approached the cradle cautiously. I took his hand and placed it over the baby's. The child opened his fingers and curled them around Bartolomé's thumb.

'Oh,' Bartolomé breathed. And for the first time since the dreadful day of his arrest, he smiled.

The next morning in the convent my aunt Beatriz made her surprise announcement.

'Visit the court!' I said in astonishment. 'What a crazy idea! Whatever for? And where would the money come from for me to do that?'

Aunt Beatriz smiled a knowing smile.

'Ah!' I said, understanding coming to me. 'Was it here that Papa deposited the secret amount of money that Lorena told me about when she was dying?'

My aunt nodded. 'He made me swear not to tell you until the time approached for you to take your final vows. And then I was to let you know, so that you could choose whether you wanted to remain in the convent or live outside, modestly but independently.'

I took a minute to digest this information – how I had misjudged my father's intentions towards me, I thought – and then I said, 'But even if I have funds to finance the trip, why would I wish to visit the royal court?'

'I feel it is your duty to let Ramón know that he has a son.'

'It may be that he doesn't want to know,' I pointed out. I'd been surprised by my own reaction on hearing Lorena's secret. Of course I'd felt shock and disappointment at Ramón's betrayal. But it wasn't having the long-term devastating effect on me that it might have had previously. Where once I might have given way to seething anger and despair, now I viewed the matter in a different way. I suspected that my relationship with Ramón had been superficial; our mutual attraction based on looks and possessions. The troubles we had encountered at the time of my mama's death hadn't drawn us together; on the contrary, we'd grown apart. Afterwards I was so much taken up with my feud with Lorena to appreciate what was happening between us and to realize the implications of the change in his manner. And indeed I'd been too immature to properly assess his character, for, although Lorena had seduced him, using the wiles of an older woman to flatter a younger man, Ramón had been a willing partner.

'Most men like to know that they are capable of fathering a son,' said my aunt. 'They think that they can establish a dynasty through the male line. It is curious, for it's the women who bind a family together and women who keep the household on a steady course. So it may be that Ramón wouldn't acknowledge him publicly, but it would be wrong for us to conceal the child's birth from his father.'

I thought about this. What complications might arise from the news that the child was not Papa's? If things were left as they were, then the boy would inherit the estate. I didn't mind this. I would have sufficient money to live well enough whether I chose to remain in the convent or leave it. I was unsure that telling Ramón was the correct thing to do. Perhaps my aunt was right, perhaps not. But in any case, I did want to see Ramón Salazar again. There was unfinished business between us.

'You should go within the week,' my aunt said. 'A new year beginning will mark a new stage in your own life, Zarita. While the court is outside Granada it's less than a day's journey from here. I'll contact an old friend who will find you accommodation and escort you to functions.'

'An old friend?' I teased her. 'Would this be a man?'

'I had many gallants who wooed me,' Aunt Beatriz countered, but there was a hint of something unsaid in her eyes, so I persisted.

'Did you favour any of them in a special way?'

Her cheeks dimpled. 'Oh, I could speak the language of the fan as well as any señorita at court.' She paused. 'Yes, there was one. But he was not a courtier. He was of such lowly birth that my father, your maternal grandfather, would not countenance any liaison, so my gallant went away. He was killed in the War of Succession when the Portuguese tried to claim the Spanish crown. I thought I would die of a broken heart. I expect my father was thinking only of my welfare, but I judged him harshly, as no doubt you have your own father.'

Less harshly, I thought, now that I'd learned the reasons for his actions.

'We are not so different, you and I, Zarita,' my aunt continued. 'I was very like you before I learned more of the ways of the world. My father arranged an affluent marriage for me. He wanted me to have a secure position and income so that I could manage my own house, but I was young and wilful so I ran away.'

'You ran away!'

'Oh, don't be so shocked,' she laughed. 'I only ran as far as the nearest nunnery. So initially mine wasn't a true religious vocation. I didn't seek out the Lord. But sometimes now I think perhaps He sought me out, for this is where I have found love and abiding peace.'

Yes, we were similar, my aunt and I. And I too had discovered peace within the walls of the convent, but had I found love?

'This friend I speak of, Zarita, was like another sister to me. She decided to marry for expediency and not to follow me into the cloister. And just as well, for it would have made a merry unrest here with two of us like-minded for fun and dancing. Her name is Eloisa and I will write to her. She will receive you into her household: you may come and go within her protection and she will engineer for you a meeting with Ramón Salazar.'

'Very well,' I said meekly. 'But I will go as a nun.'

'I think not.' My aunt smiled, a light of mischief in her eyes. 'You will go as a princess.'

She led me up into the loft of the convent house to find an old wooden trunk. 'I brought this with me when I founded the order here,' she said. 'I wonder if any of these gowns will still fit me.'

She was taller than me, and despite being older she still had the slimness of a girl. Her way of life had given rise to none of the roundness of body that my mother had developed due to childbearing and a fondness for cake.

We opened up the chest, and there, swaddled in layers of silk, were the clothes my aunt had worn when she attended the royal court as a young girl. She lifted out a full-skirted red dress with a black net overskirt. 'The style must be horrendously out of date but the material is of the best quality and Eloisa will have a seamstress who can alter it.' She shook out the skirts and held it against herself. 'I used to wear this dress with a necklace of rubies round my throat.'

I put my hand to my neck. I remembered the blackened beads in my mother's jewellery box.

My aunt Beatriz must have guessed what was in my mind. 'Always remember, sweetheart,' she said, 'that a beautiful flower needs no adornment.'

Beatriz shed tears as we said goodbye. 'Send word to me when you arrive. Give my love to Eloisa. I hope things go well.'

Before I stepped into the carriage I took my aunt's hand in my own. 'It isn't just for the matter of the child that I am travelling to the court to speak to Ramón Salazar.'

My aunt gave me a farewell kiss on the cheek. 'I know, Zarita,' she said. 'I know.'

Chapter Thirty-seven
Saulo

It was the idea of Christopher Columbus that I should engage with the company of the court and try to win the favour of as many influential people as possible.

'Saulo, the ladies will swoon over you,' Columbus declared. 'You cut a striking figure, with your height and build, and the clarity of your eyes, blazing azure blue, having been at sea so long. Yet' – he paused and studied my clothes – 'perhaps you might consider whether your dress is a mite *too* attractive. After all' – he clapped me on the shoulder – 'you don't want to outshine those affluent nobles that we want to impress.'

I'd already come to something of the same conclusion regarding the elaborate suits I'd purchased from the smooth-talking tailor. What had appeared sophisticated and elegant in his shop mirror, with his tongue dripping flattery over me like oil over cheese, now appeared vain and overdressed in the looking glass Columbus had set opposite the window of his room.

I took the heavy fur capelet from around my neck and cast it aside. 'I can't imagine how one wears one of these every day,' I agreed.

'Ah, now, that's better.' Columbus nodded. 'We can see your face.'

He'd allowed me use of an alcove within his own room where I might stay until the court moved into Granada. There I discarded most of the rest of my finery and reverted to black tunic and hose, high leather boots and a loose white shirt with a minimum amount of pin-tuck stitching down the front and along the cuffs of the sleeves. I gathered up my cloak, stuck my long knife in my belt and was ready to sally forth.

On this, the night before the victory procession into Granada, the royal reception rooms were thronging with people eating and drinking and taking advantage of the monarchs' rare hospitality. Queen Isabella and King Ferdinand were usually frugal in their expenditure, for the war had depleted their treasury. It was accounted as fact that the queen had pawned her jewels to finance the siege, and neither she nor her husband dressed extravagantly. I edged my way through the crowds. I was curious to see the warrior woman of whom I'd heard so much.

And then I saw a different woman and I stopped very still.

She was standing gazing up at a tapestry. There was a serenity about her that arrested attention. The wall hanging showed a map of Spain. It was a pale green colour, with the names of the various provinces and kingdoms stitched in gold. In her dress of dark red the woman stood out against it in form and figure as a rose might stand out in a garden of ordinary grasses.

I thought her beautiful from the first second I saw her. Her hair was caught up in a black lace snood, so neatly that it completely exposed her chin, her neck, the curve of her shoulders. Her dress was very plain. No jewellery adorned her. It served to make her distinctive among the rainbow colours of the rest of the guests, in their gaudy satins and heavy velvets shot with silver lace and cloth of gold, all decorated with precious stones, their fingers heavy with rings.

The way she carried herself indicated that, although part of the room, she was aloof from it. I followed the line of her neck to her shoulder, down her arm to where her hands, holding her fan, rested in the folds of her skirt. She turned, very slowly, to survey the room, and I saw her brow, her nose, her face. She was exquisite.

I searched the room until I found what I reckoned to be the most alert servant, a young man with a keen, intelligent face. I went to him and said, 'Find out the name of that girl and I will give you a coin.' Then I returned to a vantage point from where I could watch her.

Within a few minutes the servant returned and spoke to me. 'Her name is Zarita de Marzena. She is from some village and is here only for a short visit under the protection of Señora Eloisa de Parada. It's her first time at court.' He glanced at her and grinned at me. 'Can't you tell?'

I gave him his coin. When he saw that it was gold, he said, 'Whatever else you need, señor, I, Rafael, am the man to get it for you. I'm attached to the fourth supply unit. You can call on me any time of the day or night.'

The girl's chaperon was close beside her, but my tailor's advice and instruction on the correct form of etiquette flew from my head. I decided to accost them without finding a mutual acquaintance to make the first contact. I made my way across the room. I felt the older woman appraise me closely as I introduced myself to her. But I was not watching the chaperon's face. It was the girl's eyes that I fixed upon.

And she looked back at me. Most directly, without embarrassment or any false coquettishness.

Clustered around her face, little curls of her hair escaping from the lace snood, made a frame for her features like paintings one sees in churches of angels. It was a very unusual

216

style. Most women wore their hair long, and arranged it with ornate combs to hold it in place. I thought: she isn't vain, for generally women want to show their hair and put on jewellery to enhance themselves, to bring out the colour of their eyes with sapphires, jet or emeralds.

Her eyes were steady. A tiny tremor crossed her face.

'You seem interested in this tapestry, Zarita de Marzena,' I said when her chaperon had finally made the introduction that allowed me to speak to her. 'It's a splendid exposition of the lands our monarchs hope to rule.'

'The work is very good,' she replied in a melodious voice. 'I'm glad you think so too. It would have taken long hours of toil, and embroidery is a skill that most men don't value.'

'Yet you do?' I wondered how she would know of such things. Being rich, she would surely fill her days with idleness. 'From where did you get your knowledge?'

'In the convent of my aunt.'

'You are a nun!' I felt as though I'd been struck a physical blow. That explained the hair, her manner, her disregard for finery. Disappointment swamped me. I stepped back.

'No . . .' She hesitated. 'Not quite. I took refuge there for a while when family matters overwhelmed me.'

I waited. After my first brave effort I didn't know how to continue the conversation.

'I meant no insult to men,' she went on, ignoring my gaucheness. 'But it isn't merely the fine stitching that makes this so wonderful, it's what's involved in the planning of the whole piece that perhaps men might not appreciate.'

'Oh, but I do,' I replied, more confidently now. 'For I am a navigator mariner, and setting out on a sea voyage isn't just about boarding a ship and casting off. One needs to think out the whole journey first, its purpose and its obstacles.' As I said this I remembered Captain Cosimo who, despite his bad eyesight, had been a careful planner, a fine mariner and astute in business affairs; I had learned these skills from him. And as I thought of him, I had a sudden ache inside me to escape the stuffiness and restrictions of this place and to be on the water again.

She noticed the change in me. 'You seem preoccupied. Did your session with Christopher Columbus and their majesties' advisers go well?'

'How did you know that myself and Christopher Columbus had been in conference with the court advisers today?'

'My chaperon says everyone at court knows the business of everyone else.'

'It went as well as any session would that consists of a group of men of differing opinion, each with his own agenda.'

She gave a little laugh. 'And do you think Señor Columbus will be successful in his aspirations?'

I thought of what I knew of Christopher Columbus. His confidence in his predictions, his unshakeable faith in the order of the universe under God, his love of life and the elemental forces of the sea, his skill as a mariner, his expertise in the basic navigational skills known to the Phoenicians and Greeks, his ability to improvise and think quickly.

'I am sure of it,' I replied.

'I heard that they think his calculations are in error.'

'The figures may be slightly inaccurate. The breadth of the Ocean Sea is a tremendously complicated thing to assess. But no matter the arithmetic, the principle is the same. There is land to the west, for the world is round.'

'I can follow that . . .' She spoke carefully, as if working it out. 'If there is land to the east, and we know there is, and the world is round, then by definition, there must be land to the west.'

'Bravo!' I said. 'Many learned men seem to have trouble grasping that notion.'

'Yet if it is so far away' – she tilted her head to look up at the map again and I saw her throat and wanted to reach out and touch her skin – 'and if the winds that blow you west are not strong enough to bring you back, how would you return . . .? Oh, I see!' she said before I could reply. 'You might go all the way round.'

'That would require a great deal of thought. And more planning than the construction of a tapestry,' I added to tease her.

'But it's so exciting.' Her voice quickened with interest. 'Tell me how you think it could be done.'

Chapter Thirty-eight
Zarita

Despite the cold weather the royal reception rooms were hot and full of the loud chatter of hordes of people. It was the eve of the monarchs' triumphal entry into Granada, and nobles, clergy and merchants wanted to be part of the spectacle. The noise assaulted my senses as Señora Eloisa and I stood under a wall hanging near an outer door.

Señora Eloisa took in the room before us. 'Now, if you were searching for a husband, Zarita—' she began.

'I am not,' I interrupted her.

'But if you were,' she continued, 'it would be crucial for you to meet the right people. There are those who are well connected and very rich, those who have noble blood but are penniless, and those with fabulous fortunes who are of merchant stock.' She snapped open her fan and waved it briskly before her. 'Those who have none of these attributes we will of course ignore completely.'

I was surprised by such rudeness, but then realized my aunt's friend was using sarcasm as wit.

'My days of the chase are over, so for this excursion into court society it's up to you to decide which you prefer.'

'I only came for the opportunity to have a short interview with Ramón Salazar,' I reminded her.

'Indeed, and I will arrange that as soon as I am able. But in the meantime, a woman as stunning as yourself will be the subject of curiosity.' She looked me over with approval. 'I must admit I have excelled myself in making over that dress of Beatriz's. Removing the overskirt of black net to reveal the deep red was inspired. It suits your dark colouring. You are so like her that it's as if the dress were made for you. And then my genius in covering up your shorn locks with the specially made snood of black lace. Perfect! Perfect!' she complimented herself. 'You'll find that all sorts will come clustering round us wanting to meet you; the informality of this court next to a battleground means we will have to admit them to our presence.'

Aunt Beatriz had chosen my chaperon well. Eloisa's health was not good and lately she lived mainly in her estates in the north. But to help her old friend she'd travelled south to meet me, arranged accommodation for us, and was now bravely overcoming her fatigue to escort me around the court. I noticed that she was starting to enjoy herself.

'You will not be in a room for long, Zarita,' she said, 'without attracting the attention of a young gallant. In fact I have my eye on one such person who is at this very moment studying you most intently.' She shielded her mouth with her fan and said, 'I believe you have caught the eye of the mariner who is with Christopher Columbus, the explorer-navigator who seeks royal financial backing. It's said they had a difficult interview with the clergy and courtiers this after-noon: they believe he's miscounted the miles in his proposed expedition. This companion of Columbus cannot take his eyes off you.'

'Where is he?' I asked. I swivelled round slowly.

And saw him.

He stood out among the others by virtue of his height, his bearing and his looks. Where once I would have raised my hand and spread my fan to cover the lower part of my face, now I did not. I met his direct gaze with one of my own as he approached me.

'I beg leave to introduce myself. I am Saulo de Lomas, the mariner who accompanies the explorer and navigator Christopher Columbus.' He addressed himself to my chaperon but he was looking at me.

There was something in his eyes; something exciting yet familiar, as though an inner part of me connected in some way with his soul.

Señora Eloisa glanced at me to ascertain whether I wished to accept his introduction. I indicated that I did, and she replied, 'I am pleased to make your acquaintance, Saulo the mariner. I am Señora Eloisa de Parada, widow of Don Juan de Parada.'

Eloisa then went on to chat for an interminable length of time about the weather, the state of the roads, the price of flour, the arrangements for tomorrow's procession into Granada, the difficulty in hiring an honest servant, again the condition of the roads, until I could have hit her with my fan. Eventually she halted her flow and said to him, 'Saulo the mariner, allow me to introduce the niece of a friend of mine.' Eloisa inclined her head in my direction. 'Zarita de Marzena.'

He was dressed in a very distinctive way. No hat on his head, no capelet or fancy collar around his shoulders, his hair caught back at the nape of his neck by a loosely tied strip of rough black silk, the top layer of his hair bleached by the sun. His face was tanned, with a fine pale scar showing just below his left cheekbone. His shirt shone white against the black of his tunic, hose and boots. He carried no sword, but had a long dagger of eastern origin in his belt. When he stood by me he didn't smooth his hair or adjust his cuffs as other men do while assessing the impression they are making. I couldn't imagine this man preening before a mirror, fretting about his appearance.

His lips parted and he smiled at me, and something went to my heart with that smile.

I thought to tell him as soon as I could that I was from a convent, and was ridiculously pleased by the crushed expression that came over his face. Then we fell easily into conversation, and he had humour and wit and fascinating stories and such an open mind. Beatriz would love him, I thought, for his questioning intellect.

It would have been rude to enquire, but I was sure he wasn't of noble birth; yet he was well read and knew some Latin and Greek and had travelled extensively.

We didn't move from that spot throughout the evening, and were still there when the queen and king left in procession with their attendants and advisers.

Saulo pointed out the explorer Christopher Columbus to me. 'Look,' he said. 'That is the man who will prove that the world is round.'

We'd been pushed back to allow the royals to pass and Saulo was very close to me, so close I could feel the heat from his body. I knew that he was identifying Christopher Columbus so that I could be a witness to history, and I was pleased that he thought to do this. But rather than being awed at seeing Señor Columbus, I was more thrilled by the presence of the man at my side.

Chapter Thirty-nine
Saulo

'That is Christopher Columbus.'

I said his name and pointed him out to Zarita as the procession of royals, nobles, clergy and dignitaries went past.

'Yes,' she said softly, and our faces almost touched. I felt her breath on the side of my cheek and her nearness filled all my senses.

Queen Isabella was smaller and plainer than I'd imagined, but the aura of authority was about her, in the set of her chin and the cast of her face. I could well believe every tale I'd heard of her: the fierce defence of her throne and of her right to rule Castile, despite being a woman; the call to her troops to defend their land, her kingdom, while riding out, in full armour, to show herself in the midst of battle; gathering up stones herself from the high sierras after fire destroyed the tented encampment and declaring she would build a town here before the walls of Granada rather than lift the siege. The king too looked like a man who had fought hard battles, spending long hours in the saddle galloping between Castile and Aragon to uphold the monarchs' rule in both kingdoms.

Towards the end of the retinue I saw the priest who'd questioned Columbus about the globe of the Earth and the location of Heaven and Hell. I recalled his name as Father Besian. He was staring at Zarita, his expression both surprised and angry. She was unaware of him: after ascertaining which man was Columbus, she turned back to me. My gaze followed the priest for another few seconds. After his initial reaction his face had changed. He now bestowed on Zarita a look of calculation and cruel intensity.

Her chaperon made to take her away. Impulsively I reached out to detain her, and for an instant our hands touched. The contact startled her and she dropped her fan. Quickly I picked it up and returned it to her.

I whispered, 'Look for me in the procession tomorrow.'

That night I went back to my alcove singing.

I arose early the next day, thinking that it would be a simple matter to ride out and find Zarita and her chaperon. What lay before me on the approach roads before the city of Granada was the largest gathering of people I'd ever seen in my entire life.

Queen Isabella was mounted on a white horse and dressed in full royal regalia, with a gem-studded golden dress showing tier upon tier of golden skirts caught up to reveal petticoats of silver cloth. A white ermine cloak was clasped about her shoulders, so full and luxurious it swathed the hindquarters of her horse. From her head fell a long white veil, held in place by a golden crown. She sparkled in the winter sun as she sat on her mount like the queen she was.

The king was astride a black stallion. His clothes blazed out beside her, red and gold velvet and satin, with a fitted tunic and padded coat with slashed sleeves. They were attended by their son, the crown prince Juan, and their daughters rode close behind. Then followed the clergy: cardinals, archbishops, bishops, priests, and lines of monks of different orders – Greyfriars and Blackfriars. And after these came the nobles and merchants, the court officials and servants.

Ranged on either side was the army, in splendid formation displaying their colours and flags. The air was thick with the smell of gunpowder and incense, while the shouting of orders, the chatter of a thousand people, the neighing of horses made a tumult of sound.

My heart squeezed in anxiety. I would never find Zarita!

Instead of plunging in among the throng I went in search of the fourth supply unit and the servant, Rafael. He wasn't there but the master of the stores told me where he should be. As soon as Rafael saw me he came running. When I told him whom I sought, he was off, returning just as the signal had been given for the parade to move off. He apologized for the delay and gave me a fix on Zarita's probable location within the ranks.

She was wearing a riding habit of midnight blue, close fitting at the neck and waist, with a matching velvet hat. The way she sat on her horse told me she was a true horsewoman, whereas I, more at home on a ship, had difficulty in working my way across to her.

She acknowledged me with a look of delight, and at once I felt awkward and clumsy and had no idea how to greet her.

She stretched across her horse and pointed with her whip. 'You will find it easier to control your mount if you adjust the bit,' she advised me. 'You have him on too short a rein. If you want to guide a horse on a certain path, then gentling is the best way.'

'Does that advice hold true for women?' I asked.

She blushed. I apologized immediately. She accepted my apologies. I felt she had forgiven me. And I didn't regret my daring remark, for if she'd cared not at all for me she would have been insulted and angry, not embarrassed and excited. And she *was* excited. Not only at the spectacle before us, but also I thought, because I was by her side.

Chapter Forty
Zarita

Eloisa and I were waiting over an hour for the procession to move off and I began to despair of seeing Saulo.

I'd spent a sleepless night going over every detail of our conversation, listing the interesting things he'd said of which I wanted to know more. I relived my sensations when I first saw him approach across the reception room. I gloried in visualizing him before me. Lying in my bed, under the fur robes Eloisa insisted on piling upon me to keep me warm, I imagined the whole evening again. Now my throat constricted with worry. Did he feel for me what I felt for him? He was so very good looking. He could have his pick of women, and they'd admire him for his mind too, and for the stories he told of the places he'd travelled. His knowledge of the sea and the stars was immense. Unlike the dry learning I'd acquired from books, Saulo had true experience of what the world was like, and what was happening in it.

As we lined up with the others in the cavalcade, unhappiness crept over me. Saulo wasn't coming. He must have met many women more entertaining and sophisticated than a simple village girl. He thought nothing of our meeting. It was a flirtation, that was all. I'd misread the signs. I was an idiot, a fool.

And then he was beside me and looking at me, and the truth was in his eyes. My mood swung upwards. Instantly I was sure he'd been thinking of me since we'd been apart. He nodded in greeting, and suddenly I felt quite superior, for I saw that he was awkward and nervous and I could be in command of this situation.

I boldly leaned over and bade him loosen the rein to let his horse have some freedom of movement. I told him it was a mistake to try to bend an intelligent creature to one's will by force. I cautioned him to be gentle, saying he was more likely to get his way by kind persuasion. He tilted his head, and with his eyes smiling into mine asked if that was how he should deal with a woman!

A thrill of pleasure shot through me. I felt my face go hot. He affected contrition, saying that he hoped he hadn't offended me, that he was in so much awe of my presence that his tongue tripped him up. He made a ceremony of this humble apology, but I could see that he was watching me to judge whether he was still in my good graces and hoping for more than that.

There was a rise in tension between us but also a growing familiar ease. We both knew what was happening and were prepared to revel in it.

Chapter Forty-one
Saulo

Christopher Columbus was to lodge with the royal astronomer but accommodation was so restricted that there was no room for me. I went to the army officer in charge of billeting to ask if he could squeeze me in somewhere. Rafael appeared by my side.

'Señor Saulo, I will find you a room – perhaps even within the Alhambra Palace itself,' he said. 'I would of course need some coins with which to bribe the appropriate officials.'

I gave Rafael more money and, making arrangements to meet up later, wandered into the town.

The streets were silent and the people I saw as I passed the Jewish quarter looked at me fearfully. I'd heard some of the more thoughtful courtiers speak of settlements under Moorish rule known as the *comunistas* where all religions lived peaceably together. Did Queen Isabella and King Ferdinand know of these communities? Wouldn't it be better to accommodate people of different religions and cultures and allow them to live in this way? I thought of my parents, and now, with the wisdom of maturity, I appreciated that for one reason or another they'd been driven out from every-where they'd tried to settle. They'd been educated people, for they had taught me letters and reading and how to count numbers. I had no idea to which creed or culture they owed their loyalty for they'd never spoken of it to me, probably considering it too deadly a secret to entrust to a young boy.

What were our monarchs doing in the name of a united

Spain? If we banished the Moors we would lose their learning. A great deal of the navigational information used in the Mediterranean was of Arab origin. If rumours were true, then we were about to exile the Jews, and their skills and knowledge would go with them too.

It was late afternoon before I met again with Rafael.

'The palace is very full,' he told me, 'but I've managed to secure you space in an outbuilding.'

When we reached my attic room I gave Rafael a generous payment. 'Now that you've found me a room,' I said, 'I'd like you to find me another. Zarita de Marzena has been given quarters here. I'm minded to walk by her corridor so that we could meet by chance.'

Rafael winked at me, gathered up his money and went off whistling. I took the chance to eat and wash and change my clothes. When Rafael came back he was in a different mood.

'I know where she and her chaperon are,' he said in a worried tone of voice. 'But, Señor Saulo, it would be best if you turned your attention elsewhere. There are plenty of pretty ladies at the court. Some of them would be more accommodating of a man's needs than that one. I could arrange a liaison, very discreet—'

'How dare you!' I grabbed him by the neck and shook him until he sobbed.

'Sir! Sir! Hear me. That lady is not for you! She brings bad luck with her!'

I raised my fist.

'Oh, noble Don, I beg you, listen to what I have to say!'

I released my grip and Rafael crashed to the floor. I went to stand by the window, my father's begging voice echoing in my ears. 'I am not a don,' I said from between clenched teeth. 'Never address me in that way.'

'No, sir.' Rafael wiped his face as he got to his feet. 'I won't make that mistake again.'

I turned away from the sight of him, sickened by my own brutality.

'Sir,' Rafael went on, 'I don't mean to insult the lady. Last night she was regarded as sweet and innocent, but when I made enquiries about her, I heard some talk that she is dangerous.'

'Dangerous!' I scoffed. 'She's a very gentle girl.'

'She is, she is,' he agreed. 'It's not that she is dangerous in herself, it's more that . . .'

'What?'

'I don't know,' he said miserably. 'These rumours have only just begun. Sometimes servants hear of things before they happen. It's been whispered that none of the maids want to be allocated to her rooms. They are nervous, extremely nervous, but no one can tell why. I'll try to find out more.'

Although he was reluctant to do so, I made Rafael disclose the location of Zarita's quarters, and as the sun set and the torches were being lit in the palace, I went to find her.

The Alhambra Palace consisted of the most intriguing and beauteous buildings. Courtyard led off courtyard, fountains sparkled, intricate patterns of tiles adorned walls, floors and ceilings. Arches and alcoves glowed with three-dimensional coloured plasterwork. Even in the depths of winter, blossom flowered in trees and bushes. The air was filled with the scent of rosemary and lavender. There were ornate jars and pots of plants, known and unknown: mint, fennel, basil – herbs for cooking and healing.

I came at last to an area of enclosed courtyards and had to search to find a door that led to an outside corridor. Then another door and a wall, easily climbed.

And there she was.

Zarita stood in a paved area beside a pillar covered in winter-flowering jasmine. She'd plucked a sprig of the yellow flower and held it in her fingers. As I dropped from the wall into the courtyard, she started in fright, but then, recognizing me, she glanced towards the full-length window of the inside room. Cautiously I peered across and saw Señora Eloisa standing by a table chatting to one of the foreign ambassadors.

'Would it be permitted for me to call on you formally this evening?' I whispered.

Zarita shook her head. 'It's impossible,' she whispered back. 'Someone else is coming to see us. And you shouldn't be here,' she scolded me. 'I cannot speak to you unless I am chaperoned.'

'Then *I* will speak to *you*,' I returned smartly, 'for I have no need of a chaperon. And as you may not reply, you will be forced to listen quietly to all that I have to say.'

'I meant that we mustn't talk to each other,' she said, pretending to be cross at my deliberate misunderstanding.

'I am content with that restriction too,' I said, moving closer to her. 'Let's neither of us talk then.'

She began to tremble, and bent her head. I put my finger under her chin to raise her face to mine. And she raised her head again and the light of vibrant life was in her eyes. Her lips were parted and she looked so very, very lovely I experienced an overwhelming surge of emotion. She was aware of it, and it seemed to coincide with some deep feeling of her own. She swayed in towards me. I bent my head and her lips brushed against mine.

We broke apart at once.

'I'm sorry,' I said. I stood away from her. My heart raced. I heard its thud in my ears.

Chapter Forty-two
Zarita

His lips were on mine and fire ran through me.

We sprang apart. He looked confused and stammered that he was sorry for what he'd done.

I was not at all sorry.

He kept repeating how sorry he was until, to make him stop, I asked him to tell me something about the ocean. I'd always viewed the sea as functional but he spoke of its beauty. He believed it to be Nature's greatest wonder: a work of art, a friend, a provider, a good companion – majestic, compelling, entrancing, and an awesome force when roused.

He told me that, at sea, no two days were ever the same. He described watching the morning lighting the sky, dawn dancing on the horizon; and evenings when the sun poured molten gold across the surface of the water. He loved boats and one day he meant to buy his own. He would be the sole commander and crew and he'd sail away beyond the setting sun to undiscovered countries.

'I've stood on the prow of a ship, Zarita,' he told me with eyes glowing. 'There is no sensation more uplifting than being there with the ship running before the wind. One feels the power of nature as she crests the waves. And' – he moved towards me – 'it is the most pleasurable experience imaginable. Or . . . *one* of the most pleasurable.'

Blushing, I turned from him.

He stepped much closer behind me and put his mouth to my ear. 'The sails fill out above your head. The backbone of the ship arches against the waves. And she's alive: she is with you, allowing herself to be guided, but with a spirit of her own.'

He traced his fingers down my backbone and let his hand rest lightly on the lowest curve of my spine. 'Like a woman when a man makes love to her.'

I shuddered and leaned into him and he wrapped his arms around me. I made to swivel round and face him.

'No, don't move,' he whispered. 'You must not turn round.'

'I want to.'

'I know. I know you do.' His breath was warm in my hair. 'But if you do, I am lost. And I must keep my senses now, else we will both be destroyed.'

I heard Eloisa call out my name.

And he disappeared.

A shadow in the garden, then nothing.

Eloisa came to the window and beckoned to me. 'I'm sorry to have left you on your own for so long, Zarita, but the ambassador was saying such amusing things, telling me of the latest Italian fashion and dances.' She looked at me more closely. 'You are flushed. Are you well?'

'I am very well indeed.'

'Well enough to see Ramón Salazar later this evening?'

'Yes,' I said. I wanted any business I had with Ramón Salazar to be over as quickly as possible.

There was the matter of the child: my aunt believed Ramón had a right to know about the baby. But I also needed to dispel any false memories I had of our time together. A new and different love was growing within me. Between Saulo and myself was a meeting of minds as well as strong physical attraction. It was far removed from the feelings I'd had for Ramón Salazar. I was a different Zarita from those days. Physically I had grown, my body filled out in woman-hood; but my manner and my mind were also altered. I'd been flattered by Ramón's pursuit of me, even though I knew at the time that my father's money was part of the reason he was courting me. And Papa, who wanted noble blood in his line of descendants, had allowed an informal betrothal. Yet . . . Papa had not appeared to object too much when Ramón had left Las Conchas. Indeed he'd said that he was happy that the marriage wouldn't take place. Had he come to realize that Ramón would not be a good husband to me, and set aside his own desire for noble connections for my benefit? My aunt had never spoken against Papa. In fact once she'd made a comment, saying that sometimes people could be mis-understood even though they did things with the best of intentions.

And now my personal reasons for meeting Ramón were even more urgent. I wanted to be sure that there was nothing left of the feelings of girlish love I'd had for him. It would underline the truth of the love I now felt for Saulo.

Yes, I most certainly did want to see Ramón Salazar.

Chapter Forty-three
Saulo

On the way back to my room I noticed none of the unusual architectural features of the palace or the stunning decorations on the walls. Thoughts tumbled freely in my head. Zarita and I were soul mates. I needed her as she did me. Without each other our lives would be incomplete. We must be wed without delay. She was only here for a short visit. I needed to gain enough status to be a worthy suitor for her. I'd no position in society but I had money. I could help finance the expedition across the Ocean Sea. Christopher Columbus was keen for me to join him, and if he became an admiral, then he might appoint me to a rank of one kind or another. That would give me some standing. I would have to speak to Zarita's chaperon and then her family. There would be an interview with her father. I sweated over that. What if he looked on me with disdain? If he refused me, would she abide by his wishes?

Columbus wanted to set out this year, and it was possible that could happen, for more and more of the clergy and royal advisers approved of his project. So if Zarita and I were to be married, it had to be now.

But would she accept my proposal? There was only one way to find out and that was to ask her. I decided to do this as soon as I was able. Señora Eloisa and Zarita were expecting a guest. I would wait until after the evening meal, and then I would go secretly to their apartment the way I'd done this morning, and I would tap on Zarita's window and ask her to marry me.

Chapter Forty-four
Zarita

Ramón was boring!

How could I have imagined myself in love with such a self-regarding prig? Lorena's assessment of him had been accurate. Ramón had a nondescript face with no mark of character on it; he was a silly boy who'd become a weak and vain man. I reflected on the wisdom of my papa, whom I now believed had stalled the marriage contract, realizing that the Salazar family only wanted access to his money and that Ramón was an unsuitable match for me. Whereas I'd been flattered, my head turned by the first young man who had paid me much attention.

Papa! I thought. *I wish you were here that I might thank you.* In my foolish wilfulness I hadn't seen that he was working to protect me.

Eloisa stifled a yawn behind her hand. Ramón had supped with us for over two hours. After allowing me to bring him up to date with some of the events in my life, he'd spent the rest of the time talking without listening, regaling us with tales about himself. Eloisa signalled me with her eyes and looked pointedly at the wine decanter. I guessed she was telling me to take the opportunity to speak with Ramón before he drank any more and became insensible.

'I would like to walk in the courtyard here before going to bed,' I announced, rising up from the table. 'Señora Eloisa, would you allow Señor Salazar to accompany me? As you know, he's a childhood friend from home and I will be quite safe.'

'Indeed, yes.' Eloisa was on her feet before I'd finished my request, bringing me a wrap to put around my shoulders and ushering us through the long windows that led to the paved area outside.

I began by enquiring of Ramón if he'd been in touch with Lorena just before her death. I believed him when he said he hadn't. He claimed to have been very busy at the siege of the city – to hear him one would have thought he'd single-handedly defeated the entire Moorish army. But I knew now how intimate he'd been with Lorena and thought him callous to be so unaffected by her passing.

'I heard that you were financially ruined by a terrible fire that burned your home to the ground.'

Now I saw why he was no longer interested in our fates. He thought the money gone: we were of no more use to him.

'You know I have just become betrothed to a girl who is both rich and noble,' he went on importantly.

'I am happy for you,' I said.

'And I am so glad you are secure in the convent, Zarita,' Ramón said patronizingly.

'I've decided not to make my final vows,' I said.

He looked at me with interest. 'Why not?'

I didn't want to tell him my reasons so I made do with giving him a partial truth. 'I have no true religious vocation.'

'What plans have you made?'

'None as yet.'

'Ah, Zarita' – Ramón's voice purred – 'then perhaps we could come to some kind of arrangement.' He glanced towards the apartment and lowered his voice. 'You know I've always found you most attractive.'

At first his meaning didn't register with me.

'Of course, any relationship we might have would have to

wait until after I was married.' Ramón took my hand in his.

'Do you mean that you want me to be your courtesan?'

'You would be my mistress. You would have a house and servants and I would give you money for clothes and buy you jewels. We could be together at certain times.'

'Ramón!' I pulled my hand away. And in that instant I decided I wouldn't tell him about the baby. I knew that, far from welcoming this news, it would seriously inconvenience him. Most likely he'd disown the child, and then the child's fate would be in peril – cast off, and at risk of having no inheritance whatsoever. In any case Ramón didn't deserve the gift of such an adorable baby, and certainly the innocent child didn't deserve such a shallow person as a father. 'Ramón,' I said distinctly, 'I have no wish to have any kind of relationship with you.'

'You have become very forthright, Zarita,' Ramón responded sourly. 'I warn you, men do not like such manners in a woman.'

'And I do not like your manners much either, Ramón,' I retorted.

He made one last try to win me over. 'I can't believe that you allowed your beautiful black locks to be shorn from your head.' He raised his hand and touched my hair as he used to love to do.

'You should go now,' I said coldly. 'And we will forget that this conversation ever took place.'

Chapter Forty-five
Saulo

I was already waiting behind a pillar in the garden when Zarita and a man appeared in the doorway and stepped out onto the paving.

Their conversation was too low for me to hear. He seemed to be flattering her. I didn't think her the type to respond to such an approach, but instead of seeing him off, her tone of voice suggested she was being most reasonable with him.

There was an arrogance to his stance that struck me as familiar. But perhaps all nobles had that way of holding themselves. Something stirred in my memory, something I didn't want to acknowledge. His face was obscured, but then he moved and the light from the window fell upon it. Where had I seen him before?

I flitted closer. This man I knew.

And his name was in my head, just as I heard Zarita say, 'Ramón.'

Ramón!

Ramón Salazar!

The man who had chased my father from the church in Las Conchas.

At that moment Ramón Salazar lifted his hand to touch Zarita on the head. And the manner in which he did this made me recognize something else.

Someone else.

She was the girl!

I put my knuckles to my mouth and bit hard upon them. It couldn't be!

Was it her? Was Zarita the girl who had been with Ramón Salazar on the day of my father's arrest? Was she the daughter of the magistrate? Almost eighteen months had passed. In that time I had changed beyond recognition. So might she. On that day the girl walking with Ramón Salazar had her face veiled. She'd been slight of build with beautiful long dark hair. Now Zarita's figure was that of a woman, and her hair was almost completely covered.

I ran to find Rafael.

In the deepest recess of my spirit I knew that I didn't need any verification. But I had to be absolutely certain. I waited while Rafael went to find out the answers to a series of questions I gave him. He came back in a state of high anxiety with the information.

'Señor Saulo, I implore you, stay away from this woman. They say—'

'Tell me what I sent you to find out!' I shouted at him.

Rafael threw his hands up in the air. 'The girl, Zarita, is from a small port in Andalucía called Las Conchas. She has recently adopted her mother's family name, but before that she used her father's, which is Don Vicente Alonso de Carbazón. He was the magistrate of the town until he died just before Christmas when his house caught fire.'

I gave a loud cry of anguish and fell onto my knees. I tore at my hair and beat my forehead on the floor. Rafael fled from the room. He had been right. This woman was dangerous – a courtesan of the most deceitful kind. She had caused me to forget my true purpose in being here at the court – which was not to ally myself with Christopher Columbus but to destroy the seed of the magistrate, Don Vicente Alonso de Carbazón. And not only had she made me forget, she herself was the very person on whom I sought to take my revenge! Now I believed utterly in witchcraft. She had placed an enchantment on me. She was a sorceress, a demon, a Circe who lured men to their deaths.

Needles of pain lanced behind my eyelids. Shock and disbelief became anger, and then outrage.

I knew what I had to do.

I would go back to her private courtyard and wait there until she had retired to bed. Then I would break into the apartment and kill her.

I would kill her tonight.

Chapter Forty-six
Zarita and Saulo

A man stood at the foot of my bed. In his hand there was a long knife. The candlelight shone on the blade, and I knew by the way he held the shaft that he'd used this knife before. He had killed with this knife. My breath thickened in my throat. On my tongue was the taste of my own fear.

She was very, very frightened. I could see her fear, smell it almost. And yet she did not flinch. She did not cower down, nor run to hide, nor edge away. She sat up and looked at me.

I rose up from the bed and faced him, conscious of being only in my nightclothes. It came to my mind that when he plunged the knife in, the colour of my blood would contrast vividly against the white muslin of my shift. His face was in the shadows, his eyes burning with a strange luminance. Familiar eyes. Yet I did not know him . . . 'What do you want?' I asked.

'I come for my revenge,' I said. 'Should I stab you? Or take this as a rope to hang you with?'

With my free hand I ripped down the tasselled sash that held back her bed curtains. 'I might string you up so that you can dance the same jig your father made my father dance.'

I moved nearer to her. There was a pulse beating at her throat under the golden skin, and her pupils were dilated. In one hand I held my dagger; in the other the length of silken rope.

'It is your time to die,' I told her.

I brought the knife point close to her breast.

'*Saulo?*' I whispered in terror. 'Saulo? It cannot be you.'

Had I gone mad? Was I dreaming? Living in a waking nightmare, where I could see and touch an assassin who had come to kill me? Some demon who had taken the guise of the man I loved?

'Saulo?'

'He was hungry,' I said.

'Who, Saulo? Who was hungry?'

'My father,' I told her. 'We were all of us starving, but I know that he would not have assaulted you. It was not in his nature. If he tried to snatch your purse, then it was to buy medicine for his wife, my mother, or to feed his son – me.'

'Ah,' I whimpered. 'Now I know who you are. You are the son of the beggar. I knew that one day I would face a judgement for what I did that dreadful afternoon. I thought it would be in the next world, not this one.'

'The day has come, Zarita,' I said. 'For I was here an hour or so ago and saw you with Ramón Salazar and recognized you.'

'Did you know who I was from the beginning?' she asked me. 'Was everything we did, was all you said to me . . .' And here her voice wavered. 'Was all of it a lie?'

'It was *you* who lied,' I said hoarsely, 'when you falsely accused my father of assaulting you.'

'I didn't lie. I didn't accuse him of assaulting me. He touched me, it's true, but his fingers only brushed against mine—'

As she began to speak, I held up my hand. 'Silence! I don't want to hear excuses. You have already bewitched me enough to addle my brain.'

But Zarita would not be silenced.

'You are right, Saulo, when you say that your father did nothing. He was blameless. It was my fault; my stupidity, my foolishness. It wasn't wickedness – that I can say truly. Not for hope of any mercy from you, but for the sake of truth, for you should know of the last act of your father, that he was an honourable man. And I believe he tried to save you.'

'Your words have no meaning for me,' I told her.

'To begin with,' she persisted, 'when he ran from the church, your father was only desperate to get away, to lose himself in the alleys and streets leading off the square. So he ran forward. But then he saw you, and he veered off towards the sea to take them away from you, his son. I was some distance behind and I could see the whole scene. Many times over the years I've thought about those events. I'm convinced that when he caught sight of you, he altered direction towards the docks so that you wouldn't be caught up in whatever happened; so that you would not be punished as he knew he would be.'

A clear recollection came to me.

My father *had* seen me. I could visualize him now, racing towards me in the square and then changing tack. Away from safety, towards a closed-off route – to save his son.

Tears were in my eyes. I dashed them away. 'None of this will save you from my vengeance. Do not think to ask for mercy.'

As I spoke, a shard of another memory sliced through my mind and I saw a girl pleading for mercy. Not for her life, but for mine. Zarita had knelt before her father and stopped him when he'd been about to hang me.

Saulo hesitated.

Why?

He'd come to my room intent on murdering me in revenge for the death of his father by my father's hand. Yet now he seemed unsure.

I should call for aid. But if I did so, Saulo would be arrested, and without doubt executed.

'You must leave,' I told him. 'Lest you be discovered here. I wouldn't want your blood on my hands, for I already have your father's death on my conscience.'

'As I have yours,' he replied abruptly.

There! It was said! Now she knew!

'You . . . ? My papa . . . Oh! Oh!'

Zarita covered her face with her hands and sank down upon the bed.

'Oh! I understand! That is why the tree outside my home was poisoned. It was *you* who set fire to the house. It was *you* Papa was running from when his heart gave out!'

Zarita raised a harrowed face to mine and moaned in a wretched voice. 'Such dreadful outcomes from one deed!'

There was a sudden cry of alarm, and then a thunderous knocking on the inside corridor door. For a second I thought that in some way she'd secretly summoned help. But she was as surprised as I was.

'I should answer them,' she said, her voice distraught. 'Señora Eloisa takes a strong sleeping potion each night. It will take her several minutes to wake up.'

'Ask them who they are and why they disturb you at this

hour,' I ordered her. 'But do not move from the doorway of this room.'

I stood behind her as she opened her bedroom door. 'Who are you?' Her voice was unsteady as she spoke.

No reply came. Only an increased hammering on the corridor door.

'Ask them again,' I instructed her.

She called out again in a louder voice. 'Name yourself! I will not unlock the door unless you do so!'

'You will do as we say!' came the reply. 'Open up this door in the name of the Holy Inquisition!'

Chapter Forty-seven
Saulo

The commotion succeeded in wakening Señora Eloisa.

We heard her coming from her room to open the door into the corridor.

I slipped behind the bedroom door as soldiers entered the apartment, and I hid as they arrested her: Zarita, daughter of the magistrate, Don Vicente Alonso de Carbazón.

She maintained her bearing as the captain of the soldiers unfurled a parchment, announced her name and made the declaration of her arrest. And then, as they came for her, she took a tiny step forward and opened her bedroom door to its full extent so that I was better concealed behind it. She chose not to reveal that a person who had vowed to kill her was lurking there. There was a gap between the door hinges and the wall, and I saw the scene as it happened. Zarita was calm but her hands were shaking.

'This is a mistake!' Señora Eloisa's voice was shrill.

'No mistake,' said the man who was in charge. He showed her the warrant. 'The woman known as Zarita, of Las Conchas, is to come with us, tonight, and at once.'

Señora Eloisa begged them to give Zarita time to dress, but they refused, so she took off her own long dressing gown and threw it over Zarita's shoulders. The soldiers seemed to treat Zarita with some respect as they laid hands on her, but everyone in all Spain knew that as soon as the doors of the Inquisition dungeon closed behind the arrested person, a different set of rules applied.

'I will petition the queen! I will send for your aunt!

I will, I will.' Señora Eloisa collapsed in a chair, weeping.

Just before they led her off, in a voice of great command Zarita said, 'I have something I wish to tell you.'

Ah, now! Her true character is revealed! I gripped my knife, expecting her to cry out and tell them where I was hidden. I thought: *She's had a chance to think on the situation and, as she herself is in no immediate danger of death, it might stand in her favour if she betrayed a would-be assassin to the authorities. It will be her way of ensuring I am punished for causing the death of her father.*

I heard Zarita speak up in a loud voice.

'It may be that I am not afforded the opportunity to make a statement. I wish to say that any ill I ever did to God, or man, or woman, was not by cruel intention; rather it was by thoughtless foolishness. I ask forgiveness of those I have wronged, and I freely forgive those who may have caused me offence.'

The soldier in charge made a click of impatience in his throat. It wasn't an odd thing for a prisoner to say. He'd probably heard similar declarations as he dragged protesting prisoners away to be tortured. But I knew for whom it was meant.

It was for me.

Chapter Forty-eight
Zarita

I didn't know if Saulo was still there.

I prayed that he'd taken the chance to get clear, yet I also hoped that he'd remained long enough to hear my declaration. Whether he had heard or not, it was said. And as I was taken away I was glad I'd said it.

Some courtiers gathered to point and stare as they marched me down the corridors, but most dropped their gaze or stood back and turned their faces to the wall.

Such was the terror of the Inquisition.

I was taken to an underground basement near the soldiers' barracks. I was surprised, but in no way comforted, to find that many of the rooms there were already full of prisoners.

A black-robed monk sat behind a long table. I stood before him, shivering, my feet bare on the stone floor, as he wrote down the details of my name and age and place of birth and family information. When he'd finished he raised his head. 'Do you wish to confess?'

'My arrest is a mistake,' I replied, for at that point I really thought an error had been made. 'I have nothing to confess.'

'Everyone has something to confess. It is better that you make your confession now, voluntarily, than . . . later.'

I shook my head. 'I have done nothing wrong.'

'Then you have nothing to fear.'

This interview lasted only ten or fifteen minutes before I was taken to a windowless room with a cot bed. As I lay down on it, my first feelings were of relief. The priest was right. I had nothing to fear. I was not like Bartolomé, who had appeared to ridicule the clergy, or the women who had sinned with their bodies. For almost five months of the previous year I'd lived the life of an enclosed nun, so there could be no offence on my part against Church or State.

Also, it was known that there was a limit to the number of times a suspect could be questioned by the Inquisition. Therefore I should only have one or two more sessions like that and I would be free to go.

I lay on the cot that night, not sleeping, and tried to convince myself that this was how it would be.

Chapter Forty-nine
Saulo

The fate of the girl Zarita de Marzena was of no interest to me.

That's what I told myself. True, she had not betrayed me to the soldiers of the Inquisition as she might have done, but it didn't mean that I owed her anything. Or that I cared for her at all.

But . . . what could she possibly have done that the Inquisition would feel compelled to investigate?

I'd hardly reached my room when there was a light tap on the door. Cautiously I opened it up. Rafael was there. Slipping under my arm, he came quickly inside.

'My apologies for disturbing you, señor.' He was out of breath and very agitated. 'I thought you'd want to know what's happening in the palace tonight.' He looked at my face anxiously.

I nodded.

'The woman Zarita has been arrested by the officers of the Holy Inquisition!'

I put my hand over my mouth and chin to conceal my face, for I found that I was biting down upon my lip.

'She's been taken to one of the secret rooms in the basement where she'll be interviewed by the Inquisitors. I came as soon as I could to warn you.'

'Warn me? Why should I need warning? What's it got to do with me?'

'Señor, perhaps because you have been travelling at sea, you are not familiar with how these investigations are carried out. The people associated with the arrested person often fall under suspicion too. At the very least they can be called upon to be a witness, to give testimony against the accused.'

Ah, now! That would be a fine thing indeed! I could go forward and speak out against the magistrate's daughter as she once spoke against my father.

'You must get away, sir,' Rafael went on. 'Earlier this evening the girl had supper with the nobleman, Ramón Salazar. His servants woke him in the night to tell him what was happening. Señor Salazar and his bodyguard went immediately to the stables, took their horses and left. He declared that he was going to his family estates in the east to sort out some emergency. But from there he can easily get across the border into France and take refuge until this investigation is over.'

So her childhood friend had run as soon as he thought himself in any danger. I should be glad to hear that. I *was* glad, I told myself.

'Not that she had any regard for him,' Rafael continued. 'The servant who cleared their food plates and tidied the room after he'd gone let me know that the girl told her chaperon she wanted no more to do with him. Both of them thought him vain and foolish and self-centred.'

'Well, he has proved that to be true,' I said, thinking as I did so: Zarita had dismissed his attentions. Had I misjudged her manner when I'd seen her stand close to him and he'd raised his hand to touch her hair?

'Her chaperon, Señora Eloisa, has sent messages to the queen – at least a dozen of them. She has also paid for a fast rider to go to the coast with a letter for a convent in Las Conchas to ask a relative to come to the court as soon as possible. Señora Eloisa then collapsed and a doctor was called to attend to her. She is quite ill.'

This relative in Las Conchas would be the Aunt Beatriz that Zarita had told me about. The chaperon must consider the circumstances grave to summon an enclosed nun from her convent!

'So you see how things are,' said Rafael. 'As I tried to tell you earlier, señor, deadly danger surrounds that woman.'

'You did, Rafael,' I said. 'And I thank you for it.' I put a coin in his hand and then added a few more. He'd obviously been staying alert to garner information for me, and probably had to bribe the grooms and household staff so that they would keep him up to date with anything of interest. I went to the door and began to open it for him. I should have been rejoicing at this news of Zarita's downfall but my head was throbbing and I felt sick in my stomach. I wanted to be alone.

'No, no, señor.' Rafael pushed the door closed. 'This time you should listen to me. You too must leave. I have contacts in the stables. I can arrange to have your horse saddled and waiting by one of the quieter outside gates. It would be best to do this now, before dawn. I will' – he coughed – 'need some money to pay for this to happen.'

'You think the situation is as desperate as that?'

'Where the Inquisition is concerned it's best not to take chances. If a fairly important nobleman like Ramón Salazar flees the palace, then he must have been given an indication of how her trial will turn out. By reason of his position he will have access to more information than I do. I'd take it that the charges against her are very serious.' He paused. 'Serious unto death.'

'I cannot go so quickly,' I told him. 'I must speak to the

navigator Christopher Columbus and let him know that I will be leaving.'

Rafael looked doubtful. 'Regarding Señor Columbus and his efforts to win support for his expedition, his position is not as high in favour as it was.'

'In what way?'

'It's said that he makes too many demands. He wants a grand title and a percentage of any treasure found. And also some matter about his arithmetic.' Rafael shrugged. 'No matter the reason, his petition is stalled. When he is informed of this he'll probably leave too. So you see, you do yourself no favours by waiting.'

'Yes, I understand what you are saying.'

I thought of Zarita in the basement room. I recalled her face, her mouth, her eyes when she'd confronted me and the soldiers in her bedroom. She had shown courage. She'd been afraid yet had concealed it. But how would she fare if put to the question by the officers of the Inquisition? Without a rich and powerful patron they would show her no mercy.

'She is doomed.' Rafael caught at my sleeve. 'There is nothing you can do to help her. Save yourself.'

Of course, Rafael thought me infatuated with a passing fancy that I could easily forget in the arms of another woman. He didn't know what was going through my mind; how I was trying to make myself think: *Here now is the perfect culmination of my vow of vengeance. The Inquisition will be the instrument of my final act of revenge on the family of the magistrate.*

Rafael looked at me expectantly, awaiting instructions.

'Yes,' I said again. 'Yes, you are right. I'll do what you suggest.'

I gave him some more money and we discussed our plan

of action. I told him that I would wait until morning before departing, for I wanted to explain myself to Christopher Columbus. Then Rafael went off to bribe whoever he needed to bribe to get me out of the palace and the city and on the road to freedom.

Chapter Fifty
Zarita

'Beatriz!'

I judged it to be late afternoon of the following day when the door of my cell opened and my aunt stood in the doorway.

I rushed to greet her but the gaoler ordered me to stand against the far wall. Beatriz had a bundle of clothes over her arm. The gaoler seemed prepared to let her in, but he was very suspicious about the clothing she carried.

'It's a nun's habit; all the sisters of my order wear them.' Aunt Beatriz showed it to him and then begged him in the sweetest tones to let me put it on.

'I don't know if it's allowed,' he grumbled.

'Your prisoner, this young woman, Zarita, is one of my novices. Surely no one can object to a novice nun reclaiming her habit,' my aunt replied, still keeping her voice peaceable and quiet. 'I understand that she is to be brought to trial. It would be unseemly in the eyes of God for even a novice nun to appear in public in her night shift. And' – Beatriz's voice quickened as if a thought had just occurred to her – 'she is obliged to wear this grey dress day and night. It means . . . that we do have the problem of disposing of her shift and wrap. I, as a nun with vows of poverty, cannot accept such an expensive gift. Perhaps you would take care of this matter for us?'

The gaoler looked at me. His eyes took in the heavy velvet dressing gown with its gold and green embroidery and trim of miniver around the neck and cuffs. Its worth was probably twice his annual salary. He took only a few seconds to decide.

'It is permitted,' he said.

He hovered by the open door while I changed my clothes. My aunt shielded me with her body, and as I put on the familiar grey dress of her order, I felt a measure of peace. I smoothed my hair under the coif and tied the leather sandals on my feet.

When the gaoler left clutching his booty, we sat together on the cot bed, holding each other close and talking.

I asked after Eloisa. Beatriz told me that her friend had taken some kind of seizure but was recovering. Although she wanted to stay, Beatriz had insisted that she go back to her own home.

'Eloisa wrote many notes and pleas to the queen, and also bribed everyone she could think of bribing, yet she couldn't discover why you've been arrested. Do you have any idea what the charge might be?'

'None.' I shook my head. 'And I've thought of little else since it happened.'

'Eloisa says that Ramón came to supper yesterday evening. Was anything untoward said then?'

'No. Ramón wouldn't compromise his own position. He is engaged in making a profitable marriage contract for himself. He'd allow nothing to get in the way of that.'

'Ah,' said Beatriz, 'you know about his intended wedding. So it won't break your heart to learn that he left Granada at great speed early this morning to put as much distance as possible between you and himself?'

'Not at all,' I replied. 'I found Ramón pompous, overbearing and arrogant. And I decided not to tell him anything about the baby. He would not have cared a scrap for his child. He didn't even react when I spoke about Lorena's death – yet he was obviously quite besotted by her at one time.'

'He was always more besotted by himself, that boy,' Beatriz observed.

'You knew!' I exclaimed. 'You knew that Ramón was shallow and deceitful. Yet you sent me to meet him!'

'I had faith in your good judgement, Zarita. The months you spent in the convent weren't wasted. The world believes that those who choose to shut themselves away from its influences have no knowledge of its doings. Yet in the time we spent together I saw you mature from girl to woman – a woman of grace and wisdom. I was confident that you would see Ramón for what he was, and then it was your choice if you decided that you wished to spend your life with him.' She cupped my cheek in her hand. 'Life is very, very precious. One must be careful what one does with it.'

'Well, you were right, Ramón was not for me. But,' I faltered, 'there is another.'

She listened quietly as I told her about Saulo. I began with the exciting and happy part of my great love. And then I related what had happened in my bedroom just before my arrest.

'I can see why Saulo would be angry,' Beatriz said at last. 'He would experience twofold rage. One, that you were the girl whom he blames for the death of his father. Two, and very damaging to the pride of a man, not recognizing you, he falls in love with you and then discovers your identity. His fury would be all-consuming.'

Yes, I thought. It had almost consumed me.

'And yet,' Beatriz mused, 'he had the courage to confess to you his part in the death of your father.'

The gaoler knocked upon the door. 'The visit must end now,' he said gruffly.

Beatriz spoke rapidly. 'Zarita, you should prepare yourself to face the worst possible accusation, that of heresy. Try to be strong. Once you have been charged, I may not be allowed to visit you again. I will help you all I can. I will petition the queen, and I will pray for you.'

When my aunt had gone, I stood up and let the rough grey wool of my habit fall into the natural folds of the skirt. It comforted me more than if I were wearing lace and brocade. I welcomed my rough sandals instead of fine satin slippers. I drew the veil across my face and pulled up the cowl around my head. I slid my hands inside each opposite sleeve and clasped them together. There! Now I was cocooned from the outside world. Safe.

For the moment.

Chapter Fifty-one
Saulo

'Would you grant me a few minutes of your time?'

There was a woman in the garb of a nun outside my door. By the similarity of her features I would have known that she was kin to Zarita even before she introduced herself.

'My name is Beatriz de Marzena. I am the maternal aunt of Zarita, the girl recently arrested by the Inquisition. I know you are acquainted with her for I have just visited her prison cell and spoken to her.'

She stepped inside. Before closing the door behind her, I glanced up and down the passageway. It was deserted – as were most of the lower corridors this morning when I went to see Christopher Columbus to let him know I was going away. I hadn't told him all my business, only that a girl I was courting had been seized by the Inquisition and I thought it better to leave as I didn't want to be associated with her. These words had left a bitter taste in my mouth when I said them.

Columbus had looked at me shrewdly. 'I suspect there is more to this affair, Saulo, than you wish to tell me at the moment?'

I nodded my head miserably. The twin blows of losing my chance to be an explorer and to share my life with Zarita made me too upset to speak.

Columbus said that he too was thinking of going elsewhere. He'd been told that the monarchs thought his requests for high office and personal benefit from any discoveries he might make too grandiose, and even impertinent.

'I have spent the years of my youth and middle age planning this expedition. I will not do the work and risk my life to be rewarded by some paltry bag of gold.' Columbus was already rolling up his maps, preparatory to moving on. 'I'll find another king or queen, in France or England, who'll grant me what I want.'

When I got back to my room I found Rafael waiting,

'Everything is arranged,' he told me. 'Let me know when you are ready to depart.' He'd touched my shoulder as he'd left. 'Don't delay too long.'

But I *had* delayed. My bag was packed hours ago, with the peacock jacket crushed tightly at the bottom. Now it was almost evening.

And still I waited.

I was still waiting when Zarita's aunt Beatriz came to visit me. I'd thought at first that the knock on my door was Rafael come to bid me hurry up. I ushered the nun into my room and closed the door behind her. She appraised me and I returned her gaze. Her eyes were of the same shape and hue as Zarita's, and with the skin of her face drawn back and smoothed by her coif she could have passed for an older sister.

I told myself that I would not enquire as to Zarita's condition or her spirits. 'Why have you come to see me?' I asked, affecting indifference.

'I thought you might be able to find out why Zarita has been arrested. I've petitioned the queen but I don't know if she will reply to me. My friend, Señora Eloisa, has already sent message after message imploring her majesty's intercession, but to no avail. Some time ago, as young girls, we lived at the royal court and attended court functions where we met Queen Isabella. So many years have passed, the queen may not remember me. Life has changed, and I fear Isabella too has changed. She was always very serious and attentive to her duties, but now she seems to have become more ruthless and is kept under very close advisement. It's a long time since she knew me; she may not choose to renew our acquaintance under these circumstances.' The nun paused. 'I want to help Zarita. If only I knew what was happening – any information at all . . .'

And, as I didn't respond, she prompted me further: 'Zarita told me that you are with the navigator Christopher Columbus and that he moves in the inner sanctum of the court. Perhaps . . . ?' Again she let her voice tail off.

'Has Zarita told you of the history between us?'

'She has.'

'All of it?'

'Yes indeed.'

'Why would I want to help you or her?' I said brusquely.

She blinked and didn't reply.

'Why?' I repeated angrily. 'My father was murdered by her father. My mother died too, by reason of his action. Both now lie in unmarked graves.'

'Your mother's grave is not unmarked.'

'What are you saying?'

'The place where your mother lies buried is not unmarked. It bears a wooden cross, and fresh flowers are placed there each day.'

'By whose hand?'

'By the hand of the woman I am asking you to help.'

'Zarita?'

Sister Beatriz nodded. 'In the days after your arrest and her mother's death my niece recalled that when asking her for money in the church your father had mentioned a wife. So she went into the slums and searched for your mother. She found a doctor who was caring for her, and as her end was near, she took your mother to my convent hospital, where we tended to her as she lay dying.'

'*What?*' I stared at her. I was so astounded I couldn't say another word.

'Believe me, it is true.' Sister Beatriz acknowledged my amazement. 'I am sorry to say, Saulo, that your mother's life could not be saved, but towards the end she didn't suffer. From her own purse Zarita paid for the medicine she needed. When she passed away, my sisters washed her body and laid her out.' She looked at me. 'I apologize if she wasn't of our faith, but with the best of intentions we organized a funeral mass for her. We lit candles, and there were many flowers. Zarita has paid for the grave to be tended and prayers to be said. She often does this herself.'

Zarita took care of my mother in her last days . . .

I tried to clear my thoughts, but only said, 'Your niece is guilty of the downfall of my family.'

'She played a part, yes,' Sister Beatriz agreed.

This woman was older, but her eyes had the same dark intensity as Zarita's, a steady glow of some inner strength.

'Is it your own feelings of guilt that sustain your anger, Saulo?'

'What?' I snapped. 'What's this talk of *me* being guilty?'

'You caused the death of Zarita's father. But you have acknowledged that. I was thinking more about your sense of dishonour over the death of your mother.'

I gasped. '*My* dishonour about my mother?'

'It's natural to feel anger at the loss of a parent. For whatever reason, when a mother or father dies, a child suffers the experience of being abandoned. It can be many years before that passes, or one matures enough to come to terms with it. The manner in which you were deprived of yours was both shocking and brutal, and that would affect you deeply . . . but—'

'But *what*?' I shouted.

'Why were you with your father and not your mother, even though she was so very ill? Zarita told me that when your father asked her for money he didn't ask for himself, but for his wife who was sick, and his child who was hungry. He was obviously not a professional beggar, else he would have known not to enter the church. Most of them wait outside to intercept those who are coming and going to pray and petition. Your father must have loved his wife and child very much to humble himself like that. And he must have loved you in particular, or he would have sent you to beg on the streets rather than doing it himself, for a child will always attract more charity than an adult.'

This nun moved closer without taking her eyes from mine. She was slightly taller than Zarita and her face was on a level with my own.

'Your father didn't do that. He must have known that your mother was dying, so he wouldn't have left her on her own. Did he bid you stay with her and tend her? Yet you disobeyed him . . . Then you were captured. With your father dead and you gone, you knew that she was left unable to move and with no one to help her. And since that day you've borne the burden of your mother's death.'

I stared at her. To my horror I felt tears forming in my eyes.

'You do not need to feel guilty,' Sister Beatriz said gently. 'Your mother was dying. No medicine could have saved her. In fact, by a bizarre fate, she probably had an easier death in my hospital than if the incident had not happened. But it isn't your fault that your mother died, Saulo. It may be that the reason you think you cannot forgive another is because you do not forgive yourself. I say again to you that you are not to blame.'

I swung round abruptly and went to the window. From here I could see the palace gardens. Beyond lay the city of Granada, and beyond that was Spain and the long road to the small town by the sea where I had lost my childhood and the parents who had loved me.

The nun waited in silence.

I gripped the window ledge with both hands as shame and self-revulsion threatened to overpower my senses. The nun's observations were painfully accurate. If ever I was to be at peace with myself and others, I needed to recognize this. I felt an infinitesimal easing of my mind. When I had calmed myself enough to speak, I said, 'Christopher Columbus cannot help us. His application for royal sponsorship is no longer progressing. He is making ready to leave the court.' I turned round. 'Is there nothing that you can think of that would have led to Zarita's arrest?'

Sister Beatriz frowned. 'There was something that happened after Zarita entered the convent. I'd accepted her as a novice, not because she sought a religious vocation, but because her family life became difficult and traumatic and she had nowhere else to go. On the day your father was murdered, her mama, my sister, died. Within a twelvemonth her father was married again to a woman called Lorena, who had a selfish and jealous nature. She wished ill to Zarita and conspired to have her driven from the family home. In the circumstances, entering the convent did seem the best option for Zarita, and it was of benefit to her. She matured in grace and wisdom and I enjoyed her company. I love her, but it would have been selfish of me to keep her for that reason alone. We were told that Lorena was expecting a child so I thought I'd wait until the baby arrived and then try for a reconciliation. Lorena escaped from the fire, and although she died in childbirth, the baby was delivered safely.'

'The child lived?' There was a relief. I'd not destroyed everything that Zarita held dear.

'Yes.' Sister Beatriz gave a brief smile. 'But only because Zarita summoned a doctor to help with the birth. The same doctor who'd attended your mother. He was a Jew.'

'Zarita brought a Jew into a convent?' Even I, with no affiliation to any religion, knew that some would see this as sacrilege.

'Indeed.'

'If they have discovered this, then she is doomed.'

'I cannot think that they have,' she replied. 'Only two others knew of it: myself and another nun whom I'd trust with my life.' She began to pace the floor. 'It was me who told Zarita to come to Granada. When the baby was born, I permitted her to come out of the cloister and attend the court. There was a family matter that needed dealing with – and I wanted her to see Ramón Salazar again.'

'You allowed her to come to the court to form a relationship with a man like him!'

'No. I allowed her to come for another reason, but also I thought it was time that our older, more mature Zarita met Ramón again and saw him for the weak, vain man that he is. Otherwise she might harbour a dream of a girlish romantic love that never was. So it was my idea, and it was I who encouraged her to leave the convent to come to the court.'

Sister Beatriz sobbed as she said this, and her face took on a stricken look.

'I now believe that I sent Zarita to her death.'

Chapter Fifty-two
Zarita

'Zarita de Marzena, you are once again given an opportunity to confess.'

The hood of my habit rested on my shoulders and my veil was drawn aside. I could see the face of the monk in the black robes seated at the table opposite me and he could see mine.

'Father,' I said politely, 'I do not feel the need to confess.'

The monk sighed. 'I don't wish a young woman, especially one with a connection to a religious order, to be put to any trial. But you must co-operate with me.'

'Of what am I accused?'

'You are accused of the most grievous sin against the Inquisition – that of heresy.'

I *was* to stand trial for heresy! Beatriz's fears had proved correct.

'When and how am I supposed to have committed this heresy?'

The monk picked up the paper in front of him and read from it. 'You committed heresy in acts and sayings on various occasions while residing in the house of your father, the magistrate of the town Las Conchas, he being known as Don Vicente Alonso Carbazón.'

'What!' I almost laughed. 'This is nonsense. My parents were devout people – especially my mother, who attended church almost every day of her life.'

The monk consulted the paper. 'There is no reference to your mother here.'

'Quote me the time and place of these incidents.'

Again he looked at his paper. 'There is no note of them.'

'Then where is your evidence?' I demanded.

'I cannot produce it here. It will be shown at your formal trial.'

'You cannot produce it because it does not exist,' I said firmly.

The monk's face flushed in annoyance. He leaned forward over the table to glare at me. 'I will tell you what *does* exist, my clever young miss. I have the means to make you confess. For, believe me, you *will* confess. In the end all our prisoners do. And I will remove any doubt from your mind about this. As you seem so keen on being shown evidence, then I will ensure that you are shown evidence that will convince you of what I say.'

He beckoned to my gaoler to come to him, and by gestures and whispering instructed him how to proceed.

The gaoler took me by the arm and led me off – not to my cell, but along a dank passageway that led down to the innermost area of the basement.

There he showed me the instruments of torture. The rack, and the pincers for removing fingernails. The hoist, and the pokers for burning the truth from the victim's flesh. This latter had been used to break Bartolomé in spirit and in body.

We passed cells that contained those who had been put to the question. They lay huddled in a corner of their room, whimpering and crying. Then the gaoler took me to a communal area where people hung chained to the walls. The smell was rancid – the bitter scent of urine, the stink of excrement. He stopped beside a set of empty chains.

'I am not to be left here,' I gabbled, all my resolve and

fortitude dissolving. 'I was only to be shown what might happen.'

He looked at me sadly. I'd noticed that he smelled of alcohol and I wondered if he drank to excess to stop himself thinking of the sights he must see every day. With genuine regret in his voice he said, 'I do as I'm told.'

'No!' I cried, my voice rising on a note of hysteria. 'I have done nothing wrong! Nothing, I tell you!'

'They all say that.' The gaoler sighed as he unlocked the ankle- and wrist-cuffs and opened them up.

I looked around. The rest of the chained men and women hardly lifted their heads to acknowledge my presence. One's mouth lolled open, showing gory stumps where there had been teeth. Another's hair was matted with blood.

'Please,' I whispered. 'I don't even know what I am supposed to have done.'

'You will be informed of that in due course,' someone said behind us. The voice was unpleasant yet familiar.

I turned.

Standing in front of me was Father Besian.

Chapter Fifty-three
Saulo

Holding a lighted taper before him, Rafael led the way up a narrow stone staircase. His hand shook and the light flared up, spreading our shadows on the bare wall as we passed. It had taken quite a few of my gold coins and much pleading from Sister Beatriz for him to embark on this venture.

To begin with he'd refused utterly.

'No, Señor Saulo, I won't help you spy on a tribunal of the Inquisition.' He'd shaken his head. 'It can't be done. There is no way to smuggle you into the hall. You can't disguise yourself as a servant, for they allow no servants in. Besides which, if you were discovered you'd be questioned. Under torture you'd reveal my part in it and then I would have no mercy shown to me. As a servant I'd be executed. If I was lucky it would take place quickly. But they have a particularly cruel Inquisitor here at the moment, so it would most likely be a long and painful death.'

At this point the nun had reached out and touched Rafael on the shoulder. 'I will pray for the success of our mission,' she told him.

'With respect, Sister, praying will do me no good when they apply red-hot pokers to my eyes.'

I piled some coins on the table in front of him. 'All of this,' I said. 'All of it is yours.'

He hesitated, for it was a goodly sum, much more than he could expect to earn in the course of several years.

'The nuns of the convent hospital of Las Conchas will pray for your soul in perpetuity,' said Sister Beatriz.

Rafael had scooped up the money and disappeared out of the door.

Now, standing before me at the top of the stairs, he glanced behind nervously. 'After this point,' he whispered, 'we must be very quiet.'

We nodded, and again our shadows, like dark spectres, followed our movements. The cowl covering the nun's head and the cloak I'd wrapped around myself made grotesque shapes beside us.

It had taken Rafael two whole days to find a tradesman who'd worked in the Alhambra Palace and knew all the rooms and passageways and some of the secret entrances and exits. He'd discovered that the Inquisition tribunal of Zarita de Marzena would be held today in the Sultan's Hall, and that there was a place where we might be able to secretly watch the proceedings. The corridor that opened out before us had no windows and no doors and ended with a blank wall at the far end.

I stopped. 'There's no outlet this way,' I said.

'The artisan told me to look here.' Rafael walked on and touched a wooden panel set halfway along the wall. The design was arabesque, with stylized flowers interlaced with geometric shapes.

'There is nothing,' I said in impatience.

'Don't you wonder that this wood panelling is so carefully engraved in a corridor where no one has reason to come?' Sister Beatriz asked. 'Why spend so much on beautiful carvings if they are never to be seen? Sometimes,' she added, 'as in the dress or the jewellery of a woman, the reason for an adornment is not to display, but to conceal.'

Her sensitive fingers ran over the wood. She traced one of the interlinking patterns, following the twists and spirals to its central point. There was a soft click, and the panel slid to one side to reveal a tiny balcony enclosed by draped curtains.

Rafael left us. The nun and I slipped inside and closed over the secret door behind us.

Little light penetrated the gloom, and there was barely enough room for two of us. The balcony had been designed to keep hidden a single person who might wish to spy on any meeting taking place below. The curtains in front of us were part of a hanging decorating the upper part of the chamber wall. Sister Beatriz adjusted the folds so that we stood within the heavy drapes and could hear and see what passed below us.

'Listen! They are beginning to assemble. Be warned, Saulo, however awful this becomes, we must make no sound, nor cry out to reveal our presence here.' But she herself started back as the officers of the tribunal, a priest and two monks, assembled below us. 'I recognize the Head Inquisitor,' she whispered in agitation. 'It is the priest, Father Besian. He bears ill-will towards me and mine. If his hand is behind this, then he would not have pursued Zarita without being confident of proving a gross misdeed.'

That explained the way this priest had stared at Zarita when leaving the royal reception rooms two days ago. It must be he who'd arranged her arrest and imprisonment.

They brought her in. Zarita stood almost directly beneath us in the hall. I could see the straight angle of her shoulders, the sweep of her neck, and a curl of her hair which had escaped the confines of the coif around her head.

And my heart and soul reached out to her.

Chapter Fifty-four
Zarita

'Zarita de Marzena, daughter of Don Vicente Alonso de Carbazón, you are accused of heresy, of performing certain heretical acts in your home in Las Conchas.'

'This is a false accusation,' I stated in firm voice.

'Do you deny the charge?'

'I do,' I replied. 'Bring forth the person who has accused me of this and I will deny it to them also.'

'The denouncement is in the form of a letter.'

'Written by whom?'

'Your stepmother, Lorena.'

Lorena!

'Let it be a matter of record,' Father Besian formally told the monk acting as secretary, 'that Lorena, wife of the magistrate of Las Conchas, one Don Vicente Alonso de Carbazón, wrote to me some months after I had conducted an Inquisition in the town.'

'What did she write?' I looked at the expression of gloating triumph on the face of Father Besian and my voice faded.

'Lorena said that she was afraid for her soul and that of her unborn child because of certain practices she'd witnessed taking place within the household of her husband. I offered immunity for herself and that of her child, and complete claim on the family property and goods, if she would put in writing what she knew.' Father Besian picked up a sheet of paper and waved it in the air. 'This is her reply. She stated that you and your father regularly engaged in Jewish rituals.'

I managed to smile at this ludicrous statement. 'Why on earth would we do that? Our family has no connection to the Jewish faith.'

'Not so!' Father Besian stood up. 'I too was suspicious when I visited your house. It was obvious that there was a lack of devotion in your person. While your stepmother attended to her religious duties, you preferred, with your father's approval, to study books. I took an opportunity to look at these books. They were neither religious nor devotional. Some of the texts were very suspect indeed. Then your father came and pleaded with me to be merciful to the man, the *converso*, found guilty of reverting to Jewish practices. This alerted me to your Jewish sympathies. Upon receiving your stepmother's first letter, I researched your ancestry. On your father's side there is a grandfather who turned from Judaism to Christianity. It is clear that you and your father reverted back.'

This explained why Papa had seemed anxious at the appearance of the officers of the Inquisition in our house. I recalled the words Father Besian had spoken concerning people who had things to hide, and Papa's reaction to this statement. This was why Beatriz had advised me to have pork served for our evening meal as Jews did not eat pig meat – something I'd neglected to attend to as it had been the day of Bartolomé's arrest. And finally I understood Papa's intense stare in my direction as the Jew *converso* was burned to death. I thought of the fear that must have been churning through his mind at that time. He would have been praying for me not to cry out in a protest that might bring me to investigation and torture. My papa had tried to protect me.

But he was no longer here and I must speak up for myself.

'What Lorena has written is not true. This letter—' I broke off.

The letter!

It was *this* letter that Lorena had spoken of on her deathbed. Her final words to me . . .

Zarita, you will burn . . . the letter.

Lorena had warned me. I thought she meant me to burn some letter that was among her papers, but in fact she was trying to tell me of the letter she'd sent to the Inquisition accusing me of heresy.

Zarita, you will burn.

Lorena had meant that *I* would burn.

'Go on.'

'What?' I looked up.

Father Besian was gazing at me intently. 'You were about to say something?'

'No, nothing.' I shook my head. What could I say? I could not repeat a deathbed confession. Even if it had been proper for me to do so, who knows where that might lead? I would have to betray the circumstances in which I'd heard Lorena say it – during the birth of her baby. Then it would all come out – God forbid! – the presence of the Jewish doctor attending a Christian woman in childbirth, examining her. They could find me guilty of heresy for that offence alone. And they would arrest everyone who'd been in the room at the time – perhaps everyone working in the convent. It would please Father Besian very much to have an excuse to close down my aunt's hospital and disperse her order of nuns. He would discover that I'd had contact with the Jewish doctor previously because I had met him when he'd attended Saulo's mother. Dear God! *Saulo!* Saulo would be taken! They'd find out who he really was and he'd be sent back to the galleys or worse. And there would be others implicated: Serafina, Ardelia and Garci, who'd helped me with Lorena, and Bartolomé. I thought of poor scourged Bartolomé.

I was weeping now, not only through fear for myself but for my beloved, my family, my friends, for all mankind . . . the whole world.

The monk who was scribing the records said gently, 'My daughter, perhaps you have strayed so far from the truth that you cannot see the devious paths down which you have gone. You should say all you know.'

'As Lorena, the wife of the magistrate, is now dead, then we can have no more information from that source.' Father Besian was addressing the other members of the tribunal. 'It's obvious that this woman has things that she chooses not to tell us. Putting her to the rack might make her consider her answers more carefully. A racked prisoner does tend to speak out more fully at the subsequent interrogation.'

His colleagues nodded in agreement.

Nausea rose from my stomach and my body went icy cold and then hot. I bent my head and held my hands to my face. There was a drumming in my ears and I saw the tiled floor rush up to meet me.

Chapter Fifty-five
Saulo

Below me, as Zarita began to sway, I leaned over involuntarily.

Swiftly her aunt placed herself in front of me to block my lunge forward, but for the first time she lost her own composure. At the mention of the rack she put her hand to her face. Now she gripped her fingers over her mouth so that her knuckles gleamed white.

'This man, Besian, had her condemned before trial.' With difficulty I kept my voice muted. 'It won't matter what Zarita does or does not confess to. He intends to find her guilty.'

Sister Beatriz let out a quiet sob of torment. 'What can we do? Saulo, what can we do?'

As they half carried her from the hall, the sun fell on Zarita's face. She raised her gaze to its light and dragged her feet and I thought I sensed why. Her cell would be dark so she was trying to remain in the sunlight for as long as possible. She attempted to straighten up as the soldiers hustled her from the chamber.

I turned to go.

'Stay,' Sister Beatriz quietly but forcefully commanded me.

For what? I wondered. The scribe monk had finished writing in his book, the other gathered some documents, then, with the head of the tribunal, Father Besian, they stood up to leave.

'The queen and king are using this hall for their

conferences,' Sister Beatriz whispered to me. 'If I had insight into Isabella's current mood, it would help me to judge how much, if any, sympathy she might show me.'

I thought about this woman, Isabella, Queen of Castile and Aragon and would-be Queen of all Spain. I recalled that she'd ordered the creation of the town of Santa Fe, hewn out of solid rock so that the siege could remain in place through the winter. I doubted if she was capable of showing mercy to a young girl accused of heresy.

We didn't have long to wait before Queen Isabella, King Ferdinand and their retinue arrived. Among the latter I recognized some of the advisers who'd been present at the session I'd attended with Christopher Columbus. The discussion began. It concerned the proposal to officially expel the Jews. The name of one of their chief financial advisers was mentioned, a Jew called Isaac Abravanel, who'd appealed to the monarchs not to issue the edict of expulsion. He'd offered to pay surety for the Jewish people to remain in Spain.

'Isaac Abravanel has worked very well for us and the good of Spain,' King Ferdinand declared. 'He helped to raise funds for the army. Now our siege here at Granada has been successful and the war is almost over.'

'Therefore we have no more need of him,' pointed out a sly courtier.

'In Granada the Jews have lived peaceably enough within the Muslim communities. Can we not let them do the same among us?'

'That could be termed heresy,' a nobleman interjected.

King Ferdinand stared at the man who had spoken.

'I only say this to advise your majesty,' the nobleman stammered. 'I would be a poor adviser if I didn't give advice.'

'Isaac Abravanel seeks to protect his people,' said Queen Isabella. 'It is an understandable sentiment. And the war has emptied our coffers. Our people are hungry. Perhaps we can come to some arrangement. What sum of money did he mention?'

Suddenly there was a commotion at the main doorway of the hall. A black-cowled figure strode in. His face was contorted, his manner wild and shaking. Above his head he brandished a crucifix of dark wood showing the twisted form of the agonized Christ in palest alabaster.

'What gathering of wickedness is this!' he cried out.

'It is Tomás de Torquemada, the Inquisitor General of all Spain!' Sister Beatriz said in my ear.

'Señor Tomás . . .' King Ferdinand spoke mildly. 'The queen and I convened a meeting of our council to discuss the state of the finances of the nation. It is not a matter for the Church.'

'Everything is a matter for Mother Church!' Torquemada retorted. 'Body and soul are joined inseparably, and therefore the rulers of a country must take due notice of the Church.'

The king's jaw tightened. 'The monarchs make decisions in the best interests of both. We are facing a crisis which, if not resolved, will lead to many deaths.'

'We must find the means to feed our soldiers and our citizens,' Queen Isabella interposed.

'Better they suffer the pangs of hunger than the eternal torments of Hell!'

The queen and king looked at each other.

'The hand of God is above this place, ready to smash His fist down upon the unclean and the unworthy! Betray not the sacred oaths you have taken! Hark to the words of the prophets! Those who crucified the Christ are among us! And you swore a sacred oath to make Spain a Christian country!'

King Ferdinand face set in a grim line.

Queen Isabella, devout and prayerful, allowed her hand to stray to the cross she wore on a chain around her neck. 'Isaac Abravanel has managed the affairs of the treasury with excellent skill,' she said.

'It is to be expected.' Torquemada spat these words out.

The king affected not to notice the remark. 'He has offered a sum of money as reparation to compensate the crown for losses.'

'That will make you further indebted to the Jews!'

'Not so. It is money that Isaac Abravanel has earned through his own business.'

'You are condoning usury, and usury is wrong. Money should not be used to make more money. Money should be earned by work.'

'He has offered to pay the money over as a gift.'

'Ha! A bribe!' crowed Torquemada.

'Not a bribe!' the king snapped back. 'It is a surety for his people. It is a customary and perfectly legal transaction to pay a sum of money in such a fashion.'

'What sum of money?' Torquemada demanded.

'The amount of thirty thousand ducats.'

'Why not then?' Torquemada shrieked. 'Why not accept this Jewish money? After all, was not Christ Jesus our Lord betrayed for thirty pieces of silver?'

And saying this, he raised his hand high above his head and hurled the crucifix to the floor. It smashed down upon the marble slabs, and the figure broke in two pieces. The head of Christ, with his agonized white face and blood oozing from the crown of thorns upon his forehead, broke loose and went skittering across the tiles to end up at the feet of the queen.

'*Jesu!*' Queen Isabella's complexion drained as white as the alabaster face of the dead Christ.

Torquemada strode from the room. There was a silence, then uproar in the assembly.

The queen slumped back in her chair.

A courtier summoned a servant to pick up the pieces of the crucifix, but the queen raised her hand and spoke. 'I will do this myself,' she said, and her voice shook with distress.

She went down on her knees and, lifting the face of Jesus, she kissed it. Then she gathered up the rest of the cross and took the veil from her head and wrapped the pieces therein.

The king drummed his fingers on the arm of his chair but did not intervene.

I had witnessed the power of Torquemada and hopelessness filled my heart, for this man was invincible. If the Queen and King of Spain could not gainsay him in a matter of State, then Queen Isabella would ignore any appeal made by the nun for mercy for Zarita.

'Now I see how it is with Isabella,' said Sister Beatriz. 'The queen will not act to spare Zarita's life.' She spoke my own thoughts and in her voice was the sound of my own despair.

The Inquisition would snuff out Zarita's life like a candle being extinguished.

Chapter Fifty-six
Zarita

Racked.

I was to be racked.

Put to the question as Bartolomé had been. To be made to confess to something I didn't do. I recalled his screams of agony the day I'd run to the barn to find him dangling from the rafters with a rope tied to his wrists. I saw again before me the old man led to his execution at the stake, staggering as he walked, his body like a loose-limbed puppet.

I could not bear it. I could not. I did not possess the courage of a martyr. I knew this now for certain. Even the prospect of being shackled in irons and hung from the wall had reduced me to such a fainting condition that my gaoler had to support me when taking me back to my cell.

I remembered what had happened when they'd tortured Bartolomé – the townspeople panicked into betraying each other, myself included. I was responsible for the two women being stripped and scourged, for I had pointed the Inquisition in their direction. This would be much worse. The pain would be so great that I would tell them anything, everything.

I thought of all I might say.

There was my aunt's collection of medical books depicting surgery upon the human body. They would deem these texts heretical, and brand her a heretic too, for she was studying Arabic and Hebrew in order to read these learned works. They would arrest her, and Father Besian would be glad to do it for he considered her presumptuous.

And what of the convent where my aunt had constructed her own rules to return to the true spirit of the first holy men and women of the Church? The remarks she'd made regarding this could be interpreted as heresy and double heresy. Her sisters would be brought for trial before the Inquisition.

I would betray the doctor who'd attended Lorena. He would be punished for daring to lay hands on a Christian woman even to save the life of a child. I would tell about the child. I would tell who had fathered him. It would destroy Ramón. And although Ramón was foolish, he was not wicked and didn't deserve to have his life ruined. And it would mean the child too would be at risk. Perhaps they would decide that the Jewish doctor had exchanged the baby for a different one: the innocent babe, now enjoying being spoiled by Garci and Serafina and Ardelia, would suffer too. The immunity that Lorena had been promised for her child in exchange for betraying me and my father would not withstand this damning evidence. As the relative of a heretic, the child would lose his inheritance.

And then there was Saulo. I would say that he wasn't an independent mariner and man of fortune. I would denounce him as the son of a hanged beggar, who had been sentenced to slavery.

I saw how this would go on and on and on, and it would never end, but consume all Spain.

I must remain silent.

God, let me die now, I thought, *let me die tonight*. If I had the means I would kill myself. For I believe in the goodness of God and He will give me mercy as He sees fit. I can only do what my conscience directs me to do. And if I died, then it would be over.

And then I thought, in truth, I do not care to live any

longer in this life. Saulo, whom I love, does not love me. He hates me. He came to my room to kill me. So the happiness I'd anticipated with him was impossible. The life I'd begun to hope to live on this Earth was dust in my hand.

I stayed awake that long night until my eyes burned in the darkness. When I heard the gaoler stirring in the corridors outside, I knew what I must do. I had the power to stop up a small part of the flood of destruction.

And there was only one way I could do this.

I went to the door and called to my gaoler. 'I would like to speak to Father Besian,' I said. 'I wish to confess.'

Chapter Fifty-seven
Saulo

Zarita has confessed to being a secret Jew!

It was Rafael who brought me this news early the next morning. I told him I must find Zarita's aunt, who'd left me the previous evening to search for a chapel in which to pray throughout the night.

'The nun already knows,' Rafael said. 'She spent the night in prayer on her knees outside the rooms of Father Besian. I was informed that he took great pleasure in telling her that her niece had confessed to heresy. It would seem that he bears Sister Beatriz ill-will and intends to punish her by destroying the girl she loves.'

I went and brought Zarita's aunt to my own room.

'Why would she confess?' I asked her. 'Have they tortured her? Has she gone mad?'

'No . . .' The nun spoke slowly. 'No, Zarita is not mad. I believe she is thinking about things very carefully. Confessing to heresy means she will not be interrogated again. She knows that if they put her to the question then she will betray us all.' She raised her head and looked at me directly. 'Would you care if she were being tortured?'

The idea of Zarita being tortured drove me wild. Pain clawed inside me as if a series of barbed hooks were being dragged through my brain. I put a hand on each side of my head. 'I cannot bear the thought of it.'

In a voice devoid of emotion Sister Beatriz said, 'It is small comfort to know that, as she has confessed to observing Jewish rituals, she will avoid torture. Now they will burn her as a heretic.'

'Burn her?' I whispered.

'Yes. It is the punishment for a *converso* who reverts to Judaism.'

'For this they will burn her alive?'

'That depends,' the nun said woodenly. 'If she chooses to recant, and she can do this even when the bonfire is alight, then mercy is shown by having the executioner strangle her quickly to save her the agony of death by fire.'

Sister Beatriz picked up a scrap of paper that was lying on the table and, leaning forward, brought the edge to the candle flame. It flared up and then descended into ashes. She contemplated these and then prodded them with her finger. 'Yes,' she murmured, half to herself, 'I see why they choose fire. It leaves nothing behind . . . no evidence of any kind.'

She stared at the flame and went into what appeared to be a trance-like state, and I realized that she was meditating. Then she seemed to come to a decision: she raised her head and looked at me seriously. 'I did petition the queen but, as I expected, my plea was rejected. As a mark of our previous friendship she has declared that, even though I am a relative of a heretic, I will escape arrest as long as I return to my convent and remain within its walls until I die. I've been told that I must quit the city before dawn tomorrow – though she will sign a special pass so that I may visit Zarita one last time. May I stay here for a while before doing that?'

I left the nun to rest on my bed and went to speak to Christopher Columbus. He was the only person I knew at court. I hoped he might have some advice as to what I could do.

'Would that I could help you, Saulo,' he said, 'but I no

longer have any status within the court. I am definitely leaving. It's useless to wait on here. They are wasting my time as others have done before. I am so disappointed, for I thought they were interested enough to invest in me.'

We embraced, and I wished him well in his ventures. He tried to persuade me to come with him, or at least to leave the city, as he intended to do, before the execution took place the following day.

'You may have been enamoured of this girl, but I urge you to go away now.'

'I cannot.'

'There is no hope for her.'

'I believe you. Yet I cannot leave.'

'You may put yourself in danger if you remain; if it becomes known that you sought out her company.'

'I don't care,' I said.

'Be careful, Saulo. I have heard that the monarchs are preparing a decree to expel all who hold to the Jewish faith. The Jews, and everyone associated with them, will lose their property and their goods. You risk being caught up in the purge.'

I thanked him sincerely for his patronage and support, and he made me promise to meet up with him some time in the future. So we parted, Christopher Columbus and I, he in anguish over his lost cause and me in anguish over mine.

Chapter Fifty-eight
Zarita

I am praying, or trying to pray as best I can.

Will I see Mama again, and Papa too, in Heaven? I hope so. There are many things I want to say to them, to ask their forgiveness and tell them how much I love them.

A priest came and heard my confession. After he left I made another private and more sincere apology to my Maker for the wrongs I'd done in my life. The priest said I could hope for some mercy at the end.

'I am to die. Is that not true?'

'Yes,' he agreed. 'You have been condemned to death at the stake and the sentence will be carried out tomorrow. But, in addition to your confession, there is a final act for you to make. You should call out that you recant. If you do, then, on a signal from the head of the tribunal, the executioner can quickly—' He coughed and began again. 'The executioner would end your life speedily and your suffering on this Earth would be over.'

I had not thought to die in such a way.

But I'd made my peace with my God and myself, and only looked forward to seeing my aunt Beatriz and bidding her farewell.

The gaoler told me that she would come one last time after midnight, for she must leave the city before daybreak or her own life would be forfeit. There is only one other person whose face I would want to see again.

Saulo.

My heart became heavy in my breast. I sat down.

How I had wronged him! What stupidity I'd displayed. What a coward I'd been. I should have flung myself in front of Papa and stayed his hand. Saulo's father would be alive if I had done so, and they would both have been with his mother when she died.

If I am denied Heaven for that, then it is just punishment and I will wait in Purgatory until my soul is cleansed before I enter Paradise.

I hear the keys of the gaoler and his stumbling steps outside my door.

Chapter Fifty-nine
Saulo

When I returned to my room, the nun was on her knees by the window.

I shook my head to indicate that, as we'd suspected, there was nothing that Christopher Columbus could do to help us.

Sister Beatriz stood up. 'Saulo, as I told you, I have been given safe passage signed by the queen to return to my convent, but only if I leave before daybreak tomorrow. Would you be my escort out of the palace and the city and go with me to Las Conchas?'

'Me?' I stared at her. 'You want *me* to escort you out of the city?'

'Yes,' she said. 'A woman travelling alone, even in the garb of a nun, might be at risk.'

'And why choose me for this task?'

'It was Zarita who told me that you were the one honest man in the court she would trust.'

Zarita had spoken of me as being honest and trustworthy. The truth being spoken by a woman facing death. A sudden annoyance at this nun's assumption that I would meekly do as she requested made me ask, 'What makes *you* think I am trustworthy?'

I folded my arms and stood in front of the door, deliberately blocking her exit from the room to indicate that she must answer me or I would prevent her leaving.

She pressed her lips together but did not react as most women would have done by showing fear. It was not pretence. She was truly unafraid.

'Zarita told me that the only thing of worth that had happened to her at court was her meeting with you, the young mariner who accompanied Christopher Columbus. Any other person hearing that might think it the prattle of a girl struck by the attentions of a handsome man. But I know my niece very well. She has suffered in her life and matured beyond such trivial girlish talk. She must have seen or sensed something in your character that makes you different from others – a nobility of purpose, some steadfastness of soul. And, in any case, can you bear to wait until tomorrow and watch her die?'

'No,' I said dully. I dropped my head upon my chest. 'I will do as you ask.'

'Thank you,' she replied. 'Then please arrange with Rafael to have two horses waiting, for there must be no delay. I want to leave immediately after I speak with my niece.'

I looked at the nun. She stood there before me, hands clasped together and hidden in her wide sleeves. There was a certain tension in her stance, but under the coif and cowl of her religious habit her face was serene.

'Don't you care for her?' I asked.

'Care for whom?' she replied. 'Zarita?'

'Yes. *Zarita!*' I shouted.

'She is the only child of my only sister, and possesses a good and loving spirit,' she said with a calmness that infuriated me. 'I care for her very much.'

'You cannot love her so much: the prospect of the terrible death awaiting her does not appear to upset you.'

'I love her more than I do my own life,' Sister Beatriz replied. She raised her head and looked at me directly. 'The question is, Saulo the mariner, how much do *you* love her?'

Chapter Sixty
Zarita

There is the light of a lantern outside my cell.

Hushed voices, a scrape of a key, and Beatriz was with me.

We embraced.

'I want you to take this.' She leaned forward to speak quietly in my ear, glancing, as she did so, towards the door. There was a man there, standing in the shadows.

'What is it?'

She took a tiny bottle from under her habit and withdrew the stopper. A sickly smell filled my nostrils. 'It's a calming brew. A mixture of my own devising. Camomile and some other . . . herbs. It will steady your nerves for the morning.' She held it to my lips. 'Come now. Zarita. Drink this. If only because it's the last thing I ask you to do,' she coaxed me. 'It will settle your mind and help you through your ordeal.'

I drank the thick syrup down. When I'd finished, Aunt Beatriz drew me close to her. 'Let me look at you one last time. Your face' – she reached up to touch my cheek – 'so beautiful, so beautiful you are, and good too. Never forget that you are beloved and good.'

I reached out for her.

'Ah, you are trembling. That will soon pass.' She took off her hooded outer cloak. 'Put this on. It will keep you warm.'

I shivered and then I giggled. I put my hand to my mouth, scarcely believing I'd done so. 'It seems amusing,' I tried to explain, 'that we should worry that I might catch cold, when in a few hours I am to die by fire.'

'Hush,' Beatriz chided me. 'Not so loud, Zarita. I'd rather you were silent. Can you promise me that, Zarita?'

'What?' My words were slurring. The thoughts in my head disjointed.

'That you will remain silent. Please.'

The nun's vow to maintain regular periods of silence had always been a problem for me. Again it struck me as a funny thing for her to say. There it was again. Lazy laughter bubbling up inside me as my senses whirled. I felt very faint. I mumbled something but had no idea whether I said the words aloud or not.

Beatriz was struggling with me, trying to edge my arm under the canopy of her cloak.

'Help me here,' she whispered hoarsely to the man by the doorway. 'We have so little time.'

Chapter Sixty-one
Saulo

I went forward at her command and took in my arms the woman I had vowed to kill.

'May God go with you,' the nun said in a low voice.

I hung back.

'Don't wait,' she urged me. 'All your strength is needed now. Call upon your own resources and the good Lord to help you.'

'I do not believe in the goodness of your Lord.'

'Then I will do the praying, Saulo. And you may do the fighting.' Sister Beatriz smiled and blessed me. 'Go,' she said, 'and don't look back.'

But I did look round, just once, as we left the cell.

She was already on her knees, where the glow from the lantern light bathed her features in a strange ethereal luminescence.

I hefted Zarita on my arm to support her.

'Saulo?' Her voice was hushed in disbelief. 'My beloved. You are really here?'

'I am here,' I said softly.

'I love you.'

'As I do you.' I edged her nearer the door.

'Wait,' Zarita said, slow realization of what was intended beginning to penetrate the fog of the drug Sister Beatriz had given her.

'Be quiet,' I hissed in her ear. The gaoler, although befuddled with sleep and liquor, could not be completely deaf.

Zarita pulled against me. 'She mustn't be allowed to do this. I have already caused too many deaths.'

'And you will cause more,' I told her brutally, 'if you don't silence yourself. For if this deception is discovered, then we will all surely be executed, as will the man who waits outside guarding the horses that might take us to safety.'

At that she collapsed against me, but began to weep and sob. 'She cannot die – she cannot – please don't let her die.'

Which was the most appropriate behaviour for the gaoler to witness as he escorted us away. I imagine he'd seen many similar scenes and would have expected the last visit of a relative to end with a man supporting a weeping female.

He took us through the main chamber and we ascended the stairs to the upper level. But it was a different matter at the entrance to the prison. There had been a change of guard and the new one studied us closely.

'Your eyes are very distinctive,' he commented. 'I think I know your face.'

'Most likely.' I yawned, hoping to infect him with my pretence of weariness, for a yawn can be catching and the hour was late. 'But we don't have time to chat.'

He glanced again at the papers I'd handed him.

Zarita gave a moan and leaned against me.

The guard looked at her and looked again at the papers in his hand.

A soldier who could read! This we did not want. We needed only a guard who would look at the official seal of the queen, recognize it and, as two people had passed in earlier, allow two people to pass out.

'I have definitely seen you.' He was in no hurry. Some minutes of conversation would break the monotony of a long boring spell of duty.

'I don't think so,' I assured him.

He wasn't convinced. Beside me Zarita stirred again. If we delayed much longer he would see that the girl I supported on one arm was in a drugged state and not suffering a swoon of grief.

'I am with the explorer Christopher Columbus,' I said, trying desperately to divert him. 'You would have seen me at court where we gave our petitions to the queen and king.'

'I've never been so close to court affairs.'

'But you should know that Señor Columbus has the queen's favour, so it would be better that you let us pass without delay.' I said this not too arrogantly so as not to prickle his pride. 'It is the queen's seal on this document.'

'So it is.' The guard handed it back to me and I tucked it in my doublet. 'And yet,' he went on, moving with infuriating slowness to get out of our way, 'it's not here that I've seen you before. A mariner, you say? I spent some time travelling on ships while our lieutenant looked for the best billet for us as the war progressed. Perhaps that's where I—' He broke off and brought the lantern closer to examine my face. He stared into my eyes.

'*Christu!*' he gasped. 'I have it now!'

And in the instant he recognized me, I recognized *him*.

It was the red-haired soldier. The one I'd first seen in the compound of the magistrate, Don Vicente Alonso, as he'd helped hang my father from a tree.

Chapter Sixty-two
Saulo

The soldier opened his mouth.

My knife was in my hand and up against his throat before he could utter a word. 'Do not cry out,' I warned him.

The lantern wavered but he didn't lose his composure. 'And what happens when you kill me, lad?' he said.

'I don't know,' I retorted, 'but I will not die alone.'

'And what becomes of her?' His eyes narrowed and abruptly he snatched the veil from Zarita's face. Her eyelids were closed but she was obviously not the age of the nun named on the pass before him. He looked at me in puzzlement. 'You are risking your life to rescue one of the prisoners? Why?'

'Love.' I answered the question almost before he'd asked it.

'How did you manage to smuggle her out of her prison cell?'

'An older nun, her aunt, has taken her place.'

'And if the gaoler notices an exchange has been made?'

'It's not in his interests for it to be known that he allowed a heretic to escape.'

'That's true,' said the red-haired soldier. 'Even if he realizes what's happened, he'll say nothing and hope that in the chaos of tomorrow's executions no one will notice.'

'Her aunt intends to go to the stake fully veiled, and she told me that she will not recant, for if the executioner went in to end her life more quickly, her veil might be pushed aside.'

'That's courage indeed,' marvelled the red-haired soldier.

I didn't add that Sister Beatriz had said that the only person who might be watching closely was Father Besian, and as it was her he truly hated then he would be more than happy to see her suffer. 'They have a nun to burn tomorrow,' I added. 'I've not deprived them of their sport.'

The soldier kept staring at me in amazement as I spoke, and I remembered that this guard had been the one who'd ended my father's agony by pulling sharply on his legs, the one who had given me water when I was almost dying of thirst in the hold of the ship.

'Twice before I've witnessed you cheat Death, boy.' His voice had a tone of wonder in it. 'I said that you were born under some special star.' He crossed himself.

'Be merciful,' I urged him, 'and I'll ask the sisters of this order to say a prayer for your immortal soul.'

'Make sure they say more than one.' He grinned. 'You have a charmed life, lad, and I'll not go against whatever god protects you. I'm on execution escort duty tomorrow morning. I'll make sure that the nun's head and face are properly covered.'

Rafael was waiting where he said he would be.

He'd been a great help to me but I'd kept back most of the huge payment I'd promised him to ensure that he was there. I'd told him that I would need two horses as I would be escorting Zarita's aunt out of the city. I let him know that she had permission to go but it would be better if it were done during the darkest hours and as discreetly as possible. If Rafael guessed at the truth of the situation, then he gave no sign. In the event, I had to leave one horse behind, for Zarita could not have stayed upright on hers.

I sat her on the saddle in front of me, and Rafael led the horse, its hooves muffled, through the lanes and alleyways until we came to a remote sally port. He went forward to speak to the soldier on duty and show the passes. I opened up my travel bag and pulled from it a heavy bag full of coins that I'd previously cut from the peacock jacket.

'This is yours,' I said, tossing it down to him. 'Inside you'll find silver and gold. There is enough there for you to buy a mansion house, fill it with servants to wait upon you and live like a grandee for the rest of your life.'

Chapter Sixty-three
Saulo

The sun was beginning to climb the eastern horizon as I rode down into the valley.

Zarita slept – probably from a combination of exhaustion, and the lingering effects of the potion her aunt had given her. I was forced to ride more slowly and cautiously than I wanted.

I avoided the army encampments. The road was empty, the countryside still quiet. It was with a shock that I heard the thudding of hoofbeats behind me.

There was nowhere to hide. How many riders? I squinted back along the road. Only one. I increased my pace but knew that I couldn't outrun him on a horse that carried two. Then I saw a small lake ahead; a few trees – barely enough cover to conceal us from the road. But it might do. I urged my horse on, but as I approached I saw another traveller ahead of me in the road. I was trapped between these two.

I reined in. What to do? I couldn't fight both of them, and my wits were stretched beyond where I could think clearly.

'Hola! Saulo!'

My head jerked in surprise. I was being hailed by the man in front of me. I went forward a little and saw that it was Christopher Columbus.

I trotted towards him and he came on to meet me. Neither Zarita's veil nor her hood were in place. Columbus started as he looked at her. He glanced back as the pursuing rider came into view and understood the situation immediately.

'Quickly,' he said. 'Take the girl there.' He pointed to the trees. 'Cover her with your cloak. From a distance he won't have spotted that your horse bears two persons.'

I slid down from my horse, gathering Zarita in my arms as I did so. Stooping over, I ran over to the group of trees by the water's edge and laid her gently on the shingle shore. I threw my cloak over her body. Columbus also dismounted and wrenched branches from the evergreen bushes to cover her. I piled a bundle of stones in front.

'Let's hope she doesn't awaken or cry out,' Columbus muttered. He winked and grinned at me as he straightened up, and I understood some of the reasons why he'd attracted such a significant group of supporters over the years. He was loyal to his friends, resourceful and quick-witted, and relished the challenge of the unexpected. He placed his hand on my shoulder to calm my agitation and we strolled casually back to our horses.

A minute later the rider galloped up.

Columbus walked towards him, obscuring the view of the lakeside where Zarita was hidden. My hand went to my dagger.

'Christopher Columbus' – the man spoke as he dismounted – 'I bring a missive from their majesties.' From inside his jerkin he took a letter bearing the seal of Queen Isabella.

Columbus waved it away. 'I am minded to be done with the King and Queen of Spain,' he said. 'I intend to go to France or England, where my brother is seeking patronage for us. With both of us there to plead our case, perhaps we will find a monarch who has the foresight to see the true potential of my planned expedition.'

'Sir' – the messenger got down on one knee and proffered

the letter to Columbus – 'this contains a summons to return to the court. Their majesties Queen Isabella and King Ferdinand have decided to agree to your terms, grant your demands and fund your expedition.'

Rather than the whoop of joy I expected from Columbus, I saw his face blanch. He placed his hand over his heart. 'Can it be true?' His words were barely audible. 'After all these years, can it really be true?'

I took the letter from the messenger and handed it to Columbus. With trembling fingers he tore open the seal and scanned the contents.

'It is written!' His voice broke in emotion. 'By the hand of Queen Isabella herself! I have her word that she will sponsor my venture!'

As the messenger went off to take his reply to the queen and king Columbus began, at once, to list the things he must do to prepare. 'I will equip three caravels, buy supplies and recruit a crew right away, for I intend to set off later this very year, when the winds and weather are favourable. It will be the most exciting adventure the world has ever known! Say that you'll come with me, Saulo!'

'There is something . . . someone . . . that I have to take care of,' I told him. 'I cannot join you.'

'But you must,' said a voice behind us. 'I do insist upon it.'

I spun round. Zarita had woken and was leaning against a tree.

'Señor Columbus' – she spoke slowly but distinctly – 'if the queen and king are going to support your expedition, please be advised that Saulo the mariner will be sailing with you.'

I went to her and told her that I would not be going

304

away, for I believed she would need my help over the next months.

Zarita shook her head. Her face was grey with grief and shock. 'I must go to the convent in Las Conchas and speak to my aunt's friend, Sister Maddalena,' she told me. 'We will try to comfort each other as we mourn the loss of someone we both admired and adored.'

I took her hands in mine and searched her eyes with my own. 'Is our love strong enough to survive all that has happened to us?' I asked.

'Yes,' Zarita replied, 'I believe it is.'

And from that moment I too believed.

We watched Christopher Columbus mount his horse and ride back to the city.

Atop the hill, the magnificence of the Alhambra Palace dominated the landscape. The turrets, domes and towers glowed, tinted with streams of gold from the rays of the rising sun.

The nun was like enough Zarita about the eyes to fool even close guards when wearing a veil, I thought. A little taller, but she intended to stoop as they took her out. That wouldn't have seemed unusual to the watchers, who would assume that the victim was broken in body and spirit. As she was a nun, they would not strip her, and her veil and cowl would remain in place.

I imagined the smell of fresh bread coming from the ovens of the bakers who rise before dawn to light their cooking fires. Then . . . the crow of a cockerel, and the inhabitants stir themselves awake. I think of one person who had most likely slept not at all throughout the night. I squeezed my eyes shut, as if I could somehow blot out the scene from my mind's eye.

Zarita came into my arms and we clung to each other.

The procession is assembling.

An escort of guards, among them the red-haired soldier. Now the steady beat of a drum as they move off to the place of execution. The populace, obliged to attend lest they attract suspicion upon themselves, edge back to let them through.

They reach the square. The stake is ready. Wood heaped around the foot.

She is led forward.

Chapter Sixty-four

She begged for a cross to hold.

They would not give her one.

Her body was bound fast with thick ropes to the central pole of the stake. Her arms and hands were free. She brought them together. She laid the thumb of her right hand across the forefinger of her left. She pressed her lips to the intersection of this cross and cried out in a loud voice,

'In the name of the Blessed Lord Jesus who died for our sins!'

The flames began to rise around her.

Was it true that in some cases they dampened the firewood so that the condemned would roast more slowly? Her figure became obscured by the smoke, her form a writhing shadow within the fire.

She could not be seen, but she could be heard now, screaming; and the crowd called to her: 'Recant! Recant!'

A young man shouted out, 'For the love of God, let her die! Let her die!'

It was rumoured that this man was Ramón Salazar, a nobleman and childhood friend who held the woman in high regard.

It sometimes happened that the executioner would go in and swiftly garrotte a heretic before the flames reached them. But she did not recant so she was shown no such mercy.

Her screams lessened to be replaced with worse – a croaking agonized babbling.

The man bent his head, sobbing, his hands covering his ears.

The stink of burning flesh lingered in the square for hours afterwards.

Epilogue

Just before sunrise on Friday 3 August 1492, at the town of Palos north of Cádiz, two men walked down from the chapel of St George to the nearby river.

From the high bank on one side of the estuary, a young woman watched as they made their way to where three ships, the *Niña*, the *Pinta* and the *Santa Maria*, were moored in the inlet below. The sailors in their homespun tunics and bright red caps raised the anchors, and the ships begin to stir as the flow of the outgoing tide edged them slowly in the direction of the river mouth. From the deck of the largest of these, the *Santa Maria*, Zarita saw Saulo raise his hand to her in farewell.

The chapel bell stopped pealing and the ships began to move more swiftly towards the Ocean Sea. As they crossed the Saltes sandbar, the broad square sail of the *Santa Maria*, white with a red cross emblazoned on it, billowed out before the wind.

Christopher Columbus had reckoned it could be six months or more before they came back. It would give her and Saulo time, Zarita thought; time and space to recover from the trauma of their previous lives. When Saulo returned, they would talk together and plan for the future. Perhaps there were unknown lands out there waiting to be discovered – a new place – where people might be free to worship as they chose and could live with each other in harmony and peace.

Thanks are due to…

Margot Aked
Lauren Buckland
Laura Cecil
Sue Cook
Marzena Currie
Annie Eaton
Georgia Lawe
Hanne, Tour Guide of 'Classical Spain'
Lily Lawes
Museo Naval de Madrid
Sophie Nelson
Hugh Rae
Random House staff
Family et al